Before the Storm

Maggie Hansen

M. H. Publishing

ISBN-13: 978-0-692-66788-0
ISBN-10: 0-692-66788-1

First Edition First Printing

Cover Photos courtesy of Holly Cockerham
Cover Design by Holly Cockerham and Maggie Hansen

Visit the author's webpage to order additional copies
maggiehansen.com

Published by M. H. Publishing 2016
Waynesville, Ohio

I would like to dedicate this book to
Karla Thompson

I love you mom, so much; I miss you every day.
Thanks for passing on your love of books.
I wish you could read it.

Acknowledgements

First I want to thank Aunt Patty for being my first fan. I really appreciate you reading the rough draft and loving it despite its many faults. Thank you Holly for...well...everything; you're my favorite person. I absolutely love the cover; I couldn't have done it without you. Crystal, this book wouldn't be half of what it is without your insight. Thank you to my good friends Sally and Chris for keeping me sane. Thank you to my beautiful children, Brigid and Jake, for putting up with me during the long process of writing, editing and formatting Before the Storm. It was a long and frustrating process at times. And finally, thank you to everyone, friends, family, and the local communities of Waynesville and Lebanon, for all of your love and support. You can't beat small town love!

Day 1

1

*H*e was running through the woods at the edge of his property, panting heavily. He was being chased, but he didn't know by whom; he was terrified. His heart was racing, and he was sweating profusely despite the chill in the air. A horrible stench permeated the air.

He knew that if he didn't get away from his pursuer, it meant death or possibly worse. So, he kept running. It was dark and rain was falling, making the leaves on the forest floor even more slippery than normal.

He risked a glance behind him and saw nothing but utter darkness. He heard hysterical laughter through the trees. The sound sent chills into his blood, and he knew it was the sound of insanity. He slipped and felt the sharp pain as his kneecap made contact with a tree root protruding from the ground.

He groaned as he clawed forward on his hands and knees, begging God that he would get his footing so he could flee once again. All he heard was his own ragged breathing as he strained to hear the snap of branches as his pursuer gained ground. He/it was too close now; he knew death was coming. He groped around the forest floor for some kind of weapon; even though he knew in his soul, fighting was useless.

He finally gained his footing, but it was too late; the laughter came again, this time from inside his head.

"HAHAHAHA; you will never get away from me."

He grabbed the sides of his head and let out a piercing scream.

"You can never be rid of me. You need me."

He looked around frantically for the owner of the voice, but there was no one in sight.

"It will never end." The voice sounded again in his head, so full of insanity it made his stomach curl.

Still clutching his head, he yelled as loud as possible, "What do you want? Who are you?"

The laughter came again; then in a whisper, "you know; you know who I am."

He woke up in a cold sweat. He had been hopeful the dreams had finally stopped. He hadn't had them in over a year, but they appeared to be back in full force and had been for the past two nights. He never remembered the dreams, only the stark terror with which they left him.

He looked at the clock and saw it was barely after three am. He threw back the covers and pulled on his jeans deciding it was useless to try and go back to sleep; he had to be up in less than two hours anyway to tend to the cows and do his other chores around the farm. He went into the kitchen to put some coffee on to brew.

The nightmares had started the first time not long after his wife had died fifteen years ago, about the same time the blackouts started. He'd been to the doctor for the blackouts in the past, but they had found nothing. He attributed both the headaches and blackouts to his grief over the loss of the love of his life. Mainly because they only occurred around the time of year Marie had died, when his grief was almost too much to bear. At one time, he had lost two entire days during one of his blackouts. That was one week after Marie's unexpected death.

He had been married to Marie for twelve years...the most wonderful twelve years of his life. He had fallen in love with her instantly the first time he saw her. Her family had moved to Jefferson during their junior year of high school. He could still picture the way she looked climbing the stairs to the high school her first day. She was beautiful and so young back then.

"Hey check out the fresh meat," his buddy Carl said jabbing him in the ribs with his elbow.

All he could do was stare. He was struck speechless by the site of her. She walked past him, Carl, and Mikey into the school.

"Yeah, she's all right," Mikey said. *"But, she sure ain't no Lucy McCollum."*

"I don't know what you see in Lucy." Carl snickered. *"She has a big nose and that mole on her chin."*

"Yeah, but she's got great knockers," Mikey replied cupping his hands in front of his chest.

Carl laughed then looked over at him; his smile turning into a look of concern. "Hey, you okay buddy? You look like you've seen a ghost."

He shook his head to clear it. "I'm cool. We better get to homeroom. Mr. Smythe will skin us for sure if we're late again this week."

He hadn't been able to get her out of his head all through the first three classes of the day. He may have even tanked his history quiz...all he could think about was the new girl. Hell, he didn't even know her name, but her face was etched in his mind.

He saw her again briefly between third and fourth period walking down the hall. He hurried after her but lost her at the stairwell. He had no idea if she went up or down. As he stood there contemplating which way to go, the bell rang starting fourth period.

He cursed and hurried to the third floor for Chemistry. When he ran into the classroom he was jolted by the sight of her. She was sitting in the front row scowling at him, practically scolding him for being late. He hurried to his seat at the back of the class mumbling an apology to Mr. Creech as he passed.

He sighed as he got up to pour his coffee. The trips down memory lane were always painful ones. He missed his sweet Marie so much even after all these years; sometimes he wondered how he was able to go on without her. He had never even dated in the fifteen years since his wife passed away. He'd never be happy with anyone who wasn't Marie. She was perfect; she was his life. He knew the moment he saw her they were meant to be together.

They never had any children. Not that they hadn't tried, Marie had wanted kids. She had gotten pregnant three times but was never able to carry the child to term. After three miscarriages, the third nearly to term, they decided it was best not to try again.

Marie went on birth control because she couldn't bear the loss of another unborn child. And, he insisted because she had nearly died herself the last time. A few years after the third miscarriage, they had started to discuss the possibilities of adopting a child. A few months later Marie was dead.

He became a widower at the age of thirty-two. Marie was up visiting her parents the weekend before Christmas. Her parents had moved to Wisconsin a few years before, and ever since, he and Marie would go up that weekend to celebrate the holidays. He usually went with her, but one of the horses was close to full term, and he didn't want to risk the foal being born while he was away. Sometimes things went wrong during labor. Even with all the medical advantages his wife had, he had learned that the hard way. So, he hadn't gone, and she never came back.

It was the middle of the afternoon when he found out, and surprisingly warm for a December day. He was in the barn grooming JoJo his prize mare when Chief Clawson tracked him down.

"Hey, Joe what brings you all the way out here?"

"Son, I'm afraid I have some bad news." The Chief had a habit of calling any man younger than him son.

Joe Clawson had been a cop for thirty years, and this part of it had always been the worst part of the job. He found the easiest way to break bad news was to do it quickly.

"I got a call from a sergeant Michaelson from up in Milwaukee. It seems that as Marie was heading home from her folks place she lost control of her vehicle and was involved in an accident."

"Marie? Is she hurt? Where is she? Is she in the hospital?" He started walking out of the barn, but the Chief grabbed his arm and turned him back to face him.

He jerked his arm in anger, but the Chief's grip was strong. "Let me go Joe, I have to get up there."

"I'm sorry, son; she didn't make it." He didn't let go.

"What do you mean she didn't make it?" He was baffled.

"Marie's dead," the Chief said flatly.

He laughed. "Of course she's not dead; I just talked to her this morning. She was on her way home." But he saw the reality of it on Joe's face. He jerked his arm from the older man's grasp; this time Joe released him.

"I'm sorry, son. I truly am. She was a fine woman. Is there anyone you want me to call?" he said sympathetically.

He shook his head. He couldn't believe it. Not his Marie.

"I...need to um...call Marie's folks." He just couldn't process it. He put two fingers to his temple...His head was starting to hurt.

"They have already been notified," Joe assured him. "The Milwaukee police department tried to notify you by telephone but couldn't get you on the line, so they contacted me. They already notified her parents. They found her address book in her purse and found her parents' number there. They called them right away."

"I don't know...I don't know what to do, Joe." It couldn't be real.

Joe put a hand on his shoulder, knowing what it was to lose a wife. His had died of cancer two years before. "Why don't you go on inside, and I'll call your brother; have him come over and stay with you for a bit."

He just nodded and walked the mile or so to the house, reality slow to kick in.

He never stepped foot in that barn again; he even stopped raising horses and sold the ones he already had. He couldn't bear the memory of being told about his wife's death. He had a new barn built closer to the house, but he let the old one stand as it had the day of the dreadful news.

The memory was a painful one regardless of the years since it had happened. He drank his coffee, even thought about adding a shot or two of whiskey. He tried to put his late wife out of his mind, but like most days after the nightmares came to him, she was nearly all he could think about. Hopefully a full day of hard labor would help keep the memories in the back of his mind, and if not...maybe he'd just get drunk.

By midmorning the dreams were a distant memory and the headache was fading slightly. It was unseasonably warm, and he was working up a good sweat. There were some fences that needed mending out in the back field, but he'd get to that after he ran to town. He needed some wire from the hardware store, and he also needed a few things from the grocery while he was in town.

All the cows were out to pasture in the front field and the stalls had been cleaned and new straw put down. It was dirty work, and it was hard on the back, but the physical labor sure felt good. He'd been a farmer his whole life. He was still working the farm he'd been working since he'd been a boy. He never wanted to be anything else anyway. If Marie would have wanted him to quit farming though, and become a banker or lawyer, he would have. He'd have done anything for her.

He sighed. *There I go thinking about Marie again.*

He sat down on the big boulder he and his brother used to play on as kids and took a little water break. The warm sun felt good on his face. He was glad Marie accepted him for who he was. They truly were perfect for each other. He remembered back to when she first found out he was a farmer.

They weren't really dating, but he felt like they were. They ate lunch together every day since the first day he saw her. He sought her out that day knowing they were meant to be together. He played it cool at first, lightly bumping into her in line and grabbing her elbow to steady her.

"I'm sorry ma'am I seem to be a little clumsy today." He smiled down at her. "I've never seen you here before." Even though it was a lie; he had seen her twice already that day.

"It's my first day, and there's no need to be sorry; there's no harm done." She smiled back at him. "I'm Marie." She introduced herself.

"Hello Marie." His smile lit his eyes. "I'm your new best friend."

And from that moment on, they were best friends. They became inseparable. Taking walks after school, going to football games, talking on the phone at night. He was in heaven. It was better than he could have imagined.

It was about two weeks later when he walked her home for the first time and met her parents. They lived in a big house downtown. Her father was the new manager of the bank, and that made him nervous. He was only a lowly farmer. They would never accept him.

Over the next several days, he started to draw away, but Marie wouldn't let him.

"What's the matter with you?" she asked him one day after he skipped lunch. "Why have you been avoiding me?"

"What? I haven't been avoiding you; I've just been busy, that's all." But he couldn't look her in the eye, and he couldn't lie to her either. "Okay fine, I've kind of been avoiding you a little bit, but...it's...it's for your own good trust me."

She could see he was miserable and softened a little. "Come on tell me what's going on. I'm your best friend; you can tell me anything...besides it can't be that bad." She flashed him one of the smiles that seemed to melt his heart.

He smiled back at her. "You are my best friend, but that's not all you are to me, Marie. I love you. Hell, I'm in love with you."

She gave him a crooked grin. "Is that all silly? Don't you know I'm in love with you too?"

The feeling which spread through him then was one he would never forget, but his elation was short lived. "It doesn't matter, Marie; it will never work!"

"Why on Earth not?" she asked exasperatingly.

"Because I'm a farmer!" He flung out his arms in emphasis thinking it obvious.

"Okay?" she asked, thinking there must be more. When he didn't elaborate, she asked frustratingly, "What does that have to do with anything?"

"I'm always going to be a farmer."

"And...?" She was so confused.

He looked at her in frustration. "And nothing! That's it!"

She leaned up, kissed him lightly on the lips, and said, "Then I'll always be a farmer's wife."

Was it any wonder he was in love with her?

And as it turned out, her parents didn't mind a bit. Her father told him, "What a man does with his life is his choice. The world needs farmers boy. More than it needs bankers...that's for sure," and he laughed softly at his own self-deprecating humor and slapped him on the back. "We all gotta eat!"

He got up from his rock and realized he was starving and his headache was coming back. It was time to clean up and head into town. He'd stop at the diner for a late breakfast. Too bad he couldn't catch a nap. Man his head was pounding good. It usually did when he started thinking about Marie too much. This was always a bad time of year for him. Losing your wife so close to the holidays was a son of a bitch that was for sure. Not that it would've been any better any other time of year he reckoned.

He'd have to stay busy and try to keep his mind off it. And hope the blackouts didn't come. They always made him nervous. He didn't like missing time out of his life. It was usually only a couple hours at a time, but he still didn't like it. Luckily, he'd never hurt himself too bad. He had woken up with a few scratches on occasion and some other bumps and bruises but never anything too serious.

Best not to think about it, he thought to himself

A shower, a few ibuprofens, and the drive to town would do him good. He'd play the mixed tape he made for Marie on their one year anniversary. It was one of the few things he had kept from the wreckage. He'd been surprised but pleased to find it in the tape player when he went to get her personal effects from the car before it was crushed.

He'd go to town, get his supplies, and then come back and mend some fences. He'd be so exhausted when he was done; he'd have no choice but to sleep well.

2

Once upon a time in a land far away, a man named Peter decided that it was time to do what he was born to do.

"That is ridiculous. You can't start a book like that it's a cliché." Liz was reading over Tom's shoulder.

"Exactly; that's the point." He looked back at her with a stupid grin on his face.

"You're such an idiot." Her tone was playful, but she sort of meant it.

"Yes, but you love me anyway; now quit standing over my shoulder and let me get back to work." He was already pecking away at the keyboard.

With a kiss on the top of his head, completely out of habit, Liz left Tom to his book.

As she walked down the hall, she wondered, *DO I love him?*

She had thought she did when they moved in together. Over the past few weeks, she had begun to wonder if what she had thought was love was in actuality lust, and that was definitely fading away.

At 32, Liz was supposed to be at her sexual peak, but she wasn't feeling it lately. She was not beautiful by her standards, but although she had never noticed, she did manage to make heads, male and female alike, turn when she walked by. Regardless, Tom seemed to enjoy being seen with her.

To her own eyes, she was pretty much ordinary with straight long hair, a color her stylist called a dark strawberry blond, but to her only seemed reddish brown, mostly brown anymore. Her eyes, even she with her lower than normal self-esteem, thought were her most attractive feature. They were a bright, bold blue helped set off by her straight smallish nose.

She was of average height, five foot six inches, and as far as she was concerned slightly overweight. She was not fat or even husky; she merely needed to shed ten or fifteen pounds. But if you asked anyone else, they would tell you she had a great body with spectacular curves.

Tom on the other hand was gorgeous with jet black hair he was constantly swiping out of his eyes and that brushed his collar in the back. He had big brown puppy dog eyes which offset the sharp bone structure of his face perfectly. With a strong chin and a great mouth containing wonderfully full lips, he was definitely something to look at. And at 34, he was in great shape. Long and lean as they say; six foot even and perfectly toned.

So, what was the problem? she asked herself and sighed. *Oh yeah, looks weren't everything.*

He had been trying to write a book for three years. Well, not trying to write a book, but a publishable book, she corrected herself, but as the first line in this one reminded her, he wasn't a very good writer. Writing was something he loved to do though...

Yeah and I love yoga, but I'm not going to quit my job so I can exercise all day! She wanted to punch something!

He had already finished two other books, neither of which was worth the paper it was written on. His intentions were good, but he just didn't have the...imagination, was that it? Well, whatever it was, he sure as hell didn't possess it. And now, he had quit his job to write the great American novel, another cliché. And just how the hell was she supposed to support him on her salary.

She had finally finished school. It had taken her twice as long as most people to get her Master's, but she had done it and with help from no one. And not one loan to pay back either; which was why it took so long. And now, when she was already questioning her feelings for Tom, he decided to quit his job and rely on her to support him.

It kind of pissed her off to tell you the truth. I mean, they had only been living together for a few months. She had only been with the paper for about the same amount of time. Well, not counting her internship and freelance work.

As a full time journalist, she had only been with the paper for a few months. She was beginning to think the excitement of the job offer combined with the relief of finally finishing school may have been clouding her real feelings for Tom. Since those emotions had started to settle, she had been wondering more and more if settling wasn't exactly what she was doing on the romantic front. Maybe she was simply in a slump. Maybe she was just too stressed at work. Maybe she should talk to Tom and let him know how she felt.

To hell with the maybes; I'm not happy and my feelings for Tom, or lack of feelings rather, are definitely part of the problem.

Well, she didn't have time to think about it more this morning. She sighed as she looked at the clock; she had to get to work.

Another day at the paper.

She hadn't been there long enough to be having that thought be a bad one. But as she pulled into the lot behind the building that housed The Journal, that was exactly how she felt.

"Hey, Liz!" A handsome man of about five eight with spiky blond hair and moss green eyes approached her.

"Hi Jimmy, how was your weekend?" Liz hugged her friend, already in a better mood in his presence.

"Well, honey; let me tell you…"

And he did. No one could cheer her up like Jimmy always seemed able to. He was very, very gay and not a bit shy about it. He was telling her about his escapades at a new night club in town.

"Thanks Jimmy."

He looked baffled by the statement. "For what?"

"For making me laugh, I sure as hell needed it." She was grinning ear to ear.

"What's the matter honey?" he asked, concerned.

"Oh Jimmy, I have no idea; just a case of the blahs I guess." But now there were tears shimmering in her eyes.

Jimmy reached over to give her a comforting hug, but she stepped back.

"No...no I'm okay." Liz managed to blink back the tears.

"If you say so beautiful...now let me tell you about the fine looking gentleman that took me home with him Saturday night." Since she didn't want comfort, he'd give her distraction.

As they walked into the lobby, Paul Hodges, Liz's editor, was coming off the elevator. He stopped when he saw her.

"Liz, come here a sec," he called to her authoritatively.

"Shit. I'll catch you later Jimmy." She gave him an air kiss as she headed towards Paul

"Lunch?" he whispered before she walked away.

"Sure...sure," she said over her shoulder and walked over to where Paul was waiting impatiently.

"Walk with me." It wasn't a question, and she had to hurry to catch up as he started off.

"Is something the matter, Paul?" She felt like a fool practically running after him. *God he looks pissed.*

"To be honest Liz, we need to talk about your performance the last few weeks." He glanced over and down his nose at her.

"Listen Paul, I know I've been a little behind and barely making my deadlines, but..." *Shit...shit...shit!* She racked her brain for something to say. Luckily, she was spared her response.

He stopped walking abruptly and turned to her. "Liz, I'm not looking for excuses but results. I know that if you apply yourself to your work you would be great, but frankly, I'm just not feeling it in your work like when you started." His gaze was steady and intimidating. "I saw your potential when you were interning, and your freelance work always found a spot. I know it's still in there somewhere; you just need to find it. Now, I need your article on the

Cranberry Festival by six." He didn't wait for an answer; he turned on his heel and left her standing there alone.

Right, the Cranberry Festival; how exciting. "Don't worry, I'll have it done," she called after his retreating back. She shook her head. *How embarrassing.* She looked around; fortunately, it didn't seem like anybody had been paying them any mind.

God how she missed the freelance work, and the internship was great. She could write what she wanted doing freelance, and when she was "learning", she got to work in several different departments. Who would have guessed she'd get stuck in current events? It didn't sound too bad unless the events were the Cranberry Festival and car shows. The only thing that would be worse, in her mind, was Politics.

UGH, it's a foot in the door I know! She reminded herself that you had to start somewhere.

"Tom, I don't have time to talk right now; I'm already behind schedule. Let me call you back in…" She glanced at her watch, but he interrupted her. "No, I can't leave early…and I can't wait to see her either…" She rolled her eyes. "…but I can't leave early. I have to finish this article or…I really have to go, Tom…I'll call you back this afternoon. Bye"

She slammed the phone down and was tempted to throw it across the room; instead, Liz put her face in her hands and took several deep breaths.

"You okay honey?" A voice sounded behind her.

Liz jumped and turned to see Jimmy standing there. "Shit Jimmy, you scared the crap out of me." She put her hand to her chest.

He laughed a little. "You ready for lunch?"

"Damn, I forgot; I'm not going to be able to make it. I have this stupid article to write on the stupid Cranberry Festival and it has to be in by stupid six o'clock, and I can't seem to focus on getting it started let alone finished," she ranted in a huff.

Jimmy took a good look at his friend and realized she wasn't only having a bad day; she had obviously been having, at a minimum, a bad week. The makeup she was wearing did little to cover the dark circles under her eyes or the stress lines around her eyes and mouth. And right now, her eyes were very bright, the way eyes look when they are full of unshed tears. She looked dangerously close to shedding them.

So, he stepped into her cubicle and perched his hip onto the edge of her desk. "Spill it."

"There's nothing to spill." But she couldn't maintain eye contact.

"Honey, it is obvious that you haven't been sleeping right; you look exhausted, and you look like somebody just stole your dog. So, spill it."

"Gee, thanks!" She glared at him and pushed her hair behind her ear in an unconscious gesture.

He simply looked at her

"Okay fine! I just can't right now. I really do need to get this article in by six; Paul's already pissed off at me, and…" She broke off with a sigh when the hurt flashed through Jimmy's eyes. "Jimmy, I love you, and I promise that as soon as I get this article finished and turned in to Paul, I'm yours." She squeezed his leg lightly. "Six o'clock mister and you're mine; I'll meet you in the bar at Tony's, and I'll spill it all okay? I promise."

"Six o'clock. I'll just meet you in the lobby and we'll walk over together." He decided to let it go for now so she could get her work done. He pushed himself up from the desk.

"Thanks Jimmy I really do love you." She got up and hugged him.

"I know, honey; I love you too." He held her tight for a moment, and she laid her head on his shoulder.

"Now, get out of here so I can get to work!" she said jokingly but turned away quickly, so he didn't see the tear escaping down her cheek.

After Jimmy left her cubicle, Liz took a few more minutes to breathe deep and then jumped into the article full force. She would get it done damn it! Even though it was a stupid article on a boring festival.

At five after six, the phone on her desk startled Liz awake. She fumbled the receiver and managed to get it to her ear without dropping it.

"'Lo," she mumbled groggily.

"Liz?" replied a stern voice on the other end.

"Yes." She was instantly awake at the sound of Paul's voice on the line.

"I don't have your article," he pointed out obviously.

She winced and nearly groaned. "I was just on my way up with it," she lied flawlessly.

"Fine. I'll see you in two minutes." He disconnected without another word.

Shit, shit, shit!

Well, at least it's finished, and had been for close to an hour. *Thank God he had called instead of dropping by the cubicle. How humiliating; I can't believe I fell asleep at my desk.*

Liz hit print and shifted her feet anxiously, waiting for the article to do just that. She snatched it out of the printer tray and took off for the stairs; up one flight to her boss' office.

"Sorry, Paul; I was just doing a last minute proof before I came up," she lied.

"Sit down, Liz."

"Okay." She sat in one of the chairs across from his desk.

"Liz, you missed your deadline again."

She glanced at her watch and winced; it was six ten. "Paul, it's only ten after…"

"I know what time it is, and I told you six o'clock," he answered angrily. "Ten minutes late is still just that…late. I thought I made myself clear this morning that I needed this article at six this evening, and…" He glared at her. "…it clearly was not here at six."

He held up a hand to stop her before she could say anything. He came around to perch on the edge of the desk directly in front of her.

"You have been with the paper for over a year, first as an intern and most recently as a full-time journalist. You have excellent talent and great potential, but as I said this morning, you're work has been suffering these past few weeks. You have been missing deadlines left and right, and the quality of your work has been lacking. I'm not sure what the reason behind this change is, but right now, I think it would be best if you took some time away from the paper to figure things out."

She was stunned. *Is he firing me? Oh my God I'm getting canned!* "You're asking me to leave?" she managed.

"No…" He went back to his chair and the position of authority it granted him. "I'm telling you to leave. Your personal affects will be boxed up to be picked up in the morning." He began shuffling through the papers on his desk, already onto the next item on his agenda.

She was too confused and horrified to speak. *Fired? How did this happen?*

Realizing she hadn't left, Paul looked at her again. "Liz, I'm sorry about this, and I hope you can figure out what you need to get back to your old self." He didn't sound sorry. He sounded like a pompous ass.

She stood as he did and took his hand as he offered it.

"Good luck, Liz."

She left his office as if in a trance. She snapped out of it when she hit the stairwell.

Good luck! Good luck! The nerve of the man to offer her good luck after he just fired her! I can't believe I actually shook his hand! As she took the stairs back down to her cubicle to grab her jacket and purse, the reality of it still hadn't quite kicked in.

Jimmy was waiting for her in the lobby. His smile faltered as she drew closer, and he got a clear look at her face.

He closed the distance between them and grabbed her shoulders. "What is it? What's the matter, Liz?"

"I think I just got fired." She said it quietly, still not quite sure what had happened.

She was clearly in shock. He was now even more determined to take her out and make sure she had some fun. And, he was damn well sure going to make her talk.

When she got home that night, it was after eleven and the house was dark. As she pulled into the driveway, wondering why Tom wasn't still up working on his book, she took stock of her day. It was a bad one all right; it had started off bad. She woke up unhappy just like she had for the previous six weeks or so. She hadn't realized how her unhappiness had been affecting her work until the past couple of days.

As her thoughts drifted back to Tom, she put her key in the lock. That was when she remembered their hurried conversation before lunch that day. Tom's sister was in town. That was why he had called her late that morning at the office, and she had completely forgotten.

She was supposed to meet them for dinner right after work. She had told Tom she couldn't wait to see Sarah, his wonderful sister, but in reality she took a few minutes to thank God she had forgotten. She couldn't think of anything that would have made her already miserable day any worse than sitting down to dinner with that self-righteous bitch.

I hope she's not planning on staying here. The thought came even as she tripped over the suitcase sitting at the bottom of the stairs.

Trying to ignore her anger and the shame of her feelings, Liz headed into the kitchen to pour a glass of wine. She would take it into the bathroom and indulge herself with a nice long, hot bath. Her evening with Jimmy had gone a long way towards making her feel better, but now that she was alone, it all came flooding back.

She grabbed the phone, intending to check her voice mail before she put it on the charger, when it rang startling her.

"Hello," she answered, silently laughing at herself for jumping.

"Liz? Where are you?" It was Tom. "I've been worried sick. When you didn't show at the restaurant...well never mind, you're okay. Why didn't you come to dinner?"

If you were so worried, you could have called my cell phone hours ago. She didn't like to lie to him, or anyone for that matter, but said, "I had to work late; sorry I didn't call. Time just got away from me. I just now got in myself."

"Oh, okay. Well, we should be back in less than an hour; we'll see you then."

"Fine. Bye Tom." It looked like she had less than hour to relax; she better enjoy it while she could.

She tossed the phone onto the bed and proceeded to take a bath, forgetting all about charging it and checking her messages.

She awoke at around two a.m. with Tom's arm over her waist and his erection pressing into her back.

"Hey Liz, are you awake?" He started nuzzling her neck.

She didn't answer. She could smell the alcohol on him, and it was making her slightly nauseous. *Hopefully he'll think I'm asleep and go away.*

"Li-iz...I know you're awake. I can tell by your breathing. Come here baby; I have something for you."

Oh God. Why do drunken men think we find that cute and amusing? What an ASS! "I am really not in the mood, Tom; I had a really bad day; just go to sleep, okay." She pushed his arm off of her.

Tom pushed himself up in bed. "No, it's not okay. You've been blowing me off for weeks. What the hell's the matter with you? You're not sleeping around on me are you?" he asked indignantly, obviously miffed he wouldn't be getting some.

"Of course not; I have no idea what is wrong with me; if I did maybe I could fix the fact that I'm miserable." She sighed heavily; she definitely wasn't in the mood for this tonight.

"Miserable?" he asked. "What do you mean miserable?"

"I don't know." She sighed again and threw back the covers to sit on the edge of the bed. "I'm going to get a glass of water. Go back to bed; we'll talk tomorrow."

He followed her downstairs into the kitchen and grabbed her arm turning her to face him.

"No, we'll talk now." It was clearly a demand.

"For Christ's sake, Tom; it's two a.m. Do you really want to do this in the middle of the fucking night with your sister sleeping upstairs?" God, she was furious. She rarely ever cursed.

"Calm down, Liz." He rubbed a hand over his face

"Don't tell me to calm down," she said too calmly. It took every ounce of her willpower not to scream. "You're the one that comes home at two a.m. drunk as a skunk expecting to get laid, and because I'm not in the mood, you start accusing me of cheating on you?" Her volume increased with each word.

"I didn't accuse you…"

"Shut up; I'm not done." Her voice was dangerously quiet again. "You automatically assume that because I haven't given it up in two weeks that means I'm fucking someone else? Well, let me tell you something mister, the reason you haven't got laid…"

Something flashed in his eyes, and her anger changed to shock. "Wait a minute, wait a minute…" She held up both hands. "You haven't got laid in the past two weeks, right Tom?"

"What the hell is the supposed to mean? You think you can turn this around on me?" he replied defensively.

But it was too late; she had seen the truth in his eyes. "Who is it? You know what? Never mind; I don't want to know who she is, because you know what Tom? I really don't care. I'll be out of the house tomorrow."

He grabbed her arm as she turned to leave the kitchen. "Wait, Liz. Look, it only happened once…" At her steely glare, he let go of her and looked away. "Okay, maybe more than once, but she means nothing to me; I love you."

"You love me?" She spun back around angrily, but then she laughed. "You love me? Yet, you're off fucking God knows who? That's great, but you know what Tom? I *don't* love you, and I realized last night that I never really have. So, when I said I don't care…I meant…I. Don't. Care; I really don't. I'll finish out the night on the couch if you don't mind, and I think I'm going home to Jefferson tomorrow. Maybe your little side dish can move in here and support you while you finish another crappy book." *God that felt great!* She turned and headed towards the living room and the couch.

All he could do was stand there and gape.

Getting past the humiliation of being cheated on, Liz felt better than she had in months. She couldn't wait to go home and see her best friend Laura and her goddaughter Jenny. She would simply relax for a few days before she figured out what she was going to do with her life. Maybe she'd go back to doing freelance work and not just for the Journal.

Hell, not for the Journal at all, screw them! She felt a little guilty at the thought; she had learned a lot in her time there. But, the beauty about freelance work was you could sell your work to whoever wanted to buy it: newspapers, magazines, online news services, the sky was the limit. Laying on the couch thinking about the possibilities, Liz finally went back to sleep.

3

"Hello, Miss Mitchell; is Jenny home?" Melissa asked when the door was answered.

"Come on in, Melissa; she's up in her room, cleaning it I hope." Laura, Jenny's mom, shared a smile with the girl. They both knew how Jenny's room could get.

"Cool, thanks." Melissa walked up the stairs to find her best friend.

Melissa was a small girl even for her thirteen years. She had long black hair and a narrow face with a nose that was slightly too large for her face. When she reached the door to Jenny's bedroom, she didn't bother to knock on the half open door.

"Hey, Jen; what's up?" She plopped down on the foot of the bed her friend was laying on.

Jenny looked up from the book she was reading. "Howdy, Mel. Hold on a sec; I'm almost finished with this chapter."

Jenny was the only one who called her Mel. She kind of liked it. She didn't want everyone calling her that, but from Jenny it was like a best pal privilege or something.

Jenny looked like a shorter version of her mother, slim with shoulder length blond hair and bright blue eyes; she was also a book worm. She read all the time. She would rather read a book than watch TV, and she was even writing a book of her own; well, more like a compilation of short stories. She had several done already, and had only let two of her friends even see them. Melissa felt honored to have been one of them, even though she didn't really like to read.

"Whatcha reading today?" Melissa leaned over to see the cover.

"Flowers in the Attic," Jenny answered shortly, but not rudely, still trying to finish the chapter.

"Isn't that an old movie?"

"I don't know maybe." Jenny shrugged. "But, it's a damn good book." She looked towards the hall to make sure her mom wasn't in ear shot. She had only recently taken up cussing in the past couple of weeks. She still had never said the F word. She was working up to it.

Melissa, who cussed like a trucker when no adults were around, didn't even notice. "What's it about?"

"Too much to explain; it's kind of weird." Jenny held up a finger to hold her friend off for a minute. She finished the chapter and set the book face down on her desk to keep her page for later. "So, what's up?"

"Not much. I talked to Ruthie before I came over here and she said since it was so nice out they, her and Lisa, we're gonna go down to Jefferson park and just sort of hang out and shit. I guess." She had a habit of talking pretty fast. "So you wanna go hang?"

"Sure; let me ask my Mom. We goin' now?" She started searching her room for her shoes knowing they were there somewhere.

"Nothin' better to do." Melissa took over the whole bed since her friend had gotten up.

Jenny looked at her clock on the night stand. "It's already after twelve thirty now; I'll probably only be allowed out for a little bit. You know how my Mom is..." Jenny rolled her eyes. "...she doesn't think I'm old enough to be out hangin' around without an adult. Plus, I'm supposed to be cleaning my room." She looked around at the little progress she had made before she found Flowers in the Attic under a pair of sweat pants in the corner.

"I wish my Mom cared half as much as yours does," Melissa mumbled.

Jenny pretended not to hear as she walked out of the room to talk to her mom. She knew all too well the relationship Melissa had with her mother. A few times a week, Melissa would come to school with a new bruise she got bumping into the door, falling down the stairs, or any number of different reasons.

Contrary to all of her less than graceful failings, Melissa while in Jenny's company had never shown herself to be a clumsy sort. In fact, she was athletic and agile on most occasions. Jenny had even mentioned this to her, but Melissa always got real defensive and changed the subject.

Jenny had been suspicious of her friend's abuse for the past six months or so when the bruises started showing up fairly regularly.

Melissa's dad had left her mother almost two years before, and shortly after the divorce, her mother had started drinking more than normal; this Melissa confided in Jenny one night while they were spending the night together at Jenny's. After her mom lost her job a couple months ago, the bruises had started to show up more often.

Jenny didn't know what to do about what she suspected. She tried to spend as much time with Melissa as she could, inviting her to spend most non-school nights at her house when her Mom gave the okay.

Jenny was still pondering over what to do for her friend when she walked into the kitchen to ask her Mom about going to the park. She was tempted to tell her Mom her suspicions but was afraid Melissa would get mad at her if she found out.

"Mom, can I please go to the park with Mel? Ruthie and Lisa are going to meet us there." Jenny was using her sugar sweet with a cherry on top voice.

Laura looked at the clock on the microwave and gave it some thought. "What time would you be back?" she asked her daughter.

"I dunno. A couple of hours I guess." She shrugged like it was no big deal and grabbed an apple out of the bowl on the table.

Laura eyed the apple. "You need to eat a real lunch." Laura held up a finger to stop Jenny from responding. "And, there better be progress on your room." She added the last a little sternly.

"I'll make a sandwich before I go. Please, Mom. It's not that far, and I'm going to be with Mel, Ruthie, and Lisa. You can check my room..." Jenny shuffled her feet. "...it's not done..." *It's barely started* "...but there's progress..." *There will be if you give me a head start.*

Laura sighed; her baby was growing up on her. The last couple months, her physical maturity had really started to show, and that made her nervous for the next phase of her daughter's life. She sighed again; she knew she couldn't keep her daughter locked in the house, no matter how much she wanted to. Plus, it was nice outside and probably wouldn't be again for another couple months.

"Why don't you see if Melissa is hungry…" *and at least make it look like there's progress.* She knew her daughter very well. "…and while you two are eating, I'll think about it."

"Cool, thanks Mom." She knew her Mom would say yes at this point. She hurried upstairs to enlist her friend's help in a little stuff and fluff.

Twenty minutes later, as Jenny and Melissa were finishing their lunch of grilled cheese and tomato soup, Laura was still worrying over letting Jenny go to the park. She knew her fears were mostly unfounded, but she still worried. Jenny had just turned thirteen and, other than being a bit of a slob, was extremely responsible for her age…but, it wasn't Jenny she was worried about. It was everyone else.

It wasn't like it would be the first time Laura had let Jenny go to the park with her friends, but she never felt easy about it. After she got her first cell phone next week for Christmas, maybe it would make it easier. She looked over at her baby girl. She could see with her own eyes that Jenny was growing up, but she still thought of her as her *little* girl. Even though her *little* girl was already over five feet tall, was sprouting breasts, and had even started her period last month.

Laura sighed inwardly. "It's one o'clock, I want you back here at three thirty…" She held up her hand to stop the protest she anticipated. "...three thirty or you can stay home. You did promise you'd clean your room today..." She gave Jenny the stare down letting her know that she knew the state of her room was mostly a façade. "...and it still needs some work. Soooo, you'll be home at 3:30, so you can work on that."

Jenny didn't back down from her mother's stare, but she got the message. "Fine," she snapped for form's sake and turned to leave.

"Keep up the attitude, and you'll stay home anyway."

Jenny smiled at her friend then turned back to her Mom. "I'll be here. I promise," she said, knowing the routine.

"If you aren't you'll be grounded for the week, and it being Winter break from school, that's double the punishment it usually is." Laura knew Jenny wouldn't be late, but she was familiar with the routine just as well.

"Don't worry, Mom; I'll be here." All snippiness gone now, Jenny smiled at her mom.

"You know all the rules?"

Rolling her eyes in the process, she recited the rules she had been told since she was a toddler, "Don't talk to strangers, use the buddy system, don't take a ride from anyone even if I know them. And, I have my watch and will be home no later than three-thirty; I promise." *Blah, blah, blah...*

"Okay, be careful, and Jenny?" she called as Jenny headed down the hall to the front door.

Jenny looked back at her mother questioningly.

"I love you."

"I love you too, Mom." She walked back and gave her Mom a hug and kiss before heading out the door.

As they walked down the front steps, Melissa looked back at Jenny's house wistfully. "Your mom is so cool."

"My mom? You really think she's cool?" Jenny arched one eyebrow. She thought it was pretty cool that she could do it. Liz had taught her last year. "How d'ya figure?"

"I don't know." Melissa shrugged uncomfortable now. She hadn't meant to say it out loud. "She's not mean, and she likes to do stuff with you and..." She shrugged again. "I don't know...forget I said anything okay?" Still feeling a little uncomfortable, Melissa took off at full speed. "I'll race you to the corner."

Even with Mel's head start, Jenny handily beat her friend.

Barely even out of breath, Jenny turned with a grin and watched her friend take her last few strides gasping for air.

"How are you so fast?" Mel had her hands on her knees; she hoped the distraction would work.

Jenny laughed. "I can't believe it's so nice out today." She tilted her face up to the sun to bask in its heat. "Can you believe it's supposed to snow in a couple days though?"

Melissa smiled to herself. *Subject changed!*

When they got to the park, Ruthie and Lisa were already there, and so were a couple of other kids their age. Ruthie was a little on the chubby side with crazy red hair and lots of freckles and was very outgoing. Lisa, on the other hand, was pretty quiet most of the time. She was pretty with a strawberry blond tint to her hair, and she was willow thin in contrast to her cousin Ruthie.

"Hey guys; what's up?" Melissa yelled out as they approached.

The two girls waved in response.

"Hey, Jen; hey, Melissa; how's it?" Ruthie exclaimed excitedly.

Melissa merely smiled and tried to pretend she wasn't aware Joey Hamilton, Ruthie's older brother, was anywhere in the vicinity.

"So, what's on the agenda?" Jenny smiled as she approached the two girls sitting on the picnic table.

"Who cares; all that matters is that we don't have to go to school," Ruthie replied with a sly smile and did a little butt wiggle.

"True that sister," Lisa agreed, and they slapped a high five.

"So, Joey what are you and David up to?" This from Melissa, almost shyly.

"Just waiting for Billy to get off work, so we can go see the new movie over at Flynn's." He jerked his thumb across the street to indicate Flynn's Theater.

"What time does he get off?" Lisa was already plotting how she could spend some time with Billy.

"Not until 3 or 4..." He shrugged and tossed his slightly too long sandy brown hair out of his eyes (Melissa nearly swooned). "...or whenever his parents decide to spring him loose."

"I'll walk over to the store and ask him when he's getting off if you want," Lisa said slyly.

"It's cool; it'll be at least another hour." Joey shrugged again.

"I need something to drink anyway. Hey Jenny; you want to walk with me?" she asked her friend, knowing full well Ruthie would want to stay and flirt with David.

"Sure." She nudged Melissa with her elbow to get her attention. "Be back in a few minutes, Mel."

"Don't worry about me." Melissa grinned as she watched Joey and David walking towards the swings.

"So, you still have a thing for Billy, huh?" Jenny asked Lisa as they walked through the park.

Lisa blushed but shrugged. "Yeah, but I'm not sure if he likes me back."

"Have you asked him?"

"Of course not!" Lisa almost tripped. The thought was absurd! "Why would I do that!"

"Ummm...gee I don't know...." Jenny looked at her friend in exasperation. "So you'll know." *Duh!*

"I don't know? What if he doesn't?" Lisa asked unsure.

"What if he does?" Jenny responded quickly. "It doesn't matter..." She could tell her friend was uncomfortable "...let's just talk to him and we'll see what we see." Jenny winked at her friend and sprinted off towards the store.

"Jenny! Wait...." Lisa caught up to her friend waiting for her at the front of the store. "Please don't say anything"

Lisa looked very distraught. Jenny threw her arm around her friend's shoulder, and said smoothly, "Don't worry; I'm just going to observe."

They walked into the store laughing.

4

"I don't need your sympathy, Mark."

God, Laura hated it when he looked at her like that with those big sad eyes.

Mark Henderson was barely over six feet tall and slender with a lean, muscular build, dark hair and darker eyes. He was good looking in a dangerous kind of way, with sharp angular features. Not only was he one of Laura's best friends, he was also the chief of police in Jefferson.

"Look, of course I sympathize Laura; I care about you, and Jenny is missing! I feel sympathy whether you want it, need it, or not." What the Hell was he supposed to do? "I *feel* bad. I don't know what to say, damn it!" He turned and started to pace her living room.

When Laura called him at four o'clock with her concerns, he came over right away. Jenny's friend Melissa Rossi stopped by the house in a huff on her way home from the park to find out why her friend had ditched her. Laura knew right away something was wrong.

Jenny never missed her curfew regardless of the time of day, and she would absolutely never ditch her bf.

She called Mark right away and even rounded up all the kids she was with that day. They were at the house waiting to be questioned by the time he got there. He stopped pacing and looked over at Laura.

At five feet seven inches, Laura was taller than average with dark blond hair and bright blue eyes. She taught at the local middle school, and Mark often thought he would have done better in school if any of his teachers had looked like Laura. But right that minute, she looked so fragile and worn out. Rightly so too since Jenny never made it home that afternoon. She was obviously strung tight and frantic. He was proud of her for holding it together as much as she was.

Mark had been a cop in his hometown of Jefferson, Illinois for almost ten years. He graduated the academy a year and a half after he graduated high school. He worked as a cop in Chicago for five years, but shortly after he had been shot in the line of duty, an opening became available in his home town. He jumped on it. Now at thirty-five, he was the youngest chief of police Jefferson ever had. Every once in a while he missed the city and the excitement of the job in that environment, but he didn't miss the stress even a little bit.

Not that his job wasn't stressful. As the chief of police, he had a lot of responsibilities, but he didn't fear for his life on a nightly basis like he had in Chicago. Jefferson was more his pace and style anyway...a little more laid back and slower paced. Also in Jefferson, was Laura Mitchell, his best friend Jeff Post's little sister.

He'd always felt protective towards her for some reason, even more so since her husband died just over two years before. He knew

Laura was stubborn and would be severely pissed if she knew he drove by several times a night to check on the house. He had every night since Jack's passing.

Jack Mitchell, another of his good friends from way back and Laura's late husband, was a volunteer fireman. Two years prior there was a large house fire over on 3rd St. The structure was a complete loss, but minutes before it collapsed, Jack went back in to retrieve a young boy who was trapped inside.

He succeeded in the rescue attempt but died two weeks later of heart failure resulting from smoke inhalation and complications with his lungs. He had given the boy his respirator, and it had saved the boy's life but had doomed his own. Laura and Jack had been married for eleven years and had a ten year old daughter at the time of his death. Jenny was now thirteen and had been missing for over two hours.

"I'm not a kid anymore Mark, and I don't want your sympathy now or ever. Damn it! I just want you to find Jenny!" Her voice caught, but she managed to keep the tears at bay, for now at least.

Take a deep breath, she told herself and did just that. "Look, I know you're just worried about Jenny and me, and I appreciate that because I need my friends right now." And he was a really good friend. "But at this particular moment, I need Mark the police officer more, okay?" She looked at him pleadingly, needing him to understand.

"Okay." She was right. "Let's go through this one more time." She looked so miserable he simply wanted to hug her and comfort her, but right now he had to get back into cop mode for both their benefits.

He willed himself to calm down before he sat on the couch and pulled out his notebook. Not that he needed it, but it usually made the family of victims feel better...like something official was being done. He hated thinking of Jenny as a victim, but he needed to separate himself from this and get the job done.

The story hadn't changed from the previous times it had been told, and the fact was, there really wasn't much to tell. Jenny and a couple of her friends left the neighborhood to walk over to Jefferson Park to "hang out". Melissa and Ruthie, two of Jenny's friends, said sometime before two o'clock that afternoon Jenny left with Lisa Johnson, another friend, to walk over to Richardson's, the local grocery store. Lisa had wanted to see Billy Richardson who she had a crush on.

They were there for about half an hour when Lisa had to go home and check in. Jenny told Lisa she was headed back to the park, but she never made it there. So, in the mile and a half from the store to the park, something went way wrong. The problem was no one saw Jenny after she and Lisa split up, at least no one that would admit to it anyway.

"Someone had to see something. I just can't understand it!" Laura was exasperated! How could no one have seen a thing?

"Laura, I'm sorry, and I know I've asked this before, but is there any chance that Jenny may have run away?" Of course, he didn't believe it, but he had to be the cop here.

The question stung coming from Mark who had known Jenny since the day she was born. "I told you, Mark. No." She looked away from him.

"The last thing I want to do is upset you more, and I don't believe it either, but you asked me to be the cop here, and I would ask anybody else the same questions."

"I know. I'm sorry, but you know Jenny; she was happy. IS happy," she stressed.

"We'll find her," he assured her, getting up to look her in the eye. God he hoped he was right. Laura and Jenny were like part of his family. He would do everything in his power to find the girl, and he told her as much.

"I'm just so scared. I don't know what to do." The tears she had been trying so desperately to keep back finally broke free.

Mark pulled her close and held her tightly going from cop to friend instantly.

"I'm sorry," she finally managed after indulging in the tears and misery in the comforting arms of her lifelong friend. Laura pulled back and looked into Mark's eyes.

Mark got caught in her gaze for a moment. He finally blinked then cleared his throat. "Don't be," he replied taking a few steps back. "Are your folks on their way up?" He hated seeing her like this.

"Yeah, but neither of them drive very well at night anymore, so they'll probably stop halfway and sleep." She walked to the window and looked out on the empty street. "They should be here first thing in the morning."

"Good. That's good; what about Jeff?" Jeff, Laura's brother and Mark's best friend since birth, was a hotshot attorney in Chicago.

"He has a big case next week; he said he would come, but I told him not to." She needed to quit looking out the window. She kept expecting to see Jenny walk towards the house. "I know he's worried, but court might keep his mind off of it. He insisted on coming as soon as the trial is over, probably late Wednesday."

She blew out a breath on a long weary sigh and turned back towards Mark. "I think I'm going to...what?" she asked as she saw the look on Mark's face.

"Nothing," he said flatly, silently cursing his friend for not dropping everything to be there. His niece was missing! "What you need to do is try and catch a few hours of sleep."

He raised his hands to hush her as she tried to speak.

"No listen to me as a cop and a friend. You need to rest; you look like crap. I know you think you probably can't sleep, but you're not going to do Jenny or yourself any good if you get sick. I am on top of this..." He grabbed her shoulders. "...and I will not let you do this to yourself. If anything breaks you'll be the first one to know I swear it." He released her and crossed his heart "Hope to die..."

She smiled slightly at that. "Maybe you're right; I can't even think straight." She sighed. "But, I know I won't be able to sleep. Every time I close my eyes I see Jenny mutilated on the side of a road somewhere. I can't bear it, Mark; I can't." She turned away from him then, afraid the tears would come again. "It's almost Christmas." She said it so quietly he almost didn't hear her.

"I know." It was all he could say.

"I don't want to talk about it anymore right now."

"Okay, just sit here with me on the couch, and we'll talk about something else or nothing at all." He sat on the couch and patted the seat beside him.

She sat next to him and laid her head on his shoulder as he put his arm around her.

"So, how about them Bears?"

She chuckled, and the sound was music to his ears.

"We'll find her Laura. We will."

He said it with such force in his voice that she desperately wanted to believe it.

Mark sat on the couch with his arm falling asleep around Laura's shoulder. Laura was asleep next to him with her head still on his shoulder. He went over it again and again in his head, but couldn't figure it out.

How could no one have seen anything?

Every time he asked himself, the answer was the same. Someone had to, but why weren't they coming forward? Jefferson wasn't exactly a happenin' place, but it was nice that day. It had been a very mild December so far, never getting under fifty until that night.

Although the forecast for the rest of the week looked bleak, earlier that day had been sunny and sixty-two. There would have been people all over town. As a matter of fact, he had driven through town several times that day and remembered thinking exactly that each time he did.

He had gotten a list from Joyce, the cashier at Richardson's, of everyone who had been in the store within an hour before or after she had seen Jenny there. It wasn't a long list. He had already talked to all but two of the locals, which was damn near everyone on the list.

There was a couple with a small child in that day who had written a check for some lunchmeat, potato salad, and bread. They had told Joyce they were on their way home to Ohio and only passing through. The address on the check they paid with was indeed in Ohio, but he hadn't yet gotten a hold of them.

Another unfamiliar face seen by Joyce belonged to a man who used a credit card to buy a pack of cigarettes and a bottle of coke. His name was Jason Reeves according to the credit card used. He turned out to be a young man from Indiana who was apparently seeing Michelle Class, who lived in an apartment directly across from the store.

Michelle vouched for Jason's whereabouts since the cigarettes he bought were for her. And when Mark talked to him to find out if he saw anything, he claimed he was too hung-over to see anything that wasn't two inches in front of his nose. So, the only lead he had was on a young couple with a baby from Ohio, and they came into the store almost forty-five minutes after Jenny left. But still, it was possible they had seen something. Plus, he had two more interviews locally that might yield some important information.

He looked down at Laura's face as she slept. *The poor thing.*

Even in sleep she looked so miserable and unhappy. He really needed to get his last two interviews done and get back to the office. He had to finish up some paperwork on a couple other cases he had too, but if he got up, the movement would probably wake Laura.

She had been asleep for only about forty-five minutes, and he knew regardless of what he said, she probably wouldn't sleep much that night. She had fallen almost instantly to sleep after she sat with him on the couch, so Mark took the opportunity to run every detail they knew about Jenny's disappearance through his cop mind.

Even though he dreaded doing so, he might have to call in the FBI on this one. After all, kidnapping was their jurisdiction, but there was no evidence of kidnapping or foul play, and she had only been missing for a couple hours. That just wasn't long enough.

Not that he thought she wasn't really missing, but it was procedure to wait until they were missing for a certain amount of time and blah, blah, blah...it was bullshit. As a cop he didn't like the idea of the feebs getting his case, but as Laura's friend he would take all the help he could get. He had a guy he could call and maybe work it unofficially. He added that to his mental list of what he needed to do.

Laura awoke slowly as Mark tried to ease his arm from around her. "I didn't mean to wake you up, but I really need to talk to a couple more potential witnesses I couldn't track down earlier and then head back to the office and check on some things."

"How...how long was I asleep?" Her brain was still a little fuzzy from it.

Mark glanced down at his watch. "Less than an hour."

"Why did you let me...?"

He put his hands on her shoulders and brushed her lips with his casually. "Because you needed it; you should really try and get a full night tonight." He threw it out there, even though he knew it was futile. "Anyway, I'll stop by later tonight; call me if you think of anything, okay?"

"Yeah, okay." She didn't want to be left alone, but she knew Mark had plenty of other responsibilities besides finding her daughter.

As if reading her mind, he said, "Finding Jenny is my top priority Laura; give me a couple of hours then I'll come back and update you on any progress."

She was afraid the tears would come if she spoke, so she nodded and walked him to the door.

He opened the door but turned back to her. "I'll bring some Chinese back with me; you still like the sweet and sour pork right?" He wasn't ready to leave her alone.

She smiled because she knew that's what he wanted, but it didn't reach her eyes. "Yep, still my favorite."

"Are you going to be okay here by yourself?" he asked, taking in how frail she looked. "You can tag along with me if you want."

"I need to stay here in case Jenny comes back." She desperately hoped for that.

"Yeah you're right that's probably the best thing." He gave himself a mental head slap. He wasn't thinking like a cop and that needed to stop if he was going to find Jenny. He turned to walk down the porch steps before she could see the doubt in his eyes.

"I still need to call Liz and let her know what's going on." She wasn't quite ready to be alone.

"Tell her I said hi when you talk to her," he called over his shoulder. "I'll see you in a couple of hours."

She watched him get into the cruiser and drive off, knowing she was putting all of her hope and faith into a very capable person. *If anybody can find my baby, it's Mark.* She subconsciously put her fingers to her lips where she could still feel his.

She sighed a heavy sigh and shut the door. She grabbed her cell phone to call her best friend of 31 years and Jenny's godmother, Liz Metcalf.

Laura and Liz, they were practically sisters, and had pretty much been raised as such. Laura's Mom, Katlyn and Liz's Father,

Mick, had been friends since they were kids; they had even dated briefly in middle school.

When Katlyn married Michael, now her husband of 37 years, Mick had been the best man. The girls were born less than three weeks apart with Laura being older. They were practically inseparable all through school until Liz left after graduation to work her way through college.

Shortly after that, Laura had married Jack and earned her college degree taking night classes and correspondence courses. They still kept in touch regularly and visited each other as often as their schedules allowed, but over the last couple of months Liz had begun to drift away. Thinking about it Laura drifted back.

"Hi, Mr. Metcalf; is Liz home?"

"Hi, Laura; she's in her room; go on up."

"Thanks, oh and my Mom wants you to call her."

"Sure thing, Sugar." He patted her head as she walked by.

Laura giggled; she thought it was funny that he was always calling her Sugar.

"Liz?" Laura called as she went down the hall towards her room.

"Hey Laura, I didn't know you were coming over." Liz jumped up from the bed and the story she was writing and hugged her friend.

"I have a surprise," Laura whispered. "Can you come out?"

"Let me ask Dad." Liz ran downstairs and came back within minutes pulling her jacket off the bed.

"Okay let's go; I only have an hour and a half until I have to be back." They hurried down the stairs and out the front door.

Laura was eleven, and Liz's eleventh birthday was the following week. "You know today is the exact middle of our birthdays. I thought we should celebrate together."

"Laura, you are so sweet; I love you." She grabbed her friend's hand and took off running for Laura's house and the tree house in the back yard.

Laura insisted on going up first to make sure everything was exactly as she wanted it. She would never forget the look of surprise on Liz's face when she saw several of their friends among all the decorations in the little fort. And the lopsided little cake on the little table in the center.

"Oh Laura." Liz clapped her hands. "It's wonderful."

They had a nice little party. When everyone but the two of them had left, Laura gave Liz her present.

"A pocket knife?" Liz asked skeptically.

"It's actually for both of us." Laura smiled slyly.

"Okay?" Liz was obviously confused.

"I think we should become blood sisters. You know, friends forever?" Laura explained.

"Of course we will be friends forever." Liz didn't like blood.

"Well, yeah; but if we do this, it can never be broken, and then we HAVE to be friends forever."

"I don't know, Laura; can't I just promise?"

Laura laughed. "It's just a little cut, not even as bad as you scraped your knee when you fell at school last week."

"That really hurt," Liz pouted.

"You're such a wimp." But Laura hugged her close. "I don't ever want to lose you as a friend Liz; you mean too much to me. I think this is the only way. I'll cut your hand for you if you want."

"No, no, no...I'll do it myself...just give me a minute, okay?"

"I'll go first." Laura snatched the knife from her friend.

Laura opened the knife and without the slightest hesitation pulled the blade along her palm. Liz turned white but took the knife when Laura offered it.

"It didn't really hurt; it's only a little blood." Laura examined her cut curiously.

"You're such a tomboy." Liz laughed.

"You're just stalling."

Knowing her friend was right, Liz pressed the blade to her palm, closed her eyes, and cut her hand.

"Oooowwww!" Liz stifled the scream.

"It's not that bad..." Laura chided, "...and I'll bandage you up as soon as we're finished." Laura took Liz's hand. "Okay, now we say the oath of friendship and shake on it swapping our blood."

"What are the words to the oath?" Liz asked, not wanting to admit her hand didn't hurt as bad as she thought it would have.

"I don't know; let's try this...I swear by my blood mixed with your blood that we will be friends forever. How's that sound?"

"Sounds good to me; okay then on three...one...two...three." Now that the cuts were already made, Liz was actually excited about it.

They said the oath of friendship and shook on it. Laura kept her word and tenderly treated Liz's wound, she even kissed it when she was done.

The phone rang once and went to Liz's voice mail.

"Hey, Liz; it's Laura. I haven't talked to you in a few weeks. Look, I know you're busy and stuff, but I really need to talk to you. Can you call me back as soon as you get a chance? It is really important. It's about Jenny; she...just get a hold of me, okay? I'll talk to you soon. Okay anyway, I love you, and...well...bye."

Ugh! I hate leaving messages. I wonder if she'll call me back. "I miss my Lizzy Bear," she said to herself as she put the phone back on the charger. She rubbed the faint scar on her palm.

5

As Mark slid into the driver's seat of his cruiser, he pulled out his notebook to check the list of names Joyce had given him. Of the six locals that stopped in, he had already talked to four, plus all the employees and the stranger across the street. So, he had two more locals and the couple from Ohio.

He was pretty certain the couple from Ohio would be a bust, but he was going to follow all threads to the end. One of the locals left on the list lived only two blocks from Laura, so he headed there first. When he was done there, he'd go out to the country to interview the last potential witness.

He pulled up to a small cottage at the end of a dead end street and walked up to the door. He hadn't seen the resident that lived there for several years. She was reclusive and well into her eighties. Her children ran most of her errands for her, but for some reason she had gotten out earlier that day. Mark had thought her old when she taught him in Kindergarten and that was thirty years ago.

He knocked on the door, and several moments went by before it was answered.

"Hello?" She squinted up at Mark

"Hi, Mrs. Dawson; you're looking lovely this evening." Mark smiled down at the frail looking old lady.

Mrs. Dawson cackled and waved her clawed hand at Mark. "You always were a smart ass Mark Henderson! Come in out of the cold and close the door behind you." She turned and shuffled towards the living room.

After she was settled in her chair, she focused on Mark sitting across from her. "I'm assuming since you're in uniform this is an official call?" She smiled out of her overly wrinkled face, her eyes were twinkling. "Did someone file a noise complaint?" She cackled again, and it turned into a coughing fit.

Mark started to get up, but she waved him back into his chair. "I'm fine, boy-o...sit down, sit down."

Mark sat on the edge of his chair, ready to pounce back up if necessary. "Actually, we have a missing girl, Jenny Mitchell."

Before he could go on, she was interrupting. "I saw her at the store today, such a sweet girl; she helped me put my groceries on the belt. What happened?" The twinkle had left her eyes and was replaced by obvious concern.

"Actually, I'm hoping you might be able to help me figure that out...did you happen to see her talking to anyone, even someone you may know?" Mark leaned forward with his arms on his knees.

"The young grocer's boy, Billy and she were with another young girl; I'm not sure of her name. Her family is new to the area, but I've seen her around with all the others." She closed her eyes to better picture the scene from earlier. "Other than those two...I don't recall seeing her with anyone else." She opened her eyes and shook her head.

"Lisa is the girl's name and I've talked to all the kids she was with today already. Do you by any chance remember anyone who may have been at the store while you were there?" Maybe he could at least add to his list of potential witnesses.

She listed off a few names; all of whom he had already talked to.

"I appreciate your time Mrs. Dawson; I hope it wasn't an inconvenience."

"Don't apologize to me, just go find that girl...such a sweet thing...you find her Mark, and get her back to her Mama. I'm sure Laura is beside herself. They will both be in my prayers." She started to maneuver herself out of the chair.

"No don't get up." Mark got up to leave. "I can let myself out; thanks for your help." *Not that it really helped, but one more person praying for Jenny couldn't hurt.*

Heading out to the country to interview the final person on his list, Mark thought about Laura. How pretty she looked even when she was so upset. Her eyes simply glowed and her lips were so plump. He couldn't help but kiss her earlier.

Not that it was really a kiss, more like a slight brush of his lips, but he had felt the small jolt of electricity. He remembered the first time his heart fell for her; the first time he kissed her...well the only time he'd "really" kissed her.

He was 19 and home from Chicago for a quick weekend visit with Jeff. Jeff was taking pre-law courses at Northwestern, and Mark had just enrolled in the academy. One of their high school buddies was having a party back home, and Jeff wanted to go so he could break up with his girlfriend and start dating this "super-hot chick" he had met at college. Mark decided to tag along and ponder on his decision to become a cop.

When they got to Jeff's house and walked in, his heart stopped at the sight of Laura when he saw her at the top of the stairs. Man had she changed in the year or more since he'd seen her. All of a sudden, she wasn't the little girl that had always followed them annoyingly around everywhere but was a beautiful young woman. She came running down the stairs and threw herself in her brother's arms.

"I didn't know you were coming home!" she squealed excitedly. "I thought you were taking summer classes"

"I am, but we came home for the weekend to go to John's party. Don't say anything, but I'm going to break up with Missy this weekend so I can date this super-hot chick I met at college." Jeff was grinning ear to ear. "You're looking good sis; what are you doing tonight?"

Laura smirked at her brother. "Going to John's party..."

"The hell you are! You're not old enough to go to that kind of party. People will be drinking...." Jeff turned immediately into the protective older brother.

Laura interrupted, "I'm sixteen Jeff, and I was invited. I'm a junior, and besides, I hardly even drink when I go to these things. It's just fun to people watch." Jeff saw the gleam in her eye and knew she was lying.

"Fine, but you're going with us, and we're leaving early!" He knew it was pointless to argue with her; he had lived with her for sixteen years.

At the word us, Laura looked over at Mark coyly and smiled her beautiful smile with the cute little dimple. "Oh, hey Mark; I didn't see you there." The gleam was still in her eye but it had changed slightly.

Was she flirting with him? His heart skipped a beat. He swallowed and stammered, "uh…. Hey Laura…"

She looked back at her brother. "Fine I'll go with you; I'll call Liz and tell her I'll meet her there. I'll be ready in an hour." She turned and bolted back up the stairs two at a time, looking back once she reached the top. She looked right at Mark and smiled her dimply smile.

Later at the party Jeff was off with Missy, probably having some pre breakup sex. Mark had a little beer buzz going but wasn't really drunk. He felt drunker earlier when Laura smiled at him.

What had gotten into him?

Normally at these parties, he would be substantially more than buzzed by now and partying hardy with everyone, maybe even making out with a cheerleader. That made him think of Laura, and he wondered where she was for the hundredth time that night. He had only caught a couple glimpses of her throughout the night and hadn't seen her at all in over an hour.

He went outside to clear his head and came across Laura sitting on a bench under a tree crying.

"What's the matter?" He walked over and sat next to her.

She jumped at the sound of his voice and started wiping furiously at her tears. "Oh, hey Mark; I didn't hear you walk up..." She tried to smile, but her dimple didn't show. "What's going on?"

"I asked, what's the matter?" He grabbed her hand as she tried to get up from the bench.

"Nothing; I'm fine." She sat back down but wouldn't make eye contact.

"You're clearly not fine." He grabbed her chin gently and turned her head, forcing her to look him in the eye. "What's the matter?"

Laura sighed. He obviously wasn't going to let it go. "Really it's nothing; I'm just a little tipsy and got a little emotional...I'm fine." It was the truth, but the tears had begun to seep again. It really wasn't a big deal, but sometimes when she started crying she just couldn't stop.

Mark merely looked at her. Fine isn't how he would describe her. People who were fine didn't cry for no reason.

She sighed exasperatingly. "You're going to make a good cop." She wiped the tears off her cheeks. "Fine! I'll tell you. It really is nothing." She let out a long breath and just spat it out. "Pete broke up with me a couple weeks ago and I just saw him making out with Rachael in the kitchen."

Mark smiled at that. "Want me to go beat him up?"

That made her laugh and her dimples did show.

"No, I don't want you to beat him up. It really is nothing; he broke up with me, and honestly, I was going to break up with him anyway...he's really boring." She laughed again and put her head on his shoulder. "Thanks, Mark; you made me feel better." She looked up at him with the same gleam in her eye she had earlier. "Want to walk me home? I don't feel like going back in there."

"Yep, let's go." He grabbed her hand and pulled her up from the bench.

They walked in silence for the first of the two miles to her house. When they were walking by the park, she grabbed his hand and pulled him towards the path leading to the playground equipment. "Let's swing for a minute."

"What?"

"Come on, let's swing for a minute." She was showing her dimple again and he couldn't resist her. They walked hand in hand to the swing set.

They swung and talked for over an hour, about his fears of becoming a cop, about her wanting to be a teacher, about everything and nothing. They simply talked.

Mark stopped swinging suddenly and got very serious. "I better get you home before Jeff, or he'll be pissed."

"What's the matter?" Laura asked worriedly. "Why so serious all of a sudden?" She stopped swinging and looked at him intently. They had been having such a carefree and fun time she had thought.

What was he supposed to tell her, that he realized he had fallen for his best friend's little sister? No way... "Nothing, I just realized how long we'd been here and Jeff might be worried."

She could tell something was bothering him, but Laura looked at her watch and her eyes got big. "Holy shit, it got late quick." She smiled up at Mark, dimple and all. "It felt like 10 minutes not almost an hour and a half! Come on! I'll race you!" She was hoping he'd take the bait and forget about whatever popped in his head and made him turn into a sourpuss all of a sudden.

She took off at a full sprint, but Mark had much longer legs and caught her before she made it 2 blocks. He grabbed her waist with both hands and stopped her. She turned laughing into his arms. He was looking down at her. When her eyes met his, she stopped laughing, and they lost themselves in each other's eyes for a moment. Laura cleared her throat and started to say something; he'd never know what because that was when he kissed her.

He had kissed plenty of girls, but this was different. Everything stopped...as soon as their lips touched there was nothing but the two of them. It was almost unexplainable, the feeling...It was like energy coursing through his veins. His world tilted and his heart felt like it would explode out of his chest.

Their lips fit together perfectly as did their bodies. He could feel it all the way in his toes! Her tongue shyly rubbed against his lips, and he intensified the kiss. His head felt like it would explode as he explored her mouth gently with his tongue. He wouldn't have stopped, but he needed to come up for air, or he would drown in her.

He broke free and could barely think; his mind was blurry along with his vision. His head was spinning as he looked blankly down at her face. She looked so fragile looking up at him. She was breathing heavy. He shook his head to clear it, but it didn't work.

"Laura, I..." he started to say something, anything, but he was at a loss. She looked at him for several seconds then turned and ran from him. He couldn't follow her; he could barely stand up...his legs felt so weak.

He shook himself out of the memory as he turned down the long lane towards the farm house. He was nearly breathless from the memory of the long ago kiss. *What a sap!* He berated himself.

When he got back to the house, all those years ago, Laura was in her room with the light off. He and Jeff left early the next morning to go back to Chicago. He only came back once in the five or six years before he got the job in town and that was to attend Laura's wedding. They had never talked about the kiss.

He knocked on the old farmhouse door, and it was answered by a man Mark had known for years. He had bailed hay for the man when he was in high school.

"Mark? Everything okay?" the man asked when he opened the door. It wasn't often the chief of police came a knocking.

"Hey, Jim; mind if I come in?" Everything was not OK, but he wasn't going to talk about it standing on the porch. The temperature was dropping fast.

"Not at all." Jim opened the door wide. "I was just getting up from a nap; I started my day early this morning. I haven't been sleeping very well the past couple nights." Jim stepped aside so Mark could get through.

"Everything okay?" Mark asked him, noticing the dark circles under the man's eyes.

"I never sleep well this time of year..." He shook his head and waved his hand in dismissal of the subject. "It's nothing, just sinus crap from this weather...you want something to drink?"

"No thanks, and I won't keep you long; I just have a couple questions for you." Mark followed him into the kitchen where Jim got a bottle of water out of the fridge.

"Okay, have a seat and ask away." Jim pointed to a chair at the table. "You sure you don't want one?" He held out the bottle towards Mark.

"I'm good thanks." He waited for Jim to down half his bottle and join him at the table. "Well, I don't know if you heard anything or not, but Jenny Mitchell went missing this afternoon."

"What!" Jim nearly jerked out of his chair. "I just saw her this afternoon in town, what happened!"

"Well, we're not exactly sure; I was hoping you could help me figure that out." Mark had become pretty adept at reading people over the years. The absolute astonishment in Jim's eyes didn't give him much hope of finding any answers here.

"I'll try my best, what do you need to know?" Jim leaned in intently. He just couldn't believe it. He had just seen her.

"You said you saw her today, tell me about that." Maybe he had seen something and just didn't know it yet. In his fifteen years as a cop, Mark had also become pretty good at coaxing information from witnesses if it was there.

Jim rubbed a big hand over his face and tried to remember everything. "Honestly, there's really not much to tell; her and another little girl, they're fairly new to town and I don't remember her name, were at the grocery talking to Billy. We left about the same time.

"I talked to her for a few seconds, you know just small talk…like 'you sure are growing up little girl' she laughed and said 'sure beats the alternative' we laughed and that was pretty much it. I was parked right out front. I got in my truck and left. When did she come up missing?"

"As far as we can tell, pretty much right after that. Lisa, the girl she was with, and Jenny split up a couple blocks after you talked to her. Jenny was supposed to be heading back to the park to meet up with the rest of her friends. Somewhere in that mile and a half she disappeared. Did you notice anyone suspicious lurking around, or did anything seem off to you?" *Please have something for me.* He tried to will it to be true.

Jim thought hard for a minute. "I'm sorry, Mark. I've got nothin'." He shook his head. "My brain has been kind of foggy and I really wasn't paying attention. I've pretty much been asleep since then and still feel exhausted. I think I might be coming down with a sinus infection or something." He finished off his bottle of water. "But, I'll think about it and let you know if I can think of something…"

He stopped for a minute remembering something else. "You know, I did see Jacob Riley, you know old man Riley's boy, driving through town, looked like he might've been coming from the bar. He's always suspicious if you ask me; at least since he started drinking himself into the ground after his wife died."

Mark asked for a list of any other names of anyone he may have seen while he was in town. Everyone else was already on his list. He thanked Jim for his help and went out to his cruiser

Well, I added one new name to the list. He glanced at the clock on the dash. *I think it's still early enough to run over and have a chat with Jacob.*

Old man Riley's farm was only a mile or two down the road. When he pulled in, the house looked dark. Jacob had moved back into his childhood home several years ago after he had a mental breakdown after his wife died. He spent seven days in the mental health ward after having a violent episode about a week after her death. He destroyed everything in their house.

Mark was working in Chicago at the time, so he didn't remember all the details. Jacob usually seemed harmless enough though. After being released from the mental health ward all those years ago, he moved in with his father, and all he seemed to do was drink and work the farm. There hadn't been anything violent on his record since the one incident, and he had somehow never gotten a DUI, even though he frequented Hank's, the local bar, almost daily.

He was obviously a functional drunk. Old man Riley wasn't able to work the fields anymore, but the Riley farm was one of the more productive in Jefferson with livestock and crops. Mark looked at the house and hoped it wasn't too late to catch Jacob at least semi-sober.

At the very least, he may have seen something. It couldn't hurt to talk to the man.

Mark climbed onto the porch and knocked loudly on the door. A couple minutes later, old man Riley pulled open the door.

"Yup?" He was only wearing a pair of boxers and had clearly been woken up.

"Hi Mister Riley, is Jacob home?"

"Sleepin'." The old man started to shut the door in Mark's face.

Mark stopped the door with his foot. "Is there any way you could rouse him for me, sir?" The man glared at him. "It's pretty important that I talk to him."

Old man Riley looked at Mark for a long minute then gave him a slight nod, pointed to the couch, said "Give me a sec," and shuffled off down the hall.

Mark sat on the edge of the creaky couch and waited a lot more than a second. When Jacob finally came in, the smell of alcohol was very strong.

"What do you want?" Jacob asked without sitting down. "I'm trying to sleep and haven't done anything wrong."

"I just have a few questions for you, Jacob. Would you mind sitting down for a minute?" Mark motioned to the chair across from him. He was impressed that Jacob was barely slurring. Based on the smell of alcohol pouring off him, he was pretty intoxicated.

"I'll stand thanks. Let's do this so I can get back to bed; my head is killing me." He was being a little snippy, but he just wanted to sleep; he had just gotten there when his dad woke him.

"Well, I don't know if you've heard yet, but as of this afternoon, Jenny Mitchell is missing." Mark stood to look the man in the eye. "You were seen around the area about the time she came up missing."

"I wasn't anywhere today but the diner for a late breakfast. I didn't see no kids there." Jacob turned to head back down the hall, but Mark grabbed his arm.

"You know her then?" Mark responded, taking notice of his use of the word kids. He was getting a little tired of Jacob's attitude.

"Little blond girl?" Jacob shrugged. "I know who she is; but I don't really know her." He shook his arm loose from Mark's grasp.

"You were at the diner, huh?" At Jacob's blank stare, Mark continued, "Okay, well when you left the diner where did you go?"

"Maybe I stopped over at Hank's and grabbed a beer." He looked away quickly.

"Do you know about what time you left there?" The man was hiding something.

"Not exactly, but I don't like to drink and drive." He looked away again. "So, it wasn't too long after I got there; maybe noon."

"Really? I have a witness that says you were driving through town at about two p.m."

"I didn't really look at my clock."

"You didn't by any chance see two young girls walking between Richardson's and the park did you?" Mark pressed.

"Nope, I wasn't paying attention to anything but driving. Can I go back to bed?" He looked at Mark, clearly uncomfortable.

Mark held eye contact for a full minute before responding. "Yeah, but I'm going to check out your story, and I might have a few more questions for you."

"Fine." Jacob turned and practically stumbled out of the room.

Old man Riley was nowhere to be seen, so Mark let himself out. He needed to head back to the office to put everything he had (what little there was) together.

Back at the office, Mark made a couple phone calls to check on Jacob's story. Jacob lied; he was at Hank's for four hours and had not one beer, but several along with a few shots of whiskey. Hank was hesitant to tell him at first since he probably shouldn't have let the man drive away, but when he found out a missing girl was involved, he spilled it pretty quick.

Jacob most assuredly had been lying because he didn't want to admit to driving drunk. But, if he lied about that, what else might he have lied about? He'd go back out and talk to him tomorrow and see if he could persuade him to remember a little better.

After organizing all his notes, Mark slammed his hand on the desk. *There's nothing here!* He was half tempted to sweep all his papers onto the floor out of frustration.

Other than Jacob, who claimed to have seen nothing, everybody saw the same thing; which was pretty much nothing. Everyone who actually saw Jenny only saw her when she was still with Lisa. Not one person saw her after she and Lisa split up, but someone had to see her. She hadn't run away. He knew that for a fact. Jenny would never put her mother through that. She would lock herself in her room and give her the silent treatment sure, but not that.

So, what then? He tapped his fingers on his desk.

That left kidnapping, and if there wasn't a call in for ransom by now, chances are there wouldn't be. He didn't want to think about what that might mean. So, he called the local paper and had them run an article on the front page of the morning's paper offering a reward for any information leading to Jenny's whereabouts.

He scanned the picture he had of Jenny in his wallet and emailed it to Lance Stone at the paper along with information on where and when she was last seen. Maybe the article would jog some memories. It was a nice day, so there could have been any number of people out and about. Anyone could have seen something that may not have seemed suspicious at the time. He felt good about the article, but it wasn't enough.

He picked up the phone and called a buddy of his in the FBI. "Hey, Mitch; it's Mark Henderson. How's everything going?"

"Mark, long time no see brother; I'm okay. Work is a little stressful, but that goes with the territory." Mitch chuckled. "But, you know that don't you? How's small town crime treating you?"

"Actually, that's why I'm calling. I'm not asking for official help yet because it's only been a few hours." Mark looked at his watch, saw it was already almost nine o'clock, and changed his statement "Well, maybe more than a few but only about 6 or so hours." He told Mitch everything.

"You sure she isn't holed up at a friend's house?"

"I've known this girl her whole life Mitch; she's missing not hiding," Mark replied a little testily.

"I'll take your word for it, buddy. Send me her picture and I'll get the word out, unofficially, for now."

"Thanks, Mitch. This one's kind of personal for me. And, I really don't want to fuck it up."

"Sounds like you've done everything you can so far. You've talked to everyone who may have seen her at the store; what about any of the other stores downtown? Anybody see her walking or talking with anybody else through the storefronts?"

"Nope. She only passed two other stores before turning towards the park. That's when her and her friend Lisa split up. City Hall was closed since it's Saturday; then it's just the park. Her friends were on the other side of the park, and it's all trees to that point.

"There may have been other people in the park, but there's no telling who." He rubbed a hand through his hair and sighed. "I've got an article running in tomorrow's paper, front page with her picture, asking for any information, and offering a reward. I don't think there's anything else I can do tonight. I keep going over the same things again and again. It's driving me crazy." Mark got up to pace his office.

"I know how that is. Sometimes you have to take a break from it and come back at it fresh in the morning. You might miss something because you're over thinking it. Let your subconscious work on it for a while," Mitch suggested.

"I know you're right Mitch; I just don't know if I can do that with this one. I can't turn it off." He plopped back down in his chair.

"Then maybe you should turn it over. Call the county guys in. I'm sure there's someone you can trust up there. Besides, they'll be better equipped for a search if you need to do one."

"Yeah, maybe you're right. There won't be any searching until tomorrow. It's too dangerous out there when it's dark. Besides, we'd have to know where to search." It was bugging him not knowing where to even start looking. "I've already been over every inch of the park. And if she was in town, we'd know it." Mark rubbed his hand over his face as he sighed. "I appreciate your help, Mitch. Please let me know immediately if you hear anything at all."

"Of course; try to get some rest man; seriously, get some sleep tonight and come at it fresh. Call your guy at the County first thing in the morning; I know you have one. We'll find her." But, he didn't sound too convincing.

After Mark hung up the phone, he sat there for a minute tapping his fingers on the desk. He picked up the phone and ordered Chinese. He saved all his notes on the computer and headed out to go tell Laura he didn't find her daughter and pretty much had nothing more than he had earlier.

Day 2

6

He was in his old horse barn. He recognized it immediately even though he hadn't set foot in there in years. It was dingier than he had kept it, and it was dark. He was in the old storage room. The light from the main part of the barn was shining, and the room was dimly lit.

From across the room, he heard a muffled groan. The room in reality wasn't very big, but in the way of dreams, he seemed very far away. Eventually, his eyes adjusted enough to allow him to see who made the noise he had heard.

He was shocked to see his wife; his wife as she was the first time he saw her; before he had even known her name.

"Marie!" he called frantically from across the room and started to go to her, only to find he was chained to the wall. He fought against his restraints furiously, but he couldn't break free.

He kept yelling "Marie!" over and over until he realized she couldn't hear him. It was like he was watching through a two way mirror. He could see what was going on, but no one knew he was there. Now that he wasn't in a frantic attempt at escape, he noticed Marie was also chained.

Suddenly, there was someone else in the room with them. He watched his wife cower from the large man. The man slapped her face, hard; he saw blood fly from her nose on impact. He could hear the man as if from far away. It was a voice he recognized.

"Why did you leave us, Marie? You ripped our heart out. You must be punished for leaving us. Now it's time to rip your heart out, so you know how it feels."

He struggled again and started screaming. "NO! Leave her alone!" The restraints were cutting into his skin, but he didn't care. "Marie! Marie!"

Then it wasn't Marie in the room anymore; it was another woman who looked very similar to Marie, then another, and another, and another. Her face kept flashing back and forth between Marie and a dozen or so women, some only girls, until finally the man did what he had threatened, and with the help of some sharp farming implements, ripped her heart out of her chest.

The man held the heart in his hand and said, "Now you know how it feels Marie." He laughed insanely. The man turned to walk from the room, still holding the heart, and he saw his face for the first time.

He let out a blood curdling scream and then...

He sat up in bed breathing heavily and covered in a cold sweat. The scream was still echoing through his head. He didn't remember the dream, he never did, but he knew he wouldn't be sleeping again.

Two really bad ones...two nights in a row. He tried to slow his breathing.

And, he had blacked out again. He remembered getting in his truck but not getting home. He didn't tell the Chief that part of his day. He had come to in the field with the cows, which wasn't so bad. He'd come to in worse places. The worst probably being a rest area four and a half hours away with a broken nose and a shirt covered in what he assumed (hoped) was his own blood.

He needed a quick shower to get rid of the smell of terror sweat on his skin. He opened the bottle of ibuprofen in the medicine cabinet and popped four in his mouth and chewed them up, hoping they'd kick in quicker. His head was pounding again. He washed the taste down with some water, and then splashed some on his face. He looked in the mirror but quickly looked away. He definitely looked as bad as he felt.

After the very long, very hot shower, his headache had eased slightly. He got the coffee going; mentally kicking himself for not starting it before the shower, so he could already be drinking it. He went out front while he was waiting, grabbed the morning paper, and breathed in the fresh air.

Boy it sure did drop quick out here. He shivered as the cold wind bit into his skin.

He went back in to pour a cup of coffee and read the paper. He wondered if he ever got the fence mended. He had gotten what he needed the day before from the hardware store before he went to the diner. He'd have to check the truck. He cursed the blackouts knowing the chances of the work being completed were slim to none. And yesterday would have been the perfect day to do it.

The sun had been shining and the temperature may have reached sixty at its peak. He opened the paper and flipped it to the back page to the weather section and sighed. High of twenty two with a wind chill of nine.

He shivered thinking about working out in the cold. Not that he minded the cold so much, but when there's a fifty degree change in how cold it felt from one day to the next, it made it feel that much colder. He flipped the paper over so he could read it, and immediately saw a picture that made his heart jump for a second. At first glance it looked like his late wife. Then he realized it was Jenny Mitchell looking up at him from the front page.

It was an article about the girl being missing. He instantly felt bad for forgetting about the girl. For crying out loud the police had just been there the night before asking if he had seen anything. He had been up for hours unable to sleep from thinking about it; his headache worsening with each breath. Finally, he had fallen into a restless sleep.

The nightmare had erased all thoughts of Jenny though. He read the article. He hoped they found her. She really seemed like a nice girl, and she was very cute, he considered as he looked at her picture. He reflected on the similarities between her and his wife, and a pain shot through his head.

It was blinding. He fell from his chair knocking over his coffee cup, clutching his head with both hands. He was on the verge of passing out because it was simply too much, and then there was nothing.

He stood up and reached down to pick up the paper he had dropped. He looked at Jenny's picture. "Marie, you'll pay for leaving us...you'll know how it feels...soon...you'll know."

He balled up the paper and threw it across the room and walked out of the house leaving his broken mug and spilled coffee where it lay on the floor.

The walk to the back barn didn't take him long, and he barely felt the cold. Things were different when he was in charge. He entered the barn and took a deep breath. He turned on the light and looked around. He had a feeling like it was going to be a good day. He went into the old tack room to get what he needed to punish Marie. He started whistling, it was an old tune, one that was on the cassette they made for Marie that they listened to yesterday on their way back from town.

He spent a few minutes trying to decide what tool would be best to punish Marie. He finally decided on the old sickle. He tested the blade to make sure it was sharp enough. He smiled at his reflection in the blade and headed to the old storage room to have a talk with Marie.

7

Her head was pounding something fierce. She went to reach for the spot where the pain was centered, but her motion was stopped with a clank.

What the...? Realizing her hands were chained, Jenny started to jerk her hands furiously.

But it was to no avail....her wrists were bound too tightly; there was no chance at escape. When she felt the blood running down her arms, she stopped. It wasn't until then the panic began to set in.

It was pitch black, so she couldn't see anything, but that didn't stop her from trying. She searched her surroundings frantically. Nothing. Once again, she tried to free her arms. She started kicking her legs only to find they were bound as well.

Finally, exhaustion took over. The pain, gone for a moment with the adrenaline rush from the panic, started to set back in. She tried to figure out what was going on; the last thing she remembered was being at the store with Lisa, and that was pretty fuzzy.

A light suddenly appeared in the distance. After a few moments with the distant light, her eyes adjusted enough to take in some of her surroundings. And then, her other senses kicked in. She could smell old moldy hay. She could feel the cold draftiness chilling her skin, which was sweat soaked from her panic attack. She could taste dried blood and salty sweat on her lips.

I'm in some kind of old barn, Jenny reasoned. *What's that noise?* She strained to hear. *Is that whistling?*

It sounded like someone whistling a tune. She started to call out for help but stopped herself, realizing whoever was whistling could be whoever had tied her up in the first place. She sat frozen for several minutes, not knowing what she should do. She was blissfully unaware her few moments of indecision may have saved her life.

She heard creaky footsteps coming in her direction. Subconsciously, she tried to make herself smaller and curl in on herself, but her restraints limited her movement. When the light came on overhead, it momentarily blinded her (it wasn't that bright, but she was looking right at it without knowing) and caused a fresh, sharp jolt of pain in her head. She yelped and tried once more to cower closer to the corner away from the man who entered through the doorway.

"Don't worry Marie…"

Marie? He thinks my name is Marie! "My name is Jenny."

"Now Marie, let's not be silly."

Marie? Who is Marie? The name rang a bell though…all of a sudden, she remembered what happened.

She had split up with Lisa a few blocks earlier and was about halfway to the park. This part of town was eerily quiet for such a nice day. She was starting to feel a little nervous at how quiet it was, but then she heard a vehicle turn down the road from behind her and start in her direction.

She chuckled at herself and took a calming breath. She had read too many books by R.L. Stine and V.C. Andrews. The truck drove past her then stalled and veered to the side of the street until bumping the curb...the driver fell getting out of the truck and went to his knees clutching his head. She recognized the man and ran to help him.

The man was a local. She knew him, sort of, had seen him probably at least once a week for her entire life. They knew each other's names and even exchanged a few words now and again. He was up by the time she reached him, but she asked him if he was okay. He was still clutching his head like he was in pain, but he turned to her at the sound of her voice and smiled. His eyes looked different and his voice was different than she remembered.

"Hello, Marie. I thought you had left. You lied to us again." He sounded very angry.

Marie? Who...? She started to back away slowly. "Are you okay, Mr....?"

Before she could finish, he grabbed her neck and slammed her head into the side of his truck.

She tried to get herself free once more, but her attempts at escape were just as unsuccessful this time as earlier, and before too long her wrists were so raw she couldn't try anymore. The man approached her slowly from across the room.

"It's okay, Marie…I'm only going to rip your heart out like you ripped out ours." He said it so matter-of-factly; he could have been commenting on the weather.

The man, who she knew but didn't know, had a long handled sharp implement in one hand and the same creepy smile from when he kidnapped her. He stepped up close to her and leaned in.

"You shouldn't have left us Marie," the man said in a harsh angry whisper. He was close enough that her face was sprayed with spittle and she could smell mint on his breath. The man looked at Jenny curiously. "Why did you leave us?" he asked, emphasizing his anger with a sharp slap across the face.

Jenny was too scared to respond.

He stood up and started to pace, once again clutching his head like the day before when all this craziness began. There was a loose board in the floor, and every time he stepped on it, it would creak loudly. All Jenny could do was stare and hope she was dreaming. But, she knew she wasn't dreaming.

She was in too much pain to be dreaming. Her shoulders were cramping from her hands being tied above her head. Her head was still pounding, her wrists were raw, and she could taste the fresh blood dripping down her face into her mouth from where he had slapped her.

He turned to her then with the same crazy smile and said in a slow obviously insane voice, "It is time for you to pay for leaving us Marie." He laughed, and it chilled her to the bone. He raised the tool in his hand like he was going to strike but stopped suddenly, jerking his head to the right. He looked like he was listening intently.

He looked back at Jenny and said quietly, "Don't worry, Marie; we will finish this later."

He turned and walked from the room turning the light off behind him.

After a few minutes, she heard people talking faintly, but she couldn't make out what was being said. She began to think whomever he was talking to might be able to help, when she heard someone screaming. She heard, "OH MY GOD, OH MY GOD...LET ME GO!" but then it stopped abruptly and there was silence.

She had a feeling her potential savior was no longer going to be able to help, and she started to cry. She tried to do so quietly hoping the crazy man (that was how she thought of him now, not by the name she once knew him as) may have forgotten about her in the excitement. She heard his footsteps pass the room she was in, and she breathed a sigh of temporary relief.

Eventually, she heard footsteps coming towards her again. She began struggling against her restraints, even though she knew it was useless.

8

"It's cold," Billy complained as he and David made their way out of the woods.

And it was. It was the first really cold day of the year, and since the sun wasn't up yet, it was bone deep. Billy felt like an idiot.

"You're just chicken," David countered.

He may be Billy's best friend, but right that minute, David was getting under his skin. He could think of hundreds of better ways to spend the second day of his Christmas vacation (like sleeping), and none of them included farm animals.

"Nuh uh." He wasn't chicken; he was just freezing. *Can you even really tip a COW?* he wondered. He looked around and hoped, not for the first time, they wouldn't find any cows.

"Well then, come on." David picked up the pace.

"What if someone sees us?" Billy nearly whined.

"Chicken," David persisted, flapping his arms. "Bok, bok….bok."

"Fine, let's just hurry; I'm fr-freezing," Billy relented as his teeth started chattering slightly. Billy shoved his friend playfully to get him moving again.

They were the same age. Well, close enough anyway. Billy was two months three days younger than David. Billy would be thirteen next weekend. He was several inches taller than David though, and most everyone else his age, with fair skin, muddy blond hair, and bold green eyes. His Mom always told him they looked like emeralds, but Billy didn't really know for sure because he'd never seen a real emerald.

David was a stark contrast to his friend with a smooth olive toned complexion, dark, nearly black hair, and eyes a rich brown. Regardless of the differences in physical appearance, the boys had been best friends since they could remember.

Billy was quiet and laid back, where David usually couldn't stop talking for more than two minutes and was always looking to get into something. Today, that something was cow tipping. Vince, one of David's older brothers, told them how he and Pete Martin once tipped a cow, and of course, David jumped on the idea.

But, Billy couldn't get his mind off of Jenny Mitchell and the fact that she had gone missing right after he had seen her at the store the day before. "Hey, what do you think about what happened to Jenny?"

"I dunno." David shrugged. "They don't know what happened, do they?" He looked at Billy, who only shook his head. "Do you think she ran away?"

"I don't think so." He thought about it for a minute and shook his head. "No way man, I just don't see it. I mean, she has no reason to; her mom is pretty cool, and they definitely love each other..." he trailed off because David didn't seem to be listening anymore. He was used to that.

They started to creep around a large run down and seemingly unused barn. At least now, they were out of the bitter wind. They were heading towards a field on one of the local farmer's properties where the cows were hopefully (or hopefully not in Billy's mind) out to pasture. It was dark out, even though the sun should be making an appearance fairly soon. Mr. Riley, the town eccentric, said the snow was comin' in within the next couple days, but the sun was supposed to be bright until later that evening. He was rarely ever wrong about the weather.

"Chief Henderson came and talked to me again after we all left her house yesterday, since I was one of the last ones to see her." Billy wasn't done talking about it after all. It was really bothering him.

"Do you think she's dead?" David asked.

Billy couldn't imagine Jenny dead; he was having a hard enough time grasping the idea of her being missing. He'd had a crush on Jenny ever since kindergarten, but being the quiet type had never said anything to anyone about it, especially Jenny and not even David.

"I don't know; I hope not! But, I am kind of worried about her, and my Mom is being all 'don't go out alone' and 'don't talk to strangers' and all that."

"Yeah mine too; they're just doing their jobs."

At a creaking sound, Billy stopped.

"Did you hear that?" he asked in a harsh whisper.

"Quit bein' chicken and come on."

"SHHH! Listen," Billy insisted.

David did hear something, but what was it?

"It sounds kinda like a rusty porch swing," Billy reflected out loud.

"No, it sounds like..." But he never got to finish. David was interrupted by a maniacal laugh coming from inside the barn.

The boys looked at one another with a curious but uneasy gleam in their eyes.

"What was that?" Billy asked with a hushed urgency.

"I don't know," David answered in a similar tone. "But I sure as heck ain't gonna stick around to find out." They both took off running.

Billy tripped right before turning the corner of the barn towards the front. David, not realizing Billy wasn't with him anymore, kept on running around the corner. As he was about to pass the barn door, a man stepped out and David ran right into him, not even budging him as they collided. The man reached out to keep the boy from falling and grabbed hold of the shoulder of his jacket.

"What are you doing out here boy?" he demanded.

"N-n-nothin', sir," David stammered.

David was petrified, not because he was caught doing something he wasn't supposed to, that happened all the time, but because something just didn't seem right. The man, whom he had known damn near his whole life, didn't really look like he remembered. But he did at the same time; it was strange and not easily identifiable.

He was still tall and wide and rough looking like most farmers, with leathery skin and lots of unruly dark hair under his straw hat. Something wasn't right though, but he couldn't put his finger on it.

Something about his eyes? He had goose bumps all over, and it had nothing to do with the cold.

"Well, you better get on outta here boy before I need to fetch your papa and tell him you were sneakin' around on my property."

"Yessir. I-I didn't mean nothin', I just..." David turned his head and looked into the barn as he started to talk; he couldn't finish, couldn't even think anymore.

Billy landed flat on his face, and damn it, his ankle hurt like hell. He looked back to see what tripped him up and saw a large rock protruding up out of the dirt. Figured, he was always doing something like this. He hadn't quite grown into his feet at that point and was used to stumbling all over the place. But that didn't make it less embarrassing; not that David ever made fun of him or anything, but still.

It took him a few seconds, but eventually he heard the man's rough voice. He crawled towards the corner to peek around and see what was going on. He saw David standing in front of a large man. He couldn't tell who it was right away, but he could tell he had a hold of David, and he sure sounded mad. He heard David say something, but couldn't quite make out the words. He heard the man perfectly though and felt like he should recognize the voice, even though he couldn't place it right off.

"Well, you better get on outta here boy before I need to fetch your papa and tell him you were sneakin' around on my property."

He heard David start to stammer again, then stop abruptly as he looked into the barn.

What the heck is going on here? Billy wondered. *Why doesn't he just let him go?*

Then he heard David start screaming and kicking. "OH MY GOD! OH MY GOD! Let go of me. LET ME GO!"

David got a good kick into the man's right shin and broke free of his hold, but the man was too quick. Billy saw for the first time the man, whose voice he sort of recognized, was holding something in his other hand.

What is that thing called? Billy asked himself.

It was a sickle, one of those farmer's tools for cutting down wheat or some such thing. Billy wasn't entirely sure because his family were grocers not farmers. They owned the small and only grocery store in town.

Even as Billy tried to put a name to the tool, he saw the man swing the sickle at David, who at that moment turned towards Billy, crumpled to the ground.

Billy was horrified at what he thought he just saw. *This can't be happening. There is no way this is happening.*

The man was now leaning over David's limp body.

What is happening? Billy asked himself, still unable to believe what he was seeing. *Did I hit my head when I fell? This can't be real; no way is this really happening.* His mind was reeling, and the nausea was beginning to set in.

Billy had enough sense left to duck back around the corner of the barn before the man saw him as well. He was too shocked to move farther than that though. An instant before he ducked back around the corner, the man looked up and Billy recognized his face in the quickly brightening sky; he was one of the store's regulars. He had seen him yesterday, but the voice didn't quite match the face.

He could hear rustling noises from around the corner. After a few minutes, he risked another peek around the barn and saw nothing but a dark spot on the ground where David had been only a few minutes before.

He was numb, but whether it was from the cold or from shock, he had no idea. He didn't even know what shock was, but he was numb and his mind was getting fuzzy.

Did I really just see one of my regular customers, someone I've known my whole life, nearly slice David in two with that sickle or whatever the thing was called? Pretty sure it's a sickle though. Mr. Jones from up the road talked to him in the store about farming now and again. *Yeah it's a sickle, almost positive.*

"Who the heck cares what the damn thing is called? Did it really happen?" Billy muttered to himself under his breath.

After about ten minutes of huddling behind the barn, he knew he had to find out. He didn't think of himself as brave, heck, if he stopped and thought about what he was about to do, he would most likely get the hell outta there. He should go tell someone. His Dad would know what to do.

"But what if I'm wrong? What if I hit my head harder than I thought and I only *thought* I saw…?" He hoped to God that was the case.

Billy peeked around the side again. There was definitely a dark spot on the ground in front of the barn door, but that could be anything; it didn't have to be David's blood. David was probably still running on through the woods not even realizing Billy had slipped and fell. That crazy laugh really got them both movin' hadn't it?

Billy shook his head to try and clear out the fuzzy feeling; it was getting harder and harder to remember exactly what he had actually seen, or thought he'd seen anyway.

The man was nowhere in sight and neither was David. Good. Maybe it wasn't real, but then why could he still see the look of shock and pain in David's eyes and hear the sound like a gurgling stream mixed with a groan David had made before his eyes went blank.

He didn't even scream. He should have screamed, then it would seem real.

He took a deep breath then started slowly around the corner towards the still open barn door. He was still on his hands and knees, but about halfway there, he stood up and shuffled slowly the rest of the way.

Billy took several long slow breaths. *I have to go in and make sure David's not in there.* He was scared brainless.

He took the first step through the door. He looked around and noticed several stalls on either side of a large open area. There were several chains with big hooks on the end hanging from the rafters towards the back of the dilapidated old barn. It looked as if something was hanging from some of them.

Bodies? Billy froze in shock and confusion. *Are they real? Wouldn't dead bodies smell?* The stench that permeated the air wasn't what you would associate with a decomposing corpse. It was more of a musty, moldy smell.

He tried to look away, but he couldn't take his eyes off what had to be the most horrifying thing he had ever seen in his life. He and David had seen some pretty gory movies, but even good special effects couldn't have prepared him for this.

There were eight of them, eight bodies in varying stages of decay, from mostly bones to an only partially decomposed corpse. All were hanging from their chests...with their heads tilted back. As Billy walked through the barn slowly, he was unable to take his eyes off the horrific sight. A muffled sound broke his trance, and he snapped his head towards its source.

David! He remembered why he was there.

As he approached the sounds, they got louder.

Chains? It never occurred to him the man may be the one making the noises, and that if he were caught in the barn, he would surely die and be the next one hanging from a hook.

As he passed the last stall on the right and turned into an old storage area, Billy could think of nothing but finding his friend. But, what he found made him move quickly and start to think more clearly.

Jenny! He ran to the wall where Jenny was chained.

She was curled up in the corner of the small room bound in chains. Her wrists were attached to the wall, and her ankles were chained to a table which appeared to be bolted in place. There was dried blood on her wrists and face; her hair was matted with it.

"Oh my God, are you okay?" He was whispering, but his tone was urgent. "Jenny can you hear me?" He reached out to shake her, but she jerked away from his touch. "Jenny, it's okay; it's me, Billy."

She lifted her badly bruised face to look at him. The recognition was slow to come, but when it did, the relief in her eyes was evident.

"Billy, are you really here?" she asked desperately in a hoarse whisper. "Please tell me I'm not dreaming."

He wanted to kill whoever had done this to her.

"I'm really here, Jenny." He laid a comforting hand softly against her battered cheek. "I'm going to get you out of here."

"What if he comes back?" She looked petrified. "Billy, he was going to kill me. Just a few minutes ago...I...I thought he was going to kill me, but...b-b-but he left. His laugh, oh my God, that laugh." She started to cry.

Billy gathered her as best he could in his arms to comfort her. "It's okay, Jenny; you don't have to worry anymore. I'm going to get you out of here." He didn't know how yet, but he was going to help her.

He eased back from her to take a better look at her constraints. He tried to pull the chains from the wall, but they were solidly attached.

"I can't budge it. I'll be right back." Billy bolted up and out the door.

Once out the door he crept slowly, believing what he saw outside fully now but knowing he had to help Jenny.

He killed David. He maintained enough sense to keep quiet but couldn't stop the tears from falling.

He went quietly through the stalls looking for something to use to help break Jenny free. He avoided the door at the back of the barn assuming that must be where the farmer had disappeared to.

A few minutes later, he reentered the storage area and put some things on the table. His search hadn't come up completely empty handed.

"I couldn't find anything to break you out of those chains. I'm going to have to go for help unless you know where the key is."

All she could do was shake her head.

"Okay, I'm going to go get Chief Henderson. He's been looking for you." He picked up the things off the table. "I found these."

He showed her a rusty sliver of metal which could have been the blade of a knife at one time and a few dusty burlap bags.

He held up the sliver of metal. "In case he comes back before I do." He shrugged.

"What am I supposed to do with it?" Jenny wiggled her hands which were still in shackles.

"I don't know...stab him?" He felt stupid. "I can try and stick it into the wall by your hands so you don't have to try and hold onto it but can still reach it if you need it." *God I hope she doesn't need it.* It wasn't very sturdy or he would have tried to pick the locks with it.

He wedged the "knife" between two barn slats and left it protruding enough for Jenny to get ahold of if needed, but where it wouldn't be seen unless looked for. He covered her as best he could with the burlap bags. It was a lot colder today than yesterday, and she was definitely not dressed for below freezing temperatures. He pushed as much of the pile of moldy straw she was sitting in around her legs and back to try and keep her warmer.

A glint of hope edged its way into her mind. "Please hurry, Billy," she whispered, not wanting him to leave her but knowing he must.

Billy kissed her cheek and promised to hurry. As he made his way back to the front of the barn, he heard movement in the back room and what may have been whistling. He hurried out the same way he came in, and as he turned the corner of the barn, he heard that awful laugh one more time. He prayed Jenny would be safe until he made it back with help.

The woods were less than half a mile away. He didn't want the man to hear him leaving, but he didn't want to risk being seen either. He sprinted to the edge of the woods surprised he hadn't tripped on his face.

I have to help Jenny. He kept telling himself that over and over as the image of David's lifeless body kept trying to creep back into the front of his mind. *I can't think about that; I need to help Jenny.*

As he came to the edge of the woods, he had to slow down to maneuver through them. He still managed a good trot even through the woods heading...*hopefully* he thought...towards town which was nearly five miles away. Help would be there in an hour or so if he hurried.

9

Early the following morning, Liz's feeling of elation had ebbed a little, and the realization that she was jobless and now homeless came crashing in. She picked up the house phone because her cell was dead. She forgot to charge it last night.

After only one ring, a recorded message came on the line... *You have reached James Christopher with The Chicago Tribune; I am unable to take your call right now, please leave me a message and I'll get back to you as soon as I can.*

"Hey Jimmy, it's Liz. Listen, I found out last night that Tom was cheating on me, and don't worry I'm fine with it. I realized before last night that I didn't love him anymore and probably never did, but anyway, I am leaving town.

"I'm going home and that feels good; I think I need it. I just wanted to let you know I wouldn't make lunch today after all. I'm heading out here in just a few minutes. God, I'm going to miss you, call me any time okay...well not right away...my cell phone is dead, anyway, I'll talk to you soon; I love you."

She hung up the phone; it made her sad to realize that in all the years she had been in Chicago, first working and then working her way through school, Jimmy was the only person she cared enough about to say goodbye to. "I'm not going to let it get to me," she mumbled to herself as she swiped at the tears quietly streaming down her cheeks.

A couple hours later her mood was up again...she was going home!

"Black crows on the blue sky, always making a mess..." Liz sang along to her favorite band, HoneyHoney, in her very off key voice as she drove her Chevy Cavalier towards Jefferson. *Almost there. I'm almost home.*

She hadn't been back in a long time. And for the life of her, she couldn't figure out why when the feeling in her heart was an almost overwhelming joy at being home. She hadn't lived there in thirteen years, but she would always think of Jefferson as her home. She had grown up there, grown bored there, had to get away from there. She remembered how trapped she had felt at eighteen with her diploma in her hand and her sights on the city.

She laughed when she passed a familiar spot on the edge of the woods. She was remembering when she and Laura and a couple of the boys they knew, and had known most of their lives, had skipped school one day in the spring of their freshman year. Laura had insisted they go to Fox Creek to go skinny dipping. Liz wasn't thrilled at the idea, but the boys were ecstatic.

She could still picture Laura running through the woods with John and Malcolm's clothes, laughing her beautiful laugh. Liz had laughed so hard she fell and sliced her cheek open on the branch of a fallen log. She had needed stitches, and that was what inevitably got them caught skipping school. She rubbed the faint scar on her cheek.

As the memory faded, shame at the way she had treated her lifelong friend in the past few months took over. *What a bitch I have been. God I miss my Laura Bean.*

She hadn't called Laura back in over two months. She kept telling herself she was too busy and would get to it later; she even ignored her call the night before, but now as she was only a couple miles out of town, she realized she was not happy with the way her life had turned out. It hadn't turned out anything like she had planned; yeah she had gotten the job of her dreams, or would have if she wouldn't have screwed it up, but that hadn't made her as happy as it should have. It did at first, but...

As a matter of fact, the last time she talked to Laura was to tell her about the full time journalist position she was finally offered. No more freelance work. She thought that would make her happy. She realized she hadn't been truly happy in a very long time...too long.

Well, it's time that changed. She thought to herself with her infamous steely determination.

I have to help Jenny.

That thought and that alone was what kept Billy going. He was fast, but he was a clumsy kid; he fell the first time only thirty feet into the woods. He caught himself with his hands and managed to slice open his right one on a rock. He cursed the pain it brought but kept going.

I have to get help.

He fell yet again, this time down the slope to Fox Creek, striking his head on a rock. He laid there blacked out for what seemed like an hour but was actually less than five minutes. He was exhausted and didn't want to get up.

While lying there after coming to, he saw some large birds watching him from a tree across the creek. The realization they were eyeing him as potential dinner sent an ominous shiver down his spine. Everything came crashing back; knowing he had to keep going in order to help Jenny, he forced himself up.

He ran...through the pain in his ankle from his earlier fall, the throbbing headache, the terrible burning in his lungs, and the multiple cuts and scrapes from the spills he had taken on his desperate flight through the woods. He looked back only twice to make sure the man hadn't heard and pursued him. That was what caused two of his falls though, so he quit looking.

I have to get help...Jenny.

He was out of breath; other than his short nap by the creek, he had only stopped twice to try and catch it. He could see the road now, and he sped up a notch knowing he was close. He kept going as he broke out of the woods knowing he could run faster on the pavement. He didn't stop, wouldn't stop.

Jenny needs me. I have to help her.

He heard, in the back of his mind, the screeching of tires and then everything went black.

She barely had time to react. The man just came barreling out of the woods right in her path. Liz slammed on her brakes and pulled the wheel hard to the left. She thought she was going to miss him completely, but as she came to a stop, she felt the thud of her right rear fender make contact.

Breathe, you need to breathe. Before getting out to survey the scene, she took a few seconds to calm herself down.

She approached the still form with a heavy dread weighing on her chest. She crouched down next to the man.

No, he's not a man. Only a boy, she realized. The dread grew heavier, but her wits were starting to return.

She checked for a pulse; the tears coming with the relief when she felt one. She checked for breathing. When she felt the soft wind of it on her cheek, she pulled out her cell phone and called 9-1-1.

"9-1-1 operator can I help you?"

"Yes…uh…I…uh…just hit a person?" Apparently, her wits hadn't returned completely. She was sweating even though it was cold, and she was starting to feel anxious.

"Tell me exactly what happened."

"I was driving and he just ran out in front of me," Liz said hurriedly. She started to pace running her hand through her hair over and over.

"I need you stay calm please miss," the operator stated sensing the panic in Liz's voice. After she heard a long breath on the other end, she continued, "Okay," she said calmly, "where are you?"

"He's just a boy." Liz said it so quietly.

"Miss what is your name?"

"Liz Metcalf."

"Listen to me Liz, we are going to help the boy; I just need to know where you are so I can send help." The operator was used to directing conversations to where they needed to go. "Now can you tell me where you are Liz?"

"I am, uh...on..." She looked around trying to get her bearings. "I'm sorry. Give me a second." Liz closed her eyes and forced herself to calm down.

"Liz? Liz are you still there?"

"I'm here," she stated. "I am on Central just outside of Jefferson..." She was back. She could handle this. "...I was heading south into town and the boy ran out of the woods. I managed to almost avoid the collision entirely. I think I just bumped him." She took another look at the motionless boy lying at her feet.

"He looks pretty beat up, scratched and bruised, but I don't think that it's from the accident." She knelt down to look at his face.

"Do you suspect any neck or head injuries?" The operator decided to take advantage of the lucid caller while she could.

"I'm not sure; he has a pulse...it's strong," Liz answered. "And he's breathing, but he is unconscious. I haven't moved him."

"That's good. Don't; I have an ambulance on the way, as well as the Jefferson police." The operator let out a breath. "They should be there any minute."

"I can hear the sirens now. Thank you." Liz disconnected as she continued to study the boy's face.

He looked sort of familiar. He looked like John Richardson, one of the boys they had stolen clothes from all those years ago, but a little taller, with lighter hair and fairer skin. She sat next to him holding his bloody hand while she waited for help to arrive.

10

Laura was pacing her living room listening to Mark update her on Jenny's case. It was only nine o'clock in the morning, but neither of them had gotten much sleep the night before. So, the day already seemed well under way.

He had finally gotten a hold of the couple from Ohio early that morning. There was no help there; they barely remembered even being in Jefferson. He believed them; he almost wished he didn't so he would have something to work with.

"There's really nothing new I can tell you." And it pained him to know it. "We're not sitting idle though...I did call Deputy Miller, my contact from the Sherriff's office. He's circulating Jenny's picture, and he also forwarded it to Channel 8 so they can broadcast it on the news. We're taking the awareness county wide, but..." He took a deep breath. Here was the part he hated having to tell her. "They're reluctant to authorize a search because, well, where do you search? There has to be a starting point. We've been all over town..." He looked at Laura as she stopped pacing and looked him in the eye. "But we are still looking Laura, and we will find her." God, he hoped so.

Being a cop, he knew each minute that ticked by in the case of a disappearance reduced the likelihood of finding the person alive. He didn't want Laura to see the doubt on his face so he turned to look out the front window.

"I read the article this morning…. I really appreciate you doing that Mark." She knew he was worried too, and she needed to remember that. This case was more than a job to him.

She had known Mark most of her life and could read his facial expressions as clearly as her own. She knew he was trying to hide his doubt and concerns from her, but she also knew and understood the statistics as well as him. She had spent plenty of her sleepless night on the internet researching kidnappings and disappearances, so she knew, but she refused to believe they applied to her Jenny.

When he turned back to face her, his face showed nothing of his doubt, only the fierce determination he held. "Hopefully it will bring us some leads," he said, referring to the article.

"Thanks for all of your help, Mark," Laura said quietly. Oh yes, she could read his face well, and there was no mistaking the flash of anger in his eyes.

"Thanks? You don't have to thank me. That's ridiculous." It was his turn to pace. "Thanks for the help," he muttered and then turned his steely glare on Laura. "I love her too."

"I know you do Mark, and she loves you." Her heart softened a little. *I'm not the only one this is affecting.* She had to keep reminding herself of that.

They were both steeped in their own thoughts when Mark's radio chirped. Laura jumped, and Mark stepped into the kitchen to call in.

A few minutes later, he came out and headed straight for the door.

"I have to go; a pedestrian was struck out on Central." He was all cop now. "An ambulance is already on the way; I need to get over there."

He looked over at Laura as he put his hand on the doorknob. He saw the raw terror on her face.

"It was a young boy. I don't know who yet." He walked over to her and gathered her in his arms for a quick hug. "I'll be back as soon as I can." And he walked out the door.

She didn't know if she should be relieved it wasn't Jenny or upset. She would never wish that kind of an accident on her only child, but simply knowing where she was would have been a godsend. With all of her emotions gone haywire over Jenny, Laura could barely find a place for compassion or concern for the boy who was hit. Not that she wished him harm; she hoped the boy was okay. She was just so focused on Jenny.

"Laura?" her mom called out as she came in the kitchen door.

"In here Mom," she called back from the living room.

Her parents had arrived early that morning. When Mark had shown up, they ran to the store to pick up a few groceries allowing Mark and Laura to talk things over.

"Oh, I thought Mark would still be here," Laura's mom Katlyn said as she walked into the living room to find Laura alone and staring out the front window. "I've got eggs and sausage for breakfast, some lunchmeat and potato salad for lunch, and I'm going to make my famous red sauce for dinner."

"He had a call." Laura turned and tears were shimmering in her eyes.

The look on her face was so miserable...Katlyn could barely contain her worry for her daughter and granddaughter. But she knew she had to try and stay strong for her baby.

"Michael, go ahead and start browning the hamburger, will you? The sauce needs to simmer for several hours to be perfect," Katlyn called back into the kitchen where her husband was putting away groceries.

"Of course, Honey," he called back.

"I'm so glad you and Dad could come up." Laura walked to her mother and put her arms around her for an embrace she desperately needed.

Katlyn led Laura to the couch and stroked her hair as they sat together and shared their tears. The two could be twins if they were the same age. Katlyn was a little bit shorter, but other than that, the resemblance was remarkable.

"She's a tough girl Laura, just like her Mama." She continued to stroke her daughter's hair hoping it was as comforting now as it had been when she was a child.

"I know that Mom, but I can't quit thinking the worst." She sniffled as the tears dried up for the time being. "I don't want to believe any of the pictures that keep popping into my head, but...I don't know." Every time she closed her eyes, she would see Jenny in some kind of predicament or danger.

"Honey, thinking the worst is a Mother's job." Katlyn chuckled. "You have no idea how many times I stayed up late worrying that you or your brother were dead on the side of the road somewhere. But here you are." She gave her daughter another pat on the shoulder and a kiss. "I'm going to go check on your father before he burns down the kitchen." She needed a moment. She couldn't hold back her own breakdown much longer.

As she walked through the doorway into the hall, she looked back at her baby girl sitting with her elbows on her knees and her head in her hands. She looked so young and fragile. She would do everything she could to help her baby get through this, no matter the outcome.

"Go be with your girl, Michael," she said to her husband as she walked into the kitchen.

"Kat, I don't know what to do for her." He looked so miserable especially for such a big man. He was slightly over six two and quite broad, with dark hair just going gray at the temples. And big brown eyes that could make your heart melt. "I just want to make everything right."

She walked over to him standing at the stove. He was looking super cute with the pathetic look on his face and the spatula in his hand, dripping hamburger grease all over the counter. She wrapped her arms around him and kissed him full on the lips.

"What you can do is be here for her. Go talk to her; I'll take care of the sauce…" She took the spatula out of his hand. "…and breakfast." She shooed him out of the room, afraid to say another word. The damn was about to break.

When she was alone in the kitchen, she indulged in the sobs she didn't want to let loose in front of her daughter.

"Hey, Sweetheart; how are you holding up?"

Laura looked into her father's eyes as he walked into the room and saw he was suffering just as much as her.

"I'm okay, Daddy." She put on the brave front. "We'll find her. We have to." *It's as simple as that. I have to find my baby.*

"Of course we will, baby." He sat with her for a while, and they talked about work, about the Bears and the horrible season they were having, again, and they talked about Jenny. Not her being missing, but good times they had shared together as a family.

Kat walked towards the living room to the sounds of laughter. She stood in the hallway and listened outside the doorway to her husband and daughter take a walk down memory lane.

"Do you remember when Jeff brought that bitch, Melissa, call me Lissa, to Christmas when Jenny was three?"

"Yeah and my granddaughter told her flat out that she didn't like her, and she wasn't allowed back in her house ever again." He was laughing almost hysterically. "That girl is walking spitfire."

"And they had only known each other five minutes." Laura let out a sigh. "She always did say what was on her mind." She laughed. "And she was right about Lissa; she was awful. I can't believe Jeff stayed with her as long as he did." She shook her head wondering what her brother saw in some of the girls he had dated.

"Well, the boy never did have much taste in women...well, at least in the brains department; he could always pick a looker though."

"Remember Suzie the gymnast? I think she only had an IQ of fifty." Laura laughed again. "I bet she had other qualities he found more important at the time." She laid her head on her father's shoulder and they sat in silence for a moment.

"You picked a good one though sweetheart," Michael said solemnly after a moment.

The last thing Laura wanted to do right now was think about Jack. Her emotions were already in an uproar over Jenny's disappearance, but she got up and walked over to the picture of Jack and Jenny she kept on the end table next to the couch. It was the last picture taken of Jack; they were at the carnival, and Jenny was showing off the goldfish her daddy won for her.

"Remember when Jack won her the goldfish when the carnival was in town? That thing only lasted two days, but she insisted on having a full ceremony in the backyard…" She clutched the picture to her chest and turned back to her father. "…and when we found the bird with the broken wing in the backyard last year and she nursed it back to health?" Laura went on, "You know she wants to be a vet. She has even been checking out books about it from the library." The tears were running down her cheeks again.

"She's a smart girl; she can do anything she wants."

The mood in the living room had changed to a somber one, so Kat walked into the room and announced, "Breakfast is about ready."

"Okay, thanks Mom. You guys go ahead; I'll be there in a minute. I need a moment"

Reluctantly, they left Laura alone.

In the kitchen with her husband, Kat stepped into his arms and laid her head on his chest. "I don't know what to do for her, Michael."

"We just need to be here for her Kat; that's all we can do." He gently stroked his wife's hair as he held her close. Neither noticing their roles had reversed from earlier.

"God, I hope Jenny is okay," she said quietly. "Where could she be? What could have happened?" She couldn't understand how this could be happening to her family.

"Mark'll find her. I have every confidence in that boy." Michael believed it. He was worried, but he was confident Jenny would be okay when they found her.

"I hope you're right Michael." It was a mother's job to worry after all.

"Honey, after all these years you haven't figured it out yet?"

She looked up at him quizzically. "Figured what out?"

"That I'm always right," he said with a crafty look.

She playfully slapped his shoulder and chuckled a little. "I'm going to whip up the eggs." He always could make her feel better.

"I better set the table then." Michael squeezed his wife a little tighter for a second before letting her go.

Just then, Laura joined them, her eyes bloodshot and puffy from crying. "Do you need any help, Mom?"

"Yeah, go ahead and stir the sauce while I do up these eggs; we don't want it to stick." Her heart broke for her daughter and her granddaughter, wherever she may be.

"It smells wonderful." Laura inhaled deeply as she stirred the large pot on the stove.

"Hopefully, it tastes that good." She chuckled. "I haven't made red sauce in years."

"Puh-lease..." Laura rolled her eyes. "...cooking is like riding a bike; you never forget how, and you were always the best, Mom."

"Well, aren't you feeding my ego, young lady." Kat decided to try to lighten the mood. "And as I recall, you aren't too shabby in the kitchen yourself. You make a spectacular stroganoff; I never could perfect that particular dish, but you my young protégé..." Kat kissed her fingers like a French chef. "...Très magnifique!"

"It's Jenny's favorite." The tears started leaking again.

Kat nearly winced. *So much for lightening the mood.* She walked to her daughter and gathered her close. "She'll be home soon, Honey; I can feel it."

Laura sobbed in her mother's arms.

After a few moments of indulging in the tears, Laura broke free of her mother's grasp and swiped at her tear stained cheeks. "I'm sorry, Mom." She sighed heavily. "I just can't seem to stop crying."

"It's okay, baby; anytime you need my shoulder it's yours." Her heart ached for her daughter. It was killing her not knowing how to help.

"Okay, let's eat." Michael said as he brought toast to the table. "I'm starving."

Laura merely picked at the food on her plate; mostly just pushing it around with her fork.

"Honey," her mother said. "You really should eat something. You don't want to make yourself sick. I can tell you didn't sleep well."

Not that she could blame her. She knew what it was like to worry, and this was way beyond her realm.

"You sound like Mark," Laura sulked, but they were right. She needed to keep her strength up; Jenny needed her. She took a few bites.

"I always did like that boy," Kat stated. "He's a good cop and a good person." She had always considered Mark as one of her own.

"I know it, Mom." Laura took a sip of the orange juice her father had poured for her. "I feel kind of bad; I've been treating him like crap since this started." She pushed her plate away unable to stomach anymore. "He's hurting too. I know he loves Jenny; he has been kind of like a surrogate father to her since Jack died, taking her to the movies on the weekends, letting her cruise around town in his police car."

She pushed herself away from the table and stood up. "I can't eat anymore. I think I'd like to be alone for a little bit." She grabbed her coat off the hook by the kitchen door. "I'll be out back; I need some fresh air." She shrugged her coat on. "I feel like I've been cooped up in this house for days."

She walked outside into the cold air; she hoped Jenny wasn't out in the cold somewhere. She had only been wearing a light jacket the day before. And the forecast was calling for snow. She was so scared.

I wish Mark were here. The thought kind of surprised her.

She remembered how it felt to be held and comforted by him. She had missed the feel of a man's arms around her. And last night when he'd kissed her, even just that light brush of his lips, it had stirred something long dormant in her. She remembered the last and only time Mark had kissed her. Thinking about it now made her heart flutter and her breath catch.

She remembered how it had felt at the time, even though it had been fifteen years ago. At first, she had been so shocked with the feelings it stirred in her. She had been a virgin at the time of the kiss and didn't understand what was happening. Her boyfriend back then had never made her feel like that when he'd kissed her. She shook off the memory because it was causing her to get a little flustered.

She hadn't been with a man in any capacity outside of friendship in over two years. For so long, the pain of losing Jack was too strong. She had decided only a few weeks ago she should maybe start dating again. The thought made her a little nervous though because she hadn't dated anyone but Jack since high school.

She didn't even know how to date; that made her laugh. She was thirty-two years old, and only two weeks ago, her biggest worry was what to make for dinner and how to go about starting to date for the first time in fourteen years. It was crazy how everything could change so quickly.

She sat on one of the chairs on the porch and closed her eyes.

Jack, please look out for our girl. Keep her safe until I find her. She isn't ready to be with you yet; she's too young.

She wondered what Jack would think about her dating again. She drifted into a half sleep thinking about her late husband and the child they shared.

They were standing by the Ferris wheel, Jack laughing and Jenny holding her plastic bag with a goldfish swimming around in it. Laura was holding the camera, getting ready to take the picture. The same one she cried over less than an hour before. Everything in her world was right again. Her husband was alive, and her daughter was safe.

"Jack, quit laughing; you look ridiculous. Jenny, quit making your father laugh." Laura was having a hard time keeping herself from laughing.

They were such a happy family. She looked through the view finder and Jack was gone, and Jenny was alone and in tears.

She dropped the camera and called her daughter's name. "Jenny!"

She ran towards her but couldn't get any closer. She slammed into an invisible barrier. She pounded her fists against it, but it wouldn't budge.

"Jenny!" she screamed over and over again. "Jenny can you hear me?" She kept pounding and screaming for her daughter. "I'm going to find you baby! I swear I'm going to find you!"

"Hurry, Mama." She heard her daughter's voice faintly. "Please hurry, I'm scared."

Then she was alone in a field of wild flowers. She looked around frantically, searching for Jenny.

"She's not here." It was a voice she hadn't heard in over two years.

She spun around in shock and faced her husband. "Jack?"

"She's still alive Laura, but you don't have much time. I can't tell you exactly how long because I don't know, but she is safe for now. But, you need to find her before the storm." He smiled his beautiful smile. "You are still the most beautiful woman I know." His

eyes looked sad. "I miss you, Laura. Mark will help you get through this. He loves you, and he loves Jenny."

"I know that, Jack. Do you know where she is?"

"Liz can help too; you will need them both."

"Liz? I haven't talked to Liz in almost two months; she won't return my calls." She was confused and a little salty. "I have to find her, Jack. I will find her. DO YOU KNOW WHERE SHE IS?"

"I have to go now, Laura. I've taken too much time already." He brushed a fingertip over her cheek, and then he was gone.

"Jack, WAIT!" she cried. "Please come back."

11

Mark got into his cruiser outside of Laura's house and slammed his hand against the wheel. He didn't want to leave her alone. He was really struggling with his role in this situation. He considered Laura and Jenny family, and he wanted to be there for her in that capacity.

Her parents will be back any minute. She doesn't need my comfort or sympathy; she already told me as much.

The thought did nothing to change the way he felt. He wanted to be there with her. He wanted to be the one to hold her and comfort her.

Who am I trying to fool? Myself? His feelings went beyond simple family; he was in love with her.

My job is to find Jenny; my only one where Laura is concerned.

He couldn't let his feelings get in the way of helping her the best way possible, and that was to simply do his job. He knew it and hated that he had to keep reminding himself of it.

As he approached the accident scene with sirens blaring, he shifted his thoughts to the job at hand. He went over what the dispatcher had told him over the radio only minutes before.

A pedestrian had been struck. An ambulance was on the way. The injured party was a yet to be identified young man. He was alive but unconscious. The driver of the vehicle involved called it in and was borderline for shock.

When he arrived at the scene, he was in full cop mode. Since Sunday mornings were usually quiet, he only had one other officer on duty. Kyle Morgan was still a little green, but he was a decent cop. He had the road barricaded and was detouring traffic away from the scene.

"Is the scene secure?" Mark asked as he pulled up to where Kyle had his barricade erected.

"Yes sir." Kyle stood up a little straighter at Mark's approach.

Mark smiled inside and was half tempted to say 'at ease' but let the boy continue.

"The EMTs just arrived and are stabilizing Billy for transport to St. Joe's..."

"Billy?" At the mention of the boy's name, Mark jerked his head towards where the body was being lifted onto a mobile gurney.

"Yes sir, Billy Richardson...I recognized him right away, sir. The driver of the car is in the back of my cruiser; I haven't questioned her yet." Kyle reported

"Thanks, Kyle. Go ahead and stay with the traffic detail, I'll take care of the driver." Mark was anxious to check on the boy.

"Yes, sir." Kyle removed the barricade temporarily to let Mark pass.

He drove through to where Kyle had parked his cruiser. He took a cursory scan of the scene as he got out. He noticed the skid marks, and from what he could tell with just a quick glance, it appeared the pedestrian must've run out in front of the vehicle, probably from the woods. He walked to where the car had stopped and noticed the small spot of blood on the pavement.

Almost missed him completely it looks like, he thought to himself. The driver may have been speeding slightly, but not enough to even be sure. He wanted to check on Billy before he talked to the driver.

Damn kid ran right out in front of the car. He shook his head and walked around the car to where the EMT van was parked. "Hey, Pam. How is he?"

Mark had known Pam Stark a long time and knew her to be one of the best EMTs in the area. She was seven years his junior, but they had a semi-romantic history. A few years ago, they had hooked up for about a month, and even though the relationship hadn't evolved, they had parted as friends. He had never known her to lose her cool, but she looked distressed. Her report was quick and thorough though.

"His vitals are stable. We have him on a backboard just in case, but there doesn't appear to be any spinal injuries. The blood on the ground is from a gash on his leg. He has a lot of scrapes and bruises and a seriously swollen ankle." She looked over at Billy thoughtfully. "I don't think any of that is from the accident though, but that's just an observation."

She shrugged as she turned back to Mark. "It looks to me like he was tearing through the woods without a care to where he was going. He's still unconscious...he has a bump on his head, the blood is pretty tacky there...pretty sure that's not from the collision either, or it would be fresher." Pam sighed. "It's Billy Richardson, Mark. I used to babysit the kid. He's a great kid; I hope he pulls through this."

"Any reason to think he won't?" Mark frowned and leaned in, so he could see the boy for himself.

Pam bit at her lower lip. "No, I'm just worried about him." She smiled faintly. "I think he used to have a crush on me. Well, I better get him over to St. Joe's."

"I'll stop by there when I'm finished here." He put a comforting hand on Pam's shoulder. "Take care of him Pam." The job always got to him more when kids were involved.

She nodded and jumped in the back of the Ambulance, calling out for the driver to go as she shut the door.

Mark really liked Billy; everyone did. He said a silent prayer for the boy, and then walked over to Kyle's cruiser to talk to the driver of the late model Chevy that struck Billy Richardson.

He opened the rear passenger side door of the cruiser and said, in an authoritative voice, "Please step out of the vehicle ma'am."

When she did, Mark was surprised to see the tear streaked face that was looking up at him.

"Liz? I didn't know you were coming in; Laura didn't say anything about it, and I just left there." Mark was thrilled to see Laura's best friend; Laura definitely needed her right now.

Liz raised one eyebrow curiously and smirked. "You just left Laura, huh?"

Mark cleared his throat. He always suspected Liz might know how he felt about Laura.

"I've been over there as much as possible since this thing with Jenny happened...unlike some..." He broke off when he saw the look on her face.

She reached out and grabbed his wrist. "What about Jenny?"

"I figured that's why you came." He was confused.

"It's not." She shook her head. "Mark what happened to Jenny?"

"We're not sure," he said carefully. "I think I had better let Laura explain it to you." He put his hand on her shoulder to stop her from asking him again. "Look, it's not my place; if you were anyone else...but I know she would want to be the one to tell you. She needs you; I will tell you that. When we finish up here, you can go straight there if you want."

That had already been her plan. "You mean you're not going to arrest me, officer?" she asked, the sarcasm dripping off each word, but then she sighed. "I was just driving, I didn't have enough time to stop or even avoid him."

He could see the raw grief etched on her face. "I know; I already surveyed the scene. It looks to me like you did your best to avoid him. Tell me everything."

So, she took him through the agonizing steps of the incident.

"...and then I called 9-1-1. Shit, Mark! It scared me to death. I thought I killed him." She looked into his eyes pleadingly. "Is he going to be okay?"

"As soon as we're done here, I'm going to the hospital to check on him." He looked at his watch. "I need to call Richardson's and notify his parents."

"That makes sense; he looks like John," she said quietly.

"I'll let you know as soon as I know anything, okay?" He put a hand reassuringly on her shoulder.

She only nodded.

"Where will you be staying?" he asked as he walked her back to her car.

"I don't know yet. I was going to go to Laura's first anyway; I miss her so much. I'll probably be there for a little while." Liz opened the door to her car and turned to Mark.

"Okay, that's where I'm headed after the hospital, so I'll just see you there."

"Okey dokey smoky." She climbed behind the wheel.

He laughed. "You haven't changed a bit, Liz."

"I wish that were true," she said under her breath as he walked away.

12

After he hurt the boy, he brought him to the tack room and tried to undo what he had done. It was useless though because the boy had been nearly cut in two. After several moments, he gave up; the realization that he had killed the boy finally sinking in.

He hadn't meant to kill the boy. He didn't need to be punished. Marie was different; she needed to be punished for leaving them and ripping their heart out. And lying, that was the worst of all. The poor little boy had done nothing to deserve this.

He cried over the lifeless body of the boy for several minutes, feeling grief and remorse for what he had done. He was no stranger to grief, but the remorse was new. Grief was the only reason he was there.

They had a hard time dealing with grief; when Marie died, it had been too much for one of them to handle. They couldn't bear the fact that she would leave them alone. Then they realized she had lied to them as well!

He saw her that day, fifteen years ago, walking down the road when she was supposed to be dead. At first he was confused, then angry, very angry…that was when he came forward and took control; it was simply too much. She had to be punished. She deserved it.

He was driving through town, still barely able to function normally. He had buried his wife the week before and wouldn't have left the house at all except he needed to stock the liquor cabinet. He would have killed himself, had thought about it several times, but knew he would surely go to Hell and never see Marie again. She was in Heaven for sure.

He just needed to bide his time here until God decided it was time for them to meet again. The alcohol helped dull the ache in his heart. He turned onto Main St. heading towards Hank's, thinking he'd have a drink on his way out of town to the liquor store.

His heart nearly stopped when he thought he saw Marie cross the street a couple blocks ahead of him. He was confused; his wife had died last week. All thoughts of a drink left him, and he turned down the street his wife had walked down.

When he saw her again half a block ahead, he got excited…She wasn't really dead after all. A sharp pain shot through his head (it was always painful to come forward), and the excitement turned to anger…she had lied to them!

She wasn't dead…she just left them. She had put them through all that grief for nothing! She needed to be punished.

He felt no remorse for Marie because she deserved what she got. The boy though...when he realized what he had done, he had tried to fix it. It wasn't fixable, so he prayed...he dropped to his knees and asked God to forgive him for what he did. He hadn't meant to hurt the boy. He had panicked when the boy screamed and didn't know what to do; he had merely reacted.

After several minutes, it came to him that the boy must have needed punished; that must be why God placed him in his path.

He didn't rip the boy's heart out like he did all the others; the punishment needed to fit the crime, and he didn't know what the boy's crime may have been. He had faith that God had led the boy to him; therefor the punishment that was meted must be good enough.

He started to prepare himself for Marie's punishment again. He began to whistle their song again, getting excited for what was to come. She would pay for lying to them and making them hurt so badly.

All of a sudden, his stomach cramped and he doubled over in near agony. The pain was accompanied by a deep hollow feeling. It was then he realized they hadn't eaten in a long time and had suddenly become very hungry. He decided Marie's punishment could wait until after they ate. They would need all their energy for what was to come.

13

Laura bolted upright. "Jack, wait!" *It was only a dream,* she realized as she recognized her surroundings.

She had never had a dream so vibrant and life like. She could still smell him and feel where he had touched her cheek. And the colors…it had to be real.

She jumped up and ran into the kitchen. "Mom, Dad!"

"What is it, honey?" Kat hurried from the living room followed by Michael.

"Jenny's okay." Laura started to weep.

Kat reached Laura and wrapped her arms around her. "I know, honey; I'm sure she's okay." She rubbed her daughter's back trying to comfort her.

Laura pulled away. "No, Mom; she's really okay." Laura was grinning and laughing. "Jack's watching out for her." Her tears were tears of relief and joy.

"Of course he is, honey. Why don't you come in the living room and rest for a little while," she said placatingly, suddenly worried about her daughter even more.

Laura laughed. "I'm not crazy, Mom." But she let her mother lead her into the living room. "Jack just came to me." She looked excitedly between her parents as they all sat. "I dozed off and he came to me...he told me she was safe for now, but that we had to hurry; we have to find her before the storm."

She had forgotten that part of it until the words came out of her mouth. Now that she had, all the grief came rushing back. "But I still don't know where she is." She broke into racking sobs.

Kat gathered Laura in her arms again, led her to the couch from the chair she was in, and rocked with her until she fell asleep. She covered Laura with a blanket and lightly ran a finger down her cheek.

My beautiful baby girl. Kat looked to her husband then and motioned for him to follow her to the kitchen so Laura could rest.

When she entered the kitchen, Kat turned to her husband. "What are we going to do, Michael?" She didn't like to feel so helpless.

"I don't know...I'm so worried about both my girls, Kat." He rubbed both hands through his hair and started to pace. "I feel like there is nothing we can do." He stopped and turned to his wife, feeling helpless and not for the first time.

"I know how you feel." She was leaning against the counter, shaken by what her daughter had told them about Jack. "I'm so glad she is sleeping though; she needs it." The emotional roller coaster of the last twenty four hours was surely exhausting.

"Do you think Jack actually came to her?" Michael sat at the table, looking at his wife curiously; unaware his thoughts were mirroring hers

Kat thought about it for a minute before responding, wondering if she should tell her husband her true thoughts. Oddly enough, even though they had talked about nearly everything over the years, their thoughts on the supernatural had never really been discussed.

"Maybe, but how can we be sure?" She went to the table and sat across from him. "She has been so emotionally exhausted the past couple days; she could just be delusional. But..." She decided to tell him why she more than believed Jack had come to Laura.

"But?" he prodded after she hesitated.

She took a deep breath. "Do you remember when Laura was three and she had pneumonia?"

"Of course, she was in the hospital for the better part of a week." He was confused with the change of subject. "But, what...?"

She stopped him. "I'll get to that, just hear me out okay?"

He nodded, and she continued, "I hardly slept a wink the entire time. I was so exhausted..." She grabbed his hand and looked at him pleadingly. "I never told you this because I didn't want you to think I was crazy."

Michael looked at his wife closely and saw the shame she felt at keeping something she thought was important from him for almost thirty years. "I would never think you were crazy; tell me." He turned his hand so he was holding hers and gave it a reassuring squeeze.

She took a deep breath. "Okay, you know my Mom died when I was fifteen?" It still hurt her heart.

"Of course." He squeezed her hand again, knowing she still had crying spells over it even after all these years.

"Okay." She squeezed his hand in return and smiled at him, appreciating the comfort and understanding. "Well, when Laura was in the hospital, Mom came to me; I must've dozed off. I was sitting by the bed...hell, I only left that spot to go to the bathroom. You were home with Jeff..." She actually felt nervous talking about it. "...Okay, I'm getting off track here. So, Mom came to me and told me I had nothing to worry about; that Laura would be fine."

Kat started to shed silent tears. "The next day they told us the pneumonia was gone, and we could take her home." She broke contact, needing to be busy. She got up and started to pace. "At the time, I told myself it must've been a hallucination because I was so tired..." She stopped pacing and looked into his eyes. "...but deep down, I had wanted to believe my Mom was watching over our babies; I was so scared." She put her fist to her heart remembering how it had felt.

She sat back down and clutched his hand again. "I didn't tell anyone about it because I was afraid I would jinx it, and I wasn't sure if it had actually happened. And, the next day when they told us she was okay, after she had been so sick..." She smiled brightly. "...well, I was so happy and just so tired...I don't know why I never told you; I mean, I talked to my dead mother for crying out loud." She laughed. "After that next day, I never doubted it had happened, but...I guess I wanted to keep her for myself...I still missed her then...hell, I still miss her now...so much, but I know she is always with me."

"Well, not *always* I hope," Michael said in a light tone, conveying his understanding.

She laughed heartily. "I love you."

"I love you too, and I don't think you're crazy," he said seriously. "I would have believed you then too, but that's neither here nor there, apparently our baby girl inherited your..." He waved his hand in the air trying to come up with an accurate description of what his wife was describing to him. "...let's just say, special ability to communicate with the dead?"

She chuckled. "More like receptive enough to listen when they speak."

"Well, however you want to put it." He squeezed her hand again then got up from the table to make some herbal tea. He would prefer coffee, but he wasn't supposed to have it. "Has she come to you since then, or was it a one-time thing?"

"I'm not sure." She laughed quietly. "I mean I think I've had dreams of her since, but nothing like that; then again, I haven't been in a situation when I needed her either."

He thought about that for a minute then walked over and kissed the top of his wife's head. "Well, I suppose we can be grateful for that at least."

"I've wished for her to come to me again." Her eyes were leaking tears. "Sometimes, even though it has been so many years since she passed away, I still miss her so much it makes my heart ache." She rubbed a hand on her chest over her heart to try and ease the ache she was feeling.

"I know, honey, and I just hope that Jack can really help us find Jenny." He rubbed Kat's shoulders for a minute; trying to relieve the stress he could feel in them. He had a feeling they were going to need all the help they could get.

They were both startled out of their thoughts at the sound of the tea kettle's whistle.

In the living room Laura jerked awake, not from the sound of the kettle but from a knock at the door. She jumped up and ran to the door thinking it was Jenny and she forgot her key.

14

Liz pulled up to the curb at Laura's house behind a late model ford sedan with Missouri plates. That could only be Laura's parents...Michael had been transferred to St. Louis 5 years ago or so.

Why am I so nervous? she asked herself as she looked in the mirror. *Just because it's been weeks and weeks since I've talked to her doesn't mean she'll hate me; I mean we're blood sisters, right?*

She took a deep breath and looked at the faint scar on her hand; she took another and opened the door. As she walked up to the porch, she noticed some changes since the last time she was there. The tire swing was no longer hanging from the branch in the front yard, and the shrubs that used to line the walkway had been replaced by rock lined flower beds. It looked good; it opened up the yard a lot.

She knew she was stalling as she walked slowly up the walk, but when she finally reached the door, she didn't hesitate to knock.

The door was opened almost immediately by a frantic looking Laura. "Jenny?"

"Laura, what's wrong!" Liz grabbed her friend's arm; she had never seen her like this.

"Liz? Oh, Liz; you got my message." Laura pulled her into a fierce embrace and immediately started sobbing.

Liz put her arms around Laura and let her cry on her shoulder for a minute; she clearly needed it. After a moment, what Laura had said got through.

"Message?" She forgot she had ignored Laura's call the night before. "No, I never checked my messages; I just needed to come home." She hugged her friend tightly, not wanting to break contact just yet. "What's going on? Mark said something about Jenny but wouldn't tell me what was going on."

Laura pulled back from Liz. "Mark? You talked to Mark?" Laura was confused.

Katlyn called from inside the house, "Laura, who is it honey?"

Laura wiped her eyes with the neck of her shirt and grabbed Liz's hand. "Liz, come in please; it seems we have a lot to talk about."

In the living room, Michael and Katlyn were huddled together on the couch.

"Liz, it's so good of you to come so quickly." Kat got up from the couch and hugged Liz close.

"Okay, I have no idea what's going on...You guys are freaking me out!" Liz broke free of Kat and looked back at Laura.

Michael and Kat exchanged a look.

"Liz, you look great." Michael got up and gave her a one armed bear hug and a kiss on top of the head. "Come on, Kat; let's leave these girls alone to talk."

After her parents left the room, Laura turned to Liz. "If you didn't get my message, what are you doing here?"

"We can talk about that later. Laura, what in the hell is going on? Mark said..."

"Let's start there," Laura interrupted a little haughtily. "When and why did you talk to Mark?" She was curious why on Earth Liz would have gotten ahold of Mark before her. And, she was still a little hurt and angry that her friend had been avoiding her for so long.

Liz sat on the edge of couch and let out a sigh. "I just left him; there was an accident on my way into town. Billy Richardson, you know, John's boy?" She looked at Laura questioningly but didn't expect a response. "Well, he ran out of the woods in front of my car. I didn't really hit him as much as he hit me, but he's unconscious and on his way to the hospital," she said super-fast, then got up and grabbed Laura's shoulders. "We can talk about all this later, what in the hell is going on with Jenny?"

Liz had known Laura practically her entire life and could tell she was barely holding it together, so she grabbed her hand and pulled her down to sit on the couch.

Laura took a deep breath but didn't let go of Liz's hand. "She's missing."

Liz almost jumped up to pace but tried to keep calm. "What do you mean missing?" Her heart was slamming in her chest.

"She went to the park with her friends yesterday afternoon and never made it home." Laura swiped furiously at the tears that wouldn't seem to stop.

"Okay, so she's with one of her friends, we'll just go talk to them..."

Laura was shaking her head the whole time and stopped Liz. "No, we've already talked to everyone she was with." Laura was struggling not to all out cry.

Liz pulled her close and whispered, "Just let it go, just for a minute; then we can finish talking about it."

As Laura sobbed in her arms, Liz felt the tugging of a memory from high school about another missing girl. *What was her name?*

As Laura's sobs started to subside, Liz spoke what was on her mind. "Remember that girl from high school who went missing, what was it? Junior year? What was her name?"

"What...?" It took Laura a few seconds to adjust to the switch in conversation. "Oh, you mean Margery Addison? I haven't thought about her in years; what about her?"

"Nothing," Liz said storing it for later. "It just popped in my head; now tell me what's going on."

Laura had repeated it so many times going over it with Mark, the story sounded almost rehearsed in her mind.

After she was finished telling Liz everything, she merely sighed and said, "I don't know what to do Liz...But Jack, he told me you would help find her." At the memory from her dream, Laura jumped up in excitement. "He said I would need you and Mark both to find her in time."

"Laura? Are you okay? You do remember that Jack died two years ago, right?" Liz stood up and looked at her friend with concern, thinking maybe she lost her mind from the stress of everything.

"Of course, silly." Laura smiled showing her dimple. "He came to me in a dream this morning. I just woke up from it maybe 20 min before you got here. He knew you were coming even though I didn't." She grabbed Liz again and hugged her quickly. "Thank God you're here! Don't you see? She's going to be okay."

Laura's excitement didn't last long though once Liz started asking questions about what was being done to find her and trying to probe deeper to find any holes in the story.

Liz got up from the couch and started pacing the room. "I want to talk to Mark; I want to help with the investigation. I'm a trained interviewer, and maybe I can talk to some of the people he's already talked to and get some more information or do some other kind of leg work." All thoughts of a relaxing visit home flew out of her mind. "Is there a search going on? Is there any other information you can tell me?" She stopped and looked at Laura, who was now sitting on the couch.

Laura shook her head. "The County Sherriff won't authorize a search because we really have nowhere to start." She understood the reasoning but hated it still. "She was last seen in town, but she's not in town, unless it's in someone's house. If she left town on her own or was taken, there's no way to know where she would be." The tears started again, and Laura yawned. The emotional roller coaster ride she had been on already this morning coupled with the lack of sleep the night before was taking its toll.

Liz sat back on the couch next to her best friend and held her close until she fell asleep. "We'll find her Laura," she whispered after her friend dozed off.

After leaving Laura to try to rest under the watchful eye of her parents, Liz tried to call Mark but kept getting his voice mail, so she went to the library. She couldn't get Margery Addison out of her mind. She was a couple years younger than them in school, but Jefferson was a small town where everybody knew everybody. Margery was about 14 when she went missing if Liz remembered correctly...at least a year older than Jenny.

It's probably nothing. But what if it wasn't?

Liz considered for a moment, but at the same time she knew instinct and gut feeling needed to be followed. That was what made her a good reporter; she always had good instincts. She felt deep down Margery was somehow important. She took herself back to her junior year of high school.

"What do you think happened to her?" Laura asked her while they were sitting in the cafeteria eating lunch.

The mood in the room was somber; it wasn't loud and crazy like it normally would be the day before winter break. But why should it be? Everyone had just found out that Margery Addison, the cute little blonde cheerleader who had made varsity as a freshman, didn't make it home from school the day before.

"I have no idea; she's so quiet and kept to herself so much, did anybody really even know her?" Liz responded taking a bite out of her apple.

"She just moved here right before her freshman year Liz..." Laura slapped the table they were sitting at causing several people to look their way. Laura didn't notice. "...it's not like she was some sort of recluse for crying out loud!"

Laura, who was the captain of the squad as a junior, which had never happened before in school history, knew Margery better than most at the school.

"Relax, Laura; I'm not badmouthing her. I am just saying she really didn't have many friends here yet, and nobody seems to know where she was going or what she was doing yesterday, that's all." She reached over and rubbed Laura's arm knowing her best friend was only concerned for her little protégé. "Who knows, maybe she has a secret boyfriend she snuck off with for a few days to have a passionate love affair." Liz tried to lighten the mood but knew that wasn't likely the case.

"It just doesn't feel right; she was supposed to call me last night to go over some ideas she had for the new routine we've been working on." Laura sighed; she was concerned. "She was so excited, and...It's just not like her that's all, and now we find out she never made it home after school; that's just crazy."

"Yeah, I don't know. It's probably nothing though; stuff like this happens all the time. She'll be fine." But Liz didn't believe it. Even then her gut feelings were pretty accurate, and she had a bad feeling about the whole thing.

As she pulled into the library parking lot just before noon, she took a minute to study the building. The architecture was nothing spectacular, but she spent so much time there as a kid, reading and writing, and researching, that the sense of nostalgia was almost too much to bear. Again, she wondered why she'd stayed away so long. She shook her head to clear it and reflected on Margery's disappearance.

It had happened the same time of year. It just didn't feel like a coincidence.

She knew she should probably have stayed with Laura, but for God's sake, she couldn't just sit around and do nothing while her Godchild was missing.

She's asleep anyway! Besides, her folks are with her and I have my cell charged if she needs me. She checked her phone to make sure it was really charged. She was bad about that.

After exchanging pleasantries with old Mrs. Jones the librarian who was always there (Liz had wondered in the past if the woman had a cot set up somewhere), Liz got to work. The Jefferson Daily was such a small paper and had never gotten online, so Liz settled in with the microfiche machine feeling at home with the research. That was what most of journalism really was, research. Everyone thought it was about the story, and of course it was, but without unlimited patience for research, the story wouldn't ever be.

After only about fifteen minutes, she found the article about Margery that ran on the front page a couple days after the disappearance. The picture that accompanied the article was sort of how she remembered Margery, but she hardly knew the girl even then.

At closer inspection, even of such a badly pixelated copy of a picture, Liz immediately recognized the similarities between Margery and Jenny. Both were slender with blonde hair and blue eyes...and they both came up missing within days of each other even though it was 15 years apart.

After another hour of searching, Liz found out the missing person case for Margery Addison was eventually turned over to a Federal division and was still open. She was never found.

Okay so what does that accomplish? Liz ran her fingers through her hair and dove back into the research.

Within another hour, Liz had compiled a list of teenage girls in the surrounding areas that had been reported missing in the last 15 years. She narrowed it down to seven that also matched a similar description as Margery and Jenny. The most recent being a 17 year old named Sasha Livingston who went missing 2 years before at about the same time of year. She was from the neighboring town of Ross.

Jenny was the youngest by almost two years, but she definitely had blossomed early, so that didn't mean anything. Five of the seven came up missing during the same week as Margery and Jenny. It couldn't be a coincidence.

I need to go talk to Mark about this. She gathered up all the notes she had made and pulled out her cell phone.

She got Mark's voicemail again, so she left him a message. "I have something; meet me in your office in 20 minutes." She hung up hoping he would get the message. Surely a cop checked his messages regularly.

She printed off the info on the other missing girls. After paying for and picking up her prints at the desk, Liz bolted for the door. On her way to the police station she called to check on Laura.

15

On his way to the hospital, Mark called the grocery store to inform Billy's parents of the accident. He went to school with both John and Sally and had even dated Sally briefly his junior year. Jefferson was a close knit community where everyone knew everyone else. It had grown only slightly since Mark was a boy.

The phone was answered by John on the fifth ring. "Richardson's." He sounded rushed.

"John, it's Mark. I need you to meet me at the hospital; there's been an accident." He took a deep breath and just spit it out. "Billy was struck by a vehicle on Central. He's on his way to St. Joe's in an ambulance. He is stable but unconscious." There was no response on the other end. Mark looked at his phone to make sure he hadn't dropped the call. "John? John are you there?"

"There must be some kind of mistake, Mark," John finally replied, overcoming his initial shock. "Billy stayed over at David's last night; they're probably not even awake yet...listen man, we're slammed right now. With the snow supposedly coming tomorrow, people are cleaning us out." He was about to hang up.

"John, listen to me! It's Billy. I'm one hundred percent certain." He waited for that to sink in. "Call over to David's place and have Marianne check on the boys, but I'm telling you, it is Billy."

"I'll call home and have Sally meet you. I'll have to wait until I can get Joyce in here before I can leave." Owning a business was a bitch sometimes. "It's just me and Sharon right now, and she's only been here a week. There's no way I can leave her here alone."

"You call Sally and Joyce; I'll call Marianne because I'll want to talk to David to see why in the Hell Billy was running like a wild man out of the woods at 9 o'clock on a Sunday morning."

"He's okay...?" The reality of the situation was starting to sink in.

"Honestly John, the car didn't really seem to hit him. The driver managed to stop and it looked more like he hit her, like he ran right into the fender and bounced off. I think he may have hit is head on the ground though, but his pulse was strong and his breathing was regular. I'm not a doctor, but I think he'll be fine." He wasn't just saying that for John's benefit; he believed it.

John let out a long breath. "Okay, thanks Mark...I'll be there as soon as I can."

After he disconnected, Mark wondered again, *what in the hell was Billy doing in the woods alone at 9 am on a Sunday? Especially after Jenny came up missing yesterday. I know I'm not the only one that told all those kids not to go out alone until we figured out was going on. I know all their mothers would have reinforced that double time.*

He dialed the number he had for the Minelli's home, and Marianne answered on the third ring. "Hello?"

"Marianne? It's Mark Henderson; I'm sorry to bother you, but I was wondering if you could do me a favor." He checked his mirror as he changed lanes to turn off towards the hospital.

"Hi Mark, of course, what can I do for you?" Marianne asked cheerily.

"Well, there was an accident out on Central, and Billy Richardson seems to be involved." He drummed his fingers on the wheel as he sat at a light. "I just got off the phone with John, and he said Billy stayed there last night with David. Is there any chance you may know where Billy was headed when he left your house?" He was anxious to hear what she had to say.

"Billy never left the house. I've been up since before 7 and haven't heard out of Billy or David all morning. I just finished making pancakes and was getting ready to wake them up," she stated confidently.

"Would you mind checking now? I'm positive it was Billy in the accident; I saw him with my own eyes. I'm hoping maybe David might have the answers I'm looking for." Billy had obviously snuck out. He had a nagging feeling Billy wouldn't have snuck out alone.

"Of course." Marianne hurried to David's room.

Mark could hear her knock on the door and call her son's name.

"Hold on a minute, Mark; he's not answering the door."

He could hear her more loudly this time, her knocking a little more fervent.

"The door is locked; let me find something to unlock it with."

Mark heard some shuffling and then nothing for a few minutes.

"Mark, neither of them are here!" Marianne said hurriedly into the phone. "You said Billy was in an accident? What about David? Where's David?"

His suspicions had been confirmed. Now, where was David? "I don't know Marianne; I don't even know if Billy was with David...maybe he wasn't." Neither of them believed it. "I'm on my way to the hospital now; hopefully Billy will be able to answer that question. Do you think there's any chance one of David's brothers or sisters may know where they may have gone?" David was one of nine Minelli children.

"I'll be sure to find out trust me!" Marianne said furiously. "I'll let you know if I find anything out." She disconnected without waiting for a reply.

Mark pulled up outside of the emergency room and hurried inside. He saw Pam talking to Dr. Murphy near the triage counter. Pam looked over and saw him.

"Mark!" she called with deep concern in her voice. "I was just getting ready to call you. There's something I need to talk to you about."

"Is Billy okay?" Mark hurried over, responding to the concern.

"He's stable," replied Dr. Murphy, a tall skinny man with dark hair and a strong nose; he was supposedly an excellent physician.

"It's not about that; well, not exactly...." She took a deep breath. "Billy never came completely to on the ride, but he did mumble quite a bit for a minute." She looked at him soberly and spit it out. "Mark, he said, 'Jenny, I need to help Jenny,' I'm sure of it!"

Mark grabbed her arm. "Are you sure?"

"I just said I'm sure, but yes...I'm sure. There's more." She was uneasy about the rest of it. "Mark, he also screamed David at one point, and there was more, but I couldn't understand it. Something about being sick or ill...I don't know...but it scared me Mark; that scream." She shivered remembering how it had echoed inside the ambulance.

"Well, that might answer one question. Billy was supposedly at David's overnight, and David isn't home." He thought about it for a minute hoping the boy was okay. David was known for getting himself into predicaments. "I'm hoping one of his siblings might know what they were up to because Marianne didn't even know they left the house." He ran his hand through his hair and looked at Dr. Murphy. "Can I see him?"

Just then Sally, Billy's mom, came rushing in. "Where is he?" she asked, hurrying up to Mark when she saw him.

"We were just going in to see him."

They all, with the exception of Pam, walked back to the ER room where Billy was located.

Dr. Murphy began explaining Billy's condition. "He has several bruises and lacerations and a small contusion on the back of his head. Along with what might be a broken ankle; we'll need x-rays, but it is severely swollen. The contusion doesn't appear to be enough to cause an unconscious state, but with head injuries you never know. We'll need to do a CAT scan to make sure there's no internal bleeding, but based on his vitals, I think we're okay there." He looked at Billy's mom. "Of course, we'll need your consent to do any tests."

Sally couldn't take her eyes off her son's battered body. "Of course, do anything you think is necessary," she said and turned to Mark. "What in the hell happened? Did you arrest whoever did this to my boy?" She was understandably upset.

"Calm down, Sally…"

"Don't tell me to calm down while my boy is lying unconscious in a hospital bed…" She poked him in the chest.

Mark grabbed her by both shoulders and gave her a little shake. "Listen to me, Sally; we're not going to get anything accomplished if you sit here and yell at me!"

She took a deep breath and visibly pulled herself together. "You're right; I'm sorry. Tell me what happened. Please." She looked at him apologetically.

So he did, ending with, "….the driver, Liz Metcalf, was not at fault, and honestly, it looks like he hit her…like ran into the car, more than she hit him." He looked over at the Dr. "What do you think doc? Does it look like he was hit by a car?"

"Actually, except for the bump on the head, it looks more like he lost an argument with a rose bush," the doctor replied with a poor attempt at humor. He cleared his throat at his bad joke and continued. "The bump on the head doesn't seem to be bad enough to cause unconsciousness, but again, we need to run some tests." He studied the boy for a moment. "Based on the behavior Pam indicated in the ambulance and what appears to be a frantic run through the overgrown woods, I'd say it's more likely a psychological trauma that has caused it."

"His behavior in the ambulance? What does that mean?" Sally looked at both of them curiously.

Mark took a deep breath. "He apparently became restless, but never quite conscious, and started mumbling some things in the ambulance. He mentioned Jenny and needing to help her, and he screamed David's name. I don't know what's going on, but at least now I have somewhere to start." He was thinking about the woods from which Billy had emerged. They needed to get a search going as soon as possible. "We have two missing kids and another unconscious."

"Two missing kids?" Sally asked. "Jenny and…You mean David?" Her eyes got big. "He wasn't with Billy was he? And he's not at home?" David may have been a little annoying, but she loved the boy.

"No he wasn't." He hugged her close for a second. "Look, I'm sure you were going to anyway, but stay here, and contact me immediately if Billy wakes up. If David *was* with Billy and they know where Jenny might be, we have a starting point for a search." He looked at her closely. "I'm going to get that under way as soon as possible. Call me right away if anything changes."

She nodded in agreement then sat next to her son and took his hand in hers.

Mark walked out of the hospital and called Kyle. "Kyle, I need you to get ahold of Lester Vance and tell him I need his dogs. Get a hold of Frank and Jamie too. I need all of you to meet me at the office in thirty minutes." He disconnected without waiting for an answer.

Next, he called Deputy Miller and updated him on the new development. After he disconnected, he looked at his clock; it was already almost noon. The day was moving way too quickly. That left maybe five hours of daylight, and the search probably wouldn't even get well under way for another couple hours. Everything had to be organized.

He'd be damned if he'd wait for the county though. They could join in or take over if they insisted when they showed up, but he was starting as soon as physically and safely possible. He wouldn't just throw people in the woods without a plan, but the sooner the better for those kids.

He started to pull out and stopped. He ran back into the room where Billy was just minutes before. Sally was sitting there crying, but Billy was no longer in the room.

"Sally, what happened? Where's Billy!" he asked, fearing the worst.

Sally looked up at Mark through her tear filled eyes. "He's on his way for x-rays and the CAT scan." She wiped furiously at the tears on her cheeks. "What's up?" She tried to pull herself together.

"I need something of Billy's, like one of his shoes or a piece of clothing, so the dogs can retrace his steps." He hated to ask, but he didn't want to have to stop at their house and waste more time.

"Dogs?" Sally looked confused.

"I figured we'd get Lester's dogs and backtrack Billy's progress through the woods. If he was where Jenny and David are, maybe we can find them."

"That makes sense." She picked a plastic bag up off the ground by the bed. "Here's the boot they cut off his foot. His ankle was too swollen to take it off regularly." She handed Mark the bag containing the mutilated boot.

"Thanks Sally; I think he'll be okay you know. And I'm not just saying that. But right now, I've got to find those missing kids." He turned to leave the room.

"I know, Mark. I'm going to be praying for them too, along with Billy, don't worry." She couldn't hold off the tears any longer.

Mark turned back, hugged her close, and let her cry on his shoulder for a minute. It looked like he was going to be a few minutes late to his own meeting.

16

Laura woke to the sound of her cell phone. She had been having a nightmare and was glad it had been interrupted.

She groped for her phone lying on the end table, still slightly groggy from sleep. "Hello?"

"Laura. Did I wake you?" Liz didn't wait for a response. "Oh well, listen; I think I may have found something. Do you remember earlier when I brought up Margery Addison?" Liz still didn't wait for an answer and kept right on talking "Well, I couldn't stop thinking about it, so I went to the library and started digging. Margery came up missing right about the same time of year."

"Okay?" Laura was still a little fuzzy, but Liz's excitement was obvious, so she shook her head to clear the last dregs of sleep from her brain.

"Well, I kept digging, and I found several more missing persons from around this area who all look similar, like Jenny and

Margery; the resemblances are mostly superficial like hair color, eye color, skin tone, but I don't think it's a coincidence."

"They never found Margery, Liz; this isn't making me feel any better." She wasn't as excited by this information as Liz seemed to be.

"I get that, but listen; if Mark can get records from all these missing person's cases, we might be able to find a common thread...potential witnesses in common, or something. I'm on my way to the police station right now to talk to Mark. How are you holding up?"

Laura sighed. "I'm okay I guess, under the circumstances. Will you let me know if you guys come up with anything else?"

"You'll be the first. I love you, Laura...we'll find her."

"I hope so...Lizzy Bear?" She got up to stretch.

"Yeah, Laura Bean?" They both smiled at the usage of their childhood pet names.

"I'm glad you're here," Laura said quietly into the phone.

"Me too." They both disconnected with tears in their eyes.

Laura went into the kitchen to make some fresh coffee. Her little nap had done her some good, but her brain was still a little foggy. There was a note on the coffee pot; she smiled at its location. It was letting her know her parents were upstairs trying to nap.

As soon as she poured a cup of coffee, Laura's phone rang again. This time it was Mark. "Mark! Tell me you found her!" Laura was fully awake now.

"I'm sorry Laura, not yet, but we do have a new development." He told her what he'd learned and what his plans were. "I'm on my way to the police station now."

"To meet Liz, I know." Laura carried her coffee into the living room and sat down on the couch.

"Liz? What do you mean?" Mark was clearly confused.

"Oh, I just got off the phone with her a few minutes ago; she has some potentially useful information as well. She said she was on her way to the police station to meet you." Things were starting to happen, and all she could do was sit there and wait.

"That's probably the voice mail I got while I was on the phone with Lee, Deputy Miller. I'll be at the office in a few minutes or so to meet with my guys about starting a search. If Billy really did see Jenny and was trying to help her, we should be able to backtrack from the accident and find her."

He didn't tell her his main concerns were fading daylight and an incoming storm. If they didn't finish the search before the heavy stuff rolled in the next day, they may not finish it at all. He wanted to stay positive for Jenny's sake and at least appear to for Laura's.

"I want to help with the search," Laura blurted, not wanting to sit idle any longer.

"I don't know if that's a good idea; what if she comes home, or....?"

Laura didn't let him finish. "Look, Mark! She's my daughter; I can't sit here and just keep wondering and worrying. If I'm involved at least I'll feel like I'm doing something useful. Right now, I just feel like a bump on a log. All I can do is think the worst. Please, let me help." She knew she was practically begging but didn't care.

"I'll think about it. Okay? That's all I'm going to say on the matter right now. I'm pulling into the station; I'll call you as soon as we have everything organized, okay?" He didn't tell her the main reason he didn't want her involved was in case they didn't find Jenny alive. He didn't want to think about it but had to. It was his job. He didn't want her there for that if it turned out that way.

"Fine, I'll talk to you soon, but Mark?" She didn't wait for him to answer "I *am* going to help. I have to." She disconnected before he could argue.

She picked up her coffee; her mind was reeling, hopefully the caffeine would help. So much had happened already that day. Liz showed up unannounced without even knowing what happened. The only person who may know where her daughter may be was unconscious in the hospital because he was hit by Liz on her way into town. Liz found information on multiple other missing persons that may be connected to her daughter's disappearance. She had a visit from her dead husband. And, another local kid was missing. It was almost too much to think about.

She was startled from her musings by a loud insistent knock on the door. She hurried to answer it only to find another surprise waiting for her.

"Jeff!" She threw herself into her brother's arms. "I thought you weren't coming!"

Jeff was a younger and slightly smaller version of their father. He had the same dark hair and soulful brown eyes.

He hugged his sister close and very tightly. "I never said I wasn't coming," he reminded her. "Just because you told me not to didn't mean I wasn't going to." He gave her one final squeeze and then held her at arm's length. "You always did think you could boss me around," he said, trying to lighten the mood.

She hugged him close again and cried for a minute. "I'm sorry; I think I may have snotted on your shirt." She managed a small laugh.

"What! How dare you!" Jeff feigned horror. "Come on, let's go inside; it's cold." Once he had her on the couch with a blanket over her shoulders, he asked, "Where's Mom and Dad? I saw their car out front."

"They're napping. They got here super early, and I don't think either of them slept very much last night." She laid her head on his shoulder, reveling in the comfort he brought her.

"What about you? Have you slept at all?" He put his arm around her hugging her closer.

She shrugged. "A little. I've dozed a few times. Not on purpose either. I probably won't until we find her." She turned away as her eyes started to tear up again. "What are you doing here, Jeff? What about your big case?"

"Fuck my case! Laura, who cares about my case? Jenny is missing; of course I'm going to be here." He would have gotten up to pace but knew his sister needed the comfort of his embrace.

"Well, I'm glad you're here." She smiled at his outburst. "Are you going to get fired?" she teased him lightly.

"No. But I might quit. I've been so stressed out trying to make ADA, and I've been missing out on everything that's important." He'd been thinking a lot about it lately anyway. "I did find someone else to take the lead on the case. I had to have it approved by the judge and the DA, or I would have been here earlier.

"Of course, they weren't happy about it, but under the circumstances, what could they do." It was his turn to shrug. "The woman I picked to take over has been part of the team all along and is more than capable of handling it." He looked at his sister; he could tell she was struggling not to cry. "But who cares about the case. Tell me what's going on here; I want to help."

So, she told him everything. He interrupted several times to ask questions and get elaborations. He was very curious about her visit from Jack, and he thought it interesting that Liz showed up unannounced without even knowing what was going on. But, Liz always did have a knack for the story. Not that he assumed she was after a story here by any means, but even as a kid she always seemed to be in the right place at the right time.

If it weren't for her, he may not have been there himself right now, but he couldn't think about that right now. When she finished telling him everything, ending with her phone conversation with Mark only minutes before he arrived, he jumped up and said, "Grab your coat, we're going to the police station."

"What? But...what if Jenny comes home?" However, she was already getting up.

"Mom and Dad are here, so it's not like we're leaving an empty house. We'll wake them up and let them know we're leaving, but we're going to be involved." He took her by the shoulders and looked her in the eye. "I know you well enough to know that being involved is what you need whether Mark wants you to be or not.

"He's going to need volunteers for the search and can't afford to turn down any help offered." He hugged his sister again and kissed her on top of the head. "We best hurry sis, before they start without us."

It was another twenty minutes or so before they made it out the door. All of a sudden, everything was happening so fast.

Ten minutes later they hurried into the police station. When they got to the closed door of the conference room, Jeff didn't bother with knocking; he just walked right in with Laura close on his heels.

Mark looked up from the map spread out on the table. "What the...?"

"Hey buddy." Jeff smiled at his best friend. "We're here to help."

"Jeff?" Mark said in surprise. Then he looked at Laura. "What are you doing here?"

"Like Jeff said, we're here to help." Laura stated with a steely glare daring Mark to protest.

Mark looked back and forth between brother and sister for a minute before settling on Laura. "Can I talk to you for a minute?" He grabbed her hand and pulled her out of the conference room, practically dragging her towards his office. A moment later, the sound of a door slamming rang out.

Jeff saw Liz and shot her a huge grin. "He doesn't seem too happy to see us."

Liz just arched one eyebrow and smirked. "Glad you finally showed up, hotshot."

Jeff grinned just a little bit bigger. "Good to see you too, Liz."

In his office, Mark paced furiously. "What are you doing here, Laura?"

"Mark, I need to be involved! I told you that." She was determined to stand her ground. "It's my daughter that's missing! All I can do at home is sit and worry! I'm sick of crying." God, she was sick of crying. "If I'm involved, it might keep my mind from heading in the worst possible direction."

Mark's anger faded into the concern that sparked it. "Laura listen...I understand that, but we don't know what we're going to find..."

"Stop trying to protect me, Mark!" She walked up to him and shoved him backwards. "Whatever you find, whatever *we* find, won't be any different because I'm not there. I need this!" It felt good to let the anger take over the worry for a minute. "I need to not feel worthless while this is happening; I need to be a part of it." She pushed him again.

He grabbed her shoulders to stop her from pushing him again. "Calm down..."

"Don't tell me to calm down! I just need to feel..." She broke free and turned from him for a moment, not knowing how to finish. She took a few calming breaths and turned back to him, not quite as angry anymore. "I just need to feel something...something other than this worry and uncertainty...I just need to feel..." She didn't know how to finish. "I just need to feel." She let out on a near sob.

She walked up to him and surprised them both by kissing him. Not like the light kiss from the night before, she practically pounced on him. It was instantaneous, the flood of energy through his veins. He didn't question it; he just responded. He wrapped his arms around her and pulled her closer. He changed the angle slightly and took more. The feelings were more than he remembered from that long ago kiss. Stronger. Deeper. Just more.

She was feeling, all right, feeling all kinds of things. It was so intense and felt so...good. Better than good. It was like a light getting brighter inside of her; it became so powerful it felt like she might burst from it. He changed the angle again and the kiss intensified; which a moment before, she would have thought impossible. After that, all thought left, and she was lost in the sensations coursing through her.

At the same time, they broke apart gasping for air. Laura started to say something, but Mark was ready for it now, and it was his turn. He grabbed her and pulled her close. He kissed her, but it wasn't the violent mating of mouths she had initiated. He started off slowly, but it wasn't any less intense.

The air around them all but sizzled. His lips moved over hers for what seemed like an eternity of easy pleasure, and then he gently nudged her lips with his tongue. When she responded with parted lips, they're tongues met briefly.

When she would have deepened the kiss, he kept it slow but not any less passionate. The way his lips moved and his tongue brushed hers sent shivers up and down her spine. His hands were on her face now lightly stroking her cheeks as he kissed her lips. He took his lips from hers but only to use them on her jaw moving towards her neck; when he reached the spot where the jaw met the neck just behind the ear, she groaned.

The sound broke through his haze of feelings, and he pulled back, nearly panting. "I'm sorry, Laura...I didn't mean...I just..." He stopped, still trying to catch his breath.

Laura didn't respond, couldn't respond. Her head was spinning, and the bright light inside of her was slow to diminish. They just looked at each other for a few moments, both breathing heavily, neither knowing what to say.

Finally, Mark cleared his throat and turned to his desk, picking up papers to shuffle just so he had something to do. He decided the best course of action was to pretend like nothing happened and chalk it up to heightened emotions.

"Okay...let's talk about the search and what your part will be."

Realizing the moment was over and obviously hadn't had the same effect on him, she turned to look out the window.

"Okay." She was ready to focus on finding her daughter. She had needed the short reprieve from all the negativity. The kiss had given her that, and it had the added benefit of an adrenaline rush like no other. But now, it was time to get to work. She turned back to face Mark, willing to pretend like nothing had happened. "What do you have in mind?"

"We need someone to man the command center." He stopped her from interrupting. "You'll still be on site of the search; you'll just be at a set location with a map and a radio," he explained, liking the idea of having her close by now that he thought about it. "You'll be in charge of monitoring areas searched on the map and coordinating between teams to make sure we maximize the area searched." He grabbed her hand and led her back towards the conference room. "Come on, I'll show you."

When they reached the door to the conference room, he stopped and faced her. "Laura..." He wasn't sure what to say but didn't want to just forget it after all. That hadn't worked out so well for him the last time, all those years ago. "...about what happened back there." He waved towards his office.

She grabbed his hand and stopped him. "It's okay. It happened; there's nothing we can do about it now. Let's just forget about it." She turned away and reached for the doorknob.

He turned her back to face him and looked her squarely in the eyes. "There's no forgetting *that*, and I think we both know it, but we can talk about it later, okay?"

The look in his eyes was so intense it made her fluttery all over again, and all she could do was nod.

In the conference room Liz and Jeff were in a discussion concerning what Liz had found at the library.

"What did Mark have to say?" Jeff asked after she told him about the other missing girls. He trusted Liz's gut one hundred percent.

"I haven't had the chance to tell him yet. With everything that's going on, the search has to be priority. Right now, Billy is the best lead we've got, and I'm the one who put him in the hospital." She couldn't shake the guilt.

"Who knows what would've happened between there and town." He was a firm believer that everything happened for a reason. "Maybe he would have passed out from exhaustion and hypothermia before he told anyone anything, and then we wouldn't even know where to start a search. Maybe that's why you came when you did, to make sure we knew where to start..." Jeff wasn't trying to make her feel better; he believed every word.

Their conversation was interrupted by the sound of the door opening. Upon seeing her friend looking a little flushed and slightly disheveled, Liz raised an eyebrow but decided to let it go for now. Liz looked over at Jeff who obviously didn't notice his sister's freshly manhandled appearance.

Men, she thought, and silently shook her head.

"It's about time you guys joined us!" Jeff boomed. "Can we get this search started or what?"

"Mark, I just need one second." Since the meeting was already stalled, Liz decided now would be the best time to bring up what she found. She pulled him off to the side and quickly explained everything she had found at the library.

Mark didn't waste any time. "Call this number." He jotted it down real quick. "Tell him everything you found and everything you suspect. Tell him about the accident and the search. His name is Mitch, and he'll get everything we need to know about all those cases. Okay?"

Liz nodded, snatched the paper from Mark, and left the room to make the call. A few minutes later, she snuck back in and nodded at Mark. The call was made, and Mitch was on it.

It took time, longer than Mark had hoped, to organize everything and recruit several trustworthy locals to help with the search. But it couldn't be helped; the safety of the people under his watch was a priority. Not only wouldn't he risk the lives of others, but an injury or a screw up could cost them precious time. When they finally left the station and got the search underway, there were only a few hours of daylight left.

At the site of the accident, still recognizable by the spot of Billy's blood on the road, Mark and Kyle got the base set up quickly, and everything started to move rapidly. Once again, Kyle would be in charge of traffic detail. He would detour any passersby around the barricade to make room for the command center, which consisted of a six foot foldout table and a couple of chairs. His other two officers, Frank and Jamie, would be heading two of the teams searching the woods.

Teams were split and radios handed out. A quick explanation of the plan was outlined to the new recruits, and the teams were sent to their entry points into the woods. Lester would be there any minute with his two dogs, Mutt and Jeff. They were trained in search and rescue and had been used all over the state, so Lester wouldn't need much instruction. He understood the grid theory of a search.

The premise of a grid search was to section out the area to be searched into rectangles. Each team was assigned a series of rectangles. They would spread across their starting area within hearing distance of each other to allow maximum coverage without too much overlap. After a certain amount of time, the team leader would call in and that rectangle would be filled in on the map. The team would then start the next rectangle, and so on, until the entire grid was filled in. Call-ins were staggered to allow the person at command time to fill in each area and document each call. It could be a slow process, especially in overgrown woods, even with the dogs.

They had used a plot map that showed a several mile stretch of the road and the woods beyond. The map showed property lines as well as waterways and also distinguished between woods and fields, which had made it easier to grid out. Certain rectangles could be bigger than others depending on terrain.

Lester had called a few of his friends from the canine search and rescue group he belonged to, but on such short notice and with the distance some of them would have to drive, it would be at least another hour before any other dogs could join. There were several acres of woods that needed to be searched.

He sent the teams off to get started. Some had to drive to their starting points, but the search was finally under way. Mark looked to where Laura was stationed with the map in front of her.

"Do you know what to do?" he asked as he walked up behind her, having to stop himself from putting his hand on her back affectionately.

"Yes, when the team leaders check in every thirty minutes or so, I mark off the areas that have been searched." She looked up from the map into his eyes. "You'll be using one of the dogs?"

"Yeah. I've worked with Mutt before...he's a good dog." Mark couldn't take his eyes from hers. "We'll find her Laura."

His gaze was a little disconcerting, so she looked back down at the map. "Whose properties are these?" she asked, pointing to the plots on the map. There were only four butting up to this stretch of the woods.

"This is the old Johnson farm." He pointed to the plot closest to town. "It's been sitting empty for years. Their kids want too much for the land and seem fine with just sitting on it. This is Jim Cook's here; this is the Riley place..." That fact hadn't escaped him earlier when he looked up the plot numbers to make sure. "...and this is the Prewitt farm." He studied the map intensely for a moment. "Based on where Billy came out, it seems most likely he came from either Jim's place or the Riley farm." He intended to head one of the teams heading towards Jacob Riley.

Just then, Lester pulled up and jumped out of his truck with both dogs. He didn't waste any time. "Where am I starting?" he asked, grabbing a radio from the table.

Mark quickly went over the map with him and brought out the items he had of Billy's they would use for his scent, the mangled shoe and his jacket. Once the dogs became familiar with the scent, they took them to the edge of the woods.

"I'll be the head of team A. You've got B. You and I will pretty much be on the same team though because we know this is where he came out. We have a witness." He looked at Liz. "You ready?"

"I don't know. I think I'd be better off re-interviewing witnesses. Not that I don't want to help search, but the more I look at the map, the more I think maybe Jim Cook or Jacob Riley might have some more information, even if they don't know it." She looked at Jeff. "What do you think?"

Mark also looked to his trusted friend. "Jeff?"

"I think she's right, but I'll go; if it's either of them, they could be dangerous," Jeff replied, having no doubt her gut was right.

"What?" Liz exclaimed. "You'll go? I'm a trained interviewer...!"

Jeff looked at her smugly. "So am I, remember."

"Okay you two; we don't have time for this," Mark interceded before it got out of hand. "I'd go, but I need to be here. We know Billy ended up here but not where he came from, and chances are it has nothing to do with Jacob Riley or Jim Cook. The search needs to be priority because it's the best lead we have." He looked between the two and shook his head.

He made a decision. They were both trained interviewers...it would be stupid not to utilize their strengths. "Both of you go. Talk to the kids again too. Joey and Ruth Hamilton, Lisa Johnson, and Melissa Rossi; they all seem to be a pretty tight circle. Chances are one of them may know where David and Billy were supposed to be this morning." He started walking back towards where the cars were parked to move them along quicker.

"Try Marianne Minelli too. She might've gotten something out of David's brothers and sisters by now. When I talked to her earlier, she suspected one of them knew something but wasn't budging, probably a sibling loyalty thing. Play good cop bad cop if you want, but let them know how serious it is. *Do not* sugar coat it. Let's find these kids, okay?" He could tell they were reluctant to work together on this, but he didn't have time to argue.

He decided to add another layer. "Look you guys; it'll be safer with both of you. If Jacob is the bad guy here...or Jim," he added, not wanting his bias against Jacob to weigh the interviews one way or another. "I don't want either of you going alone; he could be dangerous. We have enough volunteers to cover the grid." They agreed but reluctantly. He didn't miss the look that passed between them.

As Mark walked back towards the woods, he hoped he did the right thing. But, he didn't have time to worry about that right now. He looked at Lester. "You ready?"

Lester nodded. "I was born ready; let's do this."

Mutt barked at that...The dogs also seemed anxious to get started.

17

S he was still alone, and it was dark again. *Where am I? Did Billy really come, or was that a dream?*

These thoughts and others raced through Jenny's exhausted mind, and not for the first time since Billy was there.

It was freezing, and the burlap rags Billy gave her helped but only a little. Her wrists were sore and caked with blood from struggling to free herself, but she long ago gave up on that. Her shoulders were stiff from being forced in an unnatural position. She felt along with her fingers for the shard of metal Billy left for her.

He must've been here or I wouldn't have this or the blankets. It seems like he's been gone so long; hopefully the crazy man didn't find him.

Her stomach rumbled, not for the first time, and she realized the last thing she had eaten was grilled cheese and tomato soup the day before…or had it been longer? She didn't know. Her head was throbbing and her mouth was so dry her lips were cracking. She wanted so bad to scream for help but was afraid the only person who might answer was her captor, and that could be real bad. She put her head back against the wall and dozed.

The sun was shining bright, and it wasn't cold here. She was alone in a field of wildflowers. The colors were so bright and the smells so fragrant! She didn't remember ever having a dream this vivid.

"Jenny," she heard someone call from behind her.

Her heart leapt in her throat, and she turned at the sound of her father's voice.

"Daddy," she choked out on a sob and ran to him.

He scooped her into his arms and buried his face in her golden hair.

"Daddy." She was sobbing freely now, overcome with emotion. "I've missed you so much."

Jack continued to hold his daughter but knew he only had limited time with her. He gave in to one more squeeze then held her out at arm's length, so he could look into her beautiful blue eyes.

"You are looking more and more like your mother every day." He smiled sadly for a moment but hurried on because he could feel his time there diminishing. "Honey, listen to me." He didn't want to scare her too bad, but he couldn't sugar coat the situation either.

"Rest now while you can...because the bad man is going to come back for you."

He wasn't going to tell her why she was safe for the moment. Poor David, he thought, another innocent lost to the madness inside his old friend. If only he would've known before, he could've done something about it when he was alive, and none of this would be happening to his family. He shook the thought out of his head; he couldn't think like that right now. He needed to do what he could in his limited capacity as a messenger.

"The bad man is dangerous. He's not the man you think you know. Be prepared to use the knife Billy gave you. Hopefully it won't come to that; hopefully we, I mean your mom and Mark, can find you before then."

"Billy knows where I am though," Jenny interrupted excitedly. "He said he was going to get help."

"Billy had an accident when he left here..."

"No!" she yelled. "Did the crazy man get him?" Not Billy...her eyes started to tear up.

"No honey, he's safe just unconscious at the moment." He was going to try to work on that next, but he wasn't sure if his limitations would allow him to, at least not today.

"You need to be ready to help yourself if it comes to that."

"But how?" She remembered how puny the metal shard was that was wedged in the wall. And, how was she supposed to use it with her hands bound?

"Tell him what he wants to hear; try to buy some time. Help WILL come, but he might come first. If you need to fight, go for an eye with the knife; if that doesn't work, knee the bastard in the balls if you can, but don't hesitate whatever you do." He looked at her for a moment watching his words sink in. "And then run! And don't look back...stay away from the woods. Your speed is your advantage; you'll lose that in the woods." He didn't want to scare her too bad, but she *needed to know what she was up against. "Honey, he's killed before; it could be his life or yours, just remember that"*

He set her away from him with a last kiss on the top of her head. "I need to go now honey; I've been here too long already."

Jenny started to cry again. "I don't want you to go."

"I know sweetie, but I have to. I'm going to do everything I can to help you, I promise." I just hope it's enough, he worried to himself as he faded away.

Jenny woke abruptly on a sob and felt more alone than she ever had, but oddly, she also felt stronger and ready to do what must be done if necessary. She felt again for the knife and found comfort in its coldness against her fingers. She practiced grabbing the knife and putting it back in its place over and over. She almost dropped it twice. She didn't have much room to work with since her hands were chained above her head.

Who is Marie? She wished she would have asked her dad that question. She had no doubt the dream was real and her father had really visited her. *And why does he think I'm her?*

She thought about the crazy man's earlier visit. She had thought for sure she was going to die. He seemed pretty upset with Marie. He had said something about her ripping his heart out when she left them.

And who is them? Is there someone else involved? She may never know the answers.

Maybe Marie was an ex-girlfriend or something like that. She thought about it for a while and decided if she was going to have a chance with the knife she would have to have her hands free. If he thought she was someone named Marie, maybe she could pretend she was Marie and talk him into untying her hands. It was worth a shot. She couldn't save herself if she stayed in the position she was in; she was sure of that.

Her mind was reeling, but the hunger and dehydration were exhausting her. She decided to try and rest like her father had suggested. Within minutes of leaning back, she dozed again. She dreamed.

She was in the field where she had seen her father earlier.

"Dad!" She spun around looking for him in all directions. "Daddy! Are you here?" She started to run calling for her father, desperate to see him one more time and to feel his arms wrapped around her again.

She looked around and noticed this was NOT the same field she had been in earlier. That field had been vibrant and full of colors and sunshine. These flowers were droopy and infested with insects. And the sky was dark and rumbly with thunder. She stopped running; she was panting hard, out of breath. The bugs started to crawl on her skin and she swiped furiously at her arms and legs. She had to get out of there. She ran...

Now it was snowing, and she was running through an empty field. She tripped on something she couldn't see and skidded on her hands and knees. She tried to get up but hands grabbed her from behind.

Marie...

She jolted awake and yelped from the fresh pain in her wrists. She was out of breath and searched the darkness for any sign of the crazy man.

Just a dream, she told herself and finally drifted off again, thankfully into a dreamless sleep this time.

18

"Let's hit David's house first," Liz suggested, sliding into the passenger seat of Jeff's sports car. "Who knows, he may have even shown up by now."

She had reluctantly agreed to let him drive. But in reality, she was glad; her little Chevy was low on gas and needed a little TLC. She preferred to work alone but was glad she wasn't driving, so she could write down some of her thoughts. Writing things out often helped her work through it.

Sometimes she could write it better than she could think it or even say it. Not that she had trouble having a conversation, but from time to time, her thoughts were so numerous, they would get jumbled when she would start to talk. It could be frustrating at times...but writing...? That let her organize everything and gave her a focal point.

"Should we call first?" Jeff asked as he started the car. The engine purred like a kitten, well...more like a lion.

She thought about it for a second, looking up from her notes. "No, let's just pop in. Give the kids the element of surprise." She liked the idea. "And since they're all in town too, we should probably talk to all Jenny's friends before heading out to the country."

Jeff put the car in gear and couldn't help but show off a little. He patted the dashboard. This little baby had some get up in her. He floored it, burning a little rubber before taking off like a rocket.

Liz yelped and reached for her seatbelt. "Holy shit, jerk face! You tryin' to kill us?"

Once to speed, he let off a little. "Scared you did I?" he asked with a gleam of humor in his eye.

"I just wasn't ready for it," she retorted, not willing to admit her heart was beating like a jackhammer in her chest. She checked the Minelli's address in her notes. "Take the second left; it's…"

"I know the name of the street, Liz. I'm from here too you know?" He looked at her with a sarcastic smile on his face to show he was clearly joking.

"I didn't mean it like that…" she started to defend herself then saw his smile and stopped. She rattled off the address, confident he would find it.

Jeff had always made her feel a little self-conscious. She had always seemed to feel unsure around him. He was always so perfect, almost too perfect, in every way. Everybody loved him. He was funny and smart which made him witty as well. He was also kind and considerate. Plus, he was athletic and fit; he had played varsity soccer all four years of high school and had made it to state twice in singles tennis. Not to mention, he was extremely handsome. He was a little too clean cut for her though; she wasn't really into pretty boys, but that smile could melt butter.

As they pulled to the curb in front of the Minelli house, they talked strategy for a minute.

Liz looked at Jeff. "You should definitely be good cop."

Jeff almost looked insulted. "Why?" he asked, almost huffily.

"Please, look at you; everybody likes you and trusts you on the spot, especially if you pull out that smile." Which he did as he listened to her give a play by play of what she expected. "If you start talking law and being able to work a deal and spinning your hotshot lawyer crap…" He smiled even bigger at that. "…then I can come in hard like 'Kids are missing and you want to make a deal?' You can calm me down and then I can say, 'screw the deal; we just want information. We'll forget you ever hid anything if you tell us now, otherwise we'll take you downtown and make you talk.'"

He laughed. "You watch too much TV; downtown, Liz? We're not in Chicago anymore, Toto." He laughed again. "But I get the idea; I'm sure we'll figure it out." He opened the door and got out of the car.

"Maybe I got a little carried away," she admitted as she joined him on the sidewalk in front of the Minelli house. "But, I don't want to waste any time if we're sure they don't know anything okay?"

On that they were in agreement. It was possibly his niece's life on the line. He needed to remember that, so he nodded, and they walked to the door.

Jeff took the lead when the door was answered by a small round Italian woman.

"Yes?"

"Hello Mrs. Minelli; we're here on behalf of the local police department. Mark is in the middle of the search for your son and Jenny Mitchell. We were hoping you and your children would have a few minutes to answer a couple questions."

"Of course, of course...Please, call me Marianne," she replied as she wiped her hands nervously on her apron and let them into her home. She had a real bad feeling about David.

Because she and her husband had nine children, she was a stay at home mother. The youngest of the nine was five and the oldest twenty-two, and at thirteen, David was the middle child. She was the epitome of the Italian housewife. She cooked everything from scratch, kept a very tidy house, and was clearly the boss of the home.

Mr. Minelli owned and operated Minelli's in town. It was known as a pizza joint, but it was more than that. It was a casual Italian restaurant with checkered tablecloths, the best lasagna in Illinois, and a fun family atmosphere. They had moved to town about the time Jeff had left for school. Of course, he had eaten at Minelli's numerous times when he'd come back to town. He had met Anthony, her husband, but had never met Marianne.

She led them into a sitting room with comfortable overstuffed chairs. This was clearly not the typical living room, like the one in the house he grew up in, where you weren't really allowed to sit on the furniture unless there was company. This was a very comfortable, lived in room.

She motioned into the room. "Please sit; I'll gather the children and get some refreshments."

Gathering the children consisted of going to the bottom of the stairs and yelling, very loudly, "FAMILY MEETING, NOW!" Without waiting for a response, she walked to the kitchen to put together a quick snack.

Liz and Jeff exchanged a quick grin as they heard the pounding of feet coming from multiple directions above their heads. Once everyone had made it downstairs, Marianne was coming in with a tray containing 2 glasses, a pitcher of tea, and a plate of cookies.

She set everything on the coffee table, turned to the children assembled at the bottom of the stairs, and said, "Sit." They all scrambled to find a spot on the couch. A couple of the younger ones sat on the laps of the older ones. There were six in all.

"You'll have to excuse Tony and Angela; they're at work with their father today," she explained then turned to the six children who were present. "You will not lie. They are with the police and you never, ever lie to the police." Rumor had it there was a family mob connection somewhere and that was the reason they moved from Chicago, to get away from the lies and corruption. They wanted to raise their children on honesty and morals.

Marianne nodded to Liz and Jeff indicating they could proceed.

Impressed with the display of authority, Jeff cleared his throat. "As you all know, your brother David is not here."

They all nodded in agreement. "Did he tell any of you where he and Billy were going today?"

They all responded in the negative, some shaking their heads, others verbally with a no or nope.

Liz noticed the youngest, a little girl of five, looking a little squirmy on her sister's lap. She stood up, walked over in front of the little girl, and squatted down in front of her to put them at eye level.

"What is your name?" Liz asked the little girl.

"Anna," she responded in an angelic voice.

"Anna, do you know where your brother is?"

She quickly looked at her Mother. "I didn't lie, Mama; he didn't tell me where he was going...he didn't."

Marianne smiled at her daughter. "It's okay, honey. Answer the lady."

Liz asked again, "Anna, do you know where your brother is?"

"No." But she smiled "I know what they were going to do though. I heard them talking about it, but it doesn't make any sense." The little girl shrugged her little shoulders in confusion and wrinkled her little face. It was almost too cute to handle.

Liz smiled. "Why is that?" She wanted to squeeze all that cuteness.

"Because cows are soooo big!" she said, spreading her arms out wide. Then she whispered to Liz conspiratorially with big eyes, "Have you ever seen one?"

Liz couldn't help but grin at the little girl despite her confusion. "I have, and they are very big, but what does that have to do with your brother, sweetie?"

Anna giggled. "They were going to tip them over. How do you tip over a cow? That's just silly." She emphasized this with her hands outstretched palms up.

Liz and Jeff exchanged a glance. "You're right, Anna; that is very silly." She gave the little girl a hug because she couldn't help herself.

None of the others knew anything about the adventure, and after a few more minutes, Marianne dismissed her children and walked Liz and Jeff to the door. "I knew one of them had to know something.

Sweet little thing, my Anna; I guess it proves the way you word a question is just as important as the question itself."

And I call myself a lawyer, Jeff thought to himself ironically. *That's like law 101.*

"We appreciate your help ma'am." Jeff turned to her after stepping onto the porch.

"Don't thank me; my son is missing. I want him home." She was worried. David always managed to get tangled up in something.

"We will let you know as soon as we know something," Jeff assured her.

"Now it's my turn to thank you." She smiled, but it was only fleeting. "My David…" she started, shaking her head. "Trouble is always finding that boy. He's just so curious; he has to try everything. It worries me." She looked towards the stairs and sighed. "But, when you have nine children, what doesn't worry you?"

Jeff smiled his million watt smile and hugged her for a minute. "We'll be in touch; I promise."

Liz was already in the car and calling Mark. "It keeps going right to voicemail," she said frustratingly.

Jeff climbed into the car. "Probably a dead spot in the woods; call Laura. She can get him on the radio."

She gave him the Hamilton's address then called Laura.

She answered on the first ring. "Hey Laura, we just talked to David's mom. It looks like Billy and David were going cow tipping this morning. I tried to call Mark, but it was going straight to voicemail. Will you let him know it looks like they're probably heading in the right direction? Three of the four farms are occupied, so there's a good chance there's cows on one of them." She said it all really fast so

Laura wouldn't have a chance to interrupt, but when she was done, Liz listened to Laura's update on the search.

After she disconnected, Liz turned in her seat and filled Jeff in. "It's really just starting to get well underway, sounds like, and progress is finally starting to be apparent on the map…" She sighed. "…but there hasn't been any sign of anything yet. It did seem one of the dogs was on the trail for a little bit but is having trouble picking it back up. She's going to let Mark know what we've found so far." Liz finished and turned to look out the window.

They drove the next few blocks in silence both lost in their own thoughts.

They pulled up to the Hamilton house. The wind was really starting to pick up, so they hurried to the porch. They knocked several times, but no one answered.

Jeff peered in a couple windows. "It's dark. It doesn't look like anyone is here." He knocked loudly one more time.

Finally, after it was apparent no one was home, they got back in the car and headed to see Lisa.

At Lisa's house the door was answered on the first knock.

"Patty?" Liz asked when she recognized the woman who answered the door.

"Liz!" Patty, Lisa's mom, and Liz had played softball together in high school. "Are you here about Jenny? It's awful, just awful. Lisa is beside herself about the whole thing. She was the last one to see her, and she just feels horrible for leaving her. I keep telling her that it's not her fault; she was just doing what she was told by checking in on time." Patty realized she was rambling while Liz and Jeff were out on the freezing porch. "I'm sorry. Please come in; I don't know what got into me."

She opened the door wider and led them into the kitchen. "I just don't know what to do. How is Laura? Poor thing...I couldn't imagine...there I go again rambling. I do that when I'm nervous. Is there any news?" she asked.

"Yes, but not like you mean," Liz said as she sat at the table still rubbing her hands together to warm them. *It sure did get cold quick.* She hoped Jenny wasn't outside in this.

"I just made a fresh pot of coffee. It's decaf, but it's warm if you'd like a cup," Patty offered, noticing Liz's attempt to warm her hands.

"That would be great," Jeff and Liz replied at the same time. They both looked at each other and shared a smile.

While Patty got out cups and poured everyone coffee, Liz told her about what happened with Billy when she came into town.

"Oh my God!" Patty put her hand to her mouth and almost dropped the mug she was holding. "Is he okay?"

"He's unconscious but stable." Liz still felt really horrible about what had happened. She knew there was nothing she could have done differently, but in her mind she was still responsible for him being in the hospital.

Jeff who was leaning against the counter stepped over and put a reassuring hand on Liz's shoulder. Seeing that Liz was still struggling with what happened to Billy, he took over the conversation.

"Billy is going to be fine," he said, more for Liz's benefit than Patty's. "But, David is now missing too. That's actually why we're here." Jeff accepted the cup Patty handed him. "We know they're all friends, so we're talking to all the kids to see if anyone may have known Billy and David's plans for this morning."

Taking some comfort from Jeff's hand on her shoulder and the warm mug now in her hand, Liz recovered. "Would you mind if we spoke to Lisa for a minute?"

Patty jumped up. "Of course not; I'll get her. She's been crying pretty much nonstop since we got the news about Jenny. She's napping, but I'll wake her. Just give me a few minutes." She left Jeff and Liz alone in the kitchen.

"Billy *is* going to be okay Liz." He gave her shoulder a squeeze and broke contact. "I'm going to call Melissa's house and let her know we're coming there next."

Melissa answered the phone on the third ring. "Hello?"

"Melissa? Hi, it's Jenny's Uncle Jeff..."

"Is she home?" Melissa asked excitedly, not letting him finish.

"No, she's not home, but we'll find her. We need to ask you a few questions..."

Melissa interrupted again. "I already told Mark, I mean Chief Henderson everything I know."

"I know..." He had always liked Melissa's spunk, but he spoke quickly so she couldn't interrupt him again. "...but this is actually about Billy and David. We're with Lisa now," he said as he looked up and saw Patty come in with the girl. "I just wanted to give you a call and let you know we'll be coming there next, so you're expecting us."

"Ummmm...I don't think that's a good idea; I mean...my Mom, she's in kind of a bad mood tonight, and I really don't want to make her mad."

"We won't be long. We'll be there in about fifteen minutes, okay?" He didn't wait for an answer. "See you soon." He disconnected and looked over at Patty and Lisa. "Sorry about that."

Liz looked at Lisa. "Can you answer a few questions for us?"

The girl looked at Liz through bloodshot eyes, nodded, and took an empty seat at the table. She was clearly not handling the situation well.

Not that I can blame her. She was the last person to see Jenny. *She'll be haunted by what-ifs for a while.*

Liz decided not to bring Jenny up at all. "We're trying to talk to everyone in your circle of friends to find out more information about where Billy and David may have been going today."

Lisa looked at her, obviously confused. She had clearly thought they wanted to talk to her about Jenny.

"Sorry, I told your mom, but I guess you don't know what's going on...Billy was in an accident this morning..."

At that, Lisa's eyes got wide, and her concern was obvious. "What do you mean? Is he OK?"

"He'll be fine," Liz said, not sure if it was the truth, but it was the only answer she could give. "But, David seems to be missing as well." She was watching Lisa closely. "Do you have any idea where they may have been going this morning?"

Lisa shook her head. "I haven't really talked to anybody but Ruthie since I found out about Jenny." At Jenny's name, tears started to leak from the girl's eyes, but she continued, "They, Ruthie and Joey, left this morning to go on vacation. She had to come over and get some things she left here."

She wiped the tears off her cheeks and took a deep breath. "I haven't talked to Billy since we all left Jenny's yesterday after we talked to Chief Henderson. What happened to him?" She couldn't help but ask.

"He was struck by a car, but it's not serious," she added after Lisa went completely white. "He's fine, just some bumps and bruises really." She hoped.

"Then why doesn't *he* tell you where he was?" Lisa asked curiously.

Smart girl, Liz thought and squirmed a little. "Well, he's unconscious right now, but he *is* stable. He might be better off than Jenny and David though, because we know where he is."

Lisa nodded. She obviously understood the seriousness of what was happening. "I really don't know anything; I promise. Billy and I don't really talk like that." She sighed and looked at her mother, then back at Liz. "See...I have a crush on him, I really, really like him, and every time I'm around him I get nervous and we don't really talk much."

She seemed to be slightly embarrassed but continued, "And David? He talks so much that sometimes you just end up ignoring him." She blushed and looked at her mom. "I know that's rude mom, but he just doesn't stop, and he doesn't even notice when you're not paying attention."

"It's okay, Honey. I understand." Patty rubbed her daughter's back.

Lisa started to get teary eyed again. "Can I go back to bed please? I just wanna lay down." She looked between all three adults.

Jeff walked over, squeezed her shoulder, and said, "Sure honey, get some rest."

After Lisa left the room, Liz and Jeff stood to leave, and Patty walked them through the house.

Liz hugged Patty at the door. "I'm sorry, Patty; we didn't want to upset her even more, but we have to figure this out."

"I know...and so does she. Good luck."

In the car Jeff looked over at Liz. "So much for your bad cop routine. You're just a big softie under that harsh exterior."

"Look who's talking, hotshot." But she was smiling.

"Yeah but we already knew that about me." He gave her his sarcastic smile. "So, the Hamilton's are on vacation. We can try to get them on the phone, but if they left early, chances are they won't know anything. Let's see what Mel has to say," Jeff said, using Jenny's name for her best friend.

Melissa lived with her mother in a small apartment on the edge of town. When they pulled up, the door to the apartment opened, and Melissa came running to the car. She slid in the back seat behind Liz before they even had a chance to unbuckle.

"Hey, Uncle Jeff." Since she had been Jenny's best friend forever, Melissa had known Jeff for a long time.

"Hey Mel, what's going on?" He turned to look at the small girl.

"You know...same old. Tell me what's going on. Please?" She didn't have much time; her mom could wake up at any moment.

He didn't soften it for her. He told her everything that had been going on that day.

"Stupid boys!" Melissa stated vehemently. "Why on earth would you want to go out in the freezing ass cold and try to tip over a giant animal?" She just sighed and shook her head. She didn't understand boys sometimes.

Liz raised her eyebrow at the girl with the use of the curse word. "I agree." By the girl's reaction though, she obviously didn't know about the boys' plans ahead of time.

Mel looked at Liz as if noticing her for the first time. "Oh hey, Liz; where the hell have you been? It's been a while."

"You kiss your mother with that mouth, kid?" Liz asked her jokingly but saw she may have hit a sore spot when Melissa flinched.

"Yeah, that's not how me and my mom work." Mel shrugged it off; unconsciously rubbing a fading bruise on her cheek. "So, what do we do next?"

Neither of them missed the undertones of the exchange; Liz and Jeff shared a silent look.

"We, as in Jeff and I, go and talk to a couple more people and try to figure out what's going on around here." She pointed at Melissa. "You, as in you, go back inside and call us if you hear anything," Liz responded, choosing not to bring up her suspicions right now. She'd let it stew for a while and make sure she approached it with care.

"Come on. I can help. I'm going crazy in there...Mom's passed out, I mean, asleep and all I'm doing is going crazy worrying about Jenny, and now Billy's in the hospital, and David's missing too?" Mel was getting heated. "I can't just sit here!"

Knowing how she felt but reluctant to let her help, Liz explained, "I get that, trust me, but there's nothing you can do."

At Melissa's hurt expression, she softened a little. "I'll tell you what; if nothing breaks tonight and we're still searching tomorrow, and your mom says it's okay..." She stared her down for a second letting her know she was serious about having permission. "I'll take you with me to the search and find something for you to do...Deal?"

Mel, afraid Liz might change her mind if she sat around long enough, jumped out of the back seat and said "Deal!" She slammed the car door and ran back inside.

"Well, that was a quick visit," Jeff exclaimed. "I really like that kid." He shook his head in wonder.

"Me too." Liz was still looking at the door Melissa just went through. "What do you know about her home life?"

"Not much." But, they were both more than curious now. "I know it's just her and her mom. She's at Laura's place a lot, I know. Doesn't seem like they get along very well, does it?"

"No it doesn't." Liz shook it off. She'd worry about her thoughts later. Liz looked at Jeff and smiled, wanting to change the subject for now. "Let's go for a country drive, what do you say?"

They had gotten a lot done in the little over an hour they were in town. It went a little quicker than expected. They didn't really get any new information, but they knew the search was potentially on the right track, at least with the cow connection. Now, it was time to talk to some adults and see if they could crack this wide open.

Jeff backed out of his parking spot, put the car in drive and looked at Liz. "Let's do it." He peeled out of the parking lot. This time Liz laughed.

19

He had to pull a few strings and call in a few favors, but Mitch was able to obtain all the files for the list of missing girls Liz had given him. He didn't mind cashing in on a few of his favors for Mark. After all, Mark had saved his life several years ago in Chicago. He knew Mark didn't see it like that...even considered it all part of the job...but if it hadn't been for Mark's actions, he'd surely be dead.

Taking a break before going through the files, Mitch got up to stretch. He felt like he was getting old sometimes. He was almost 43, and sitting for long periods made his bones start to ache. He grabbed a diet coke out of the mini fridge he kept in his office at home. He downed half of it then went into the bathroom to splash some water on his face to wake up a little. He looked at himself in the mirror.

He may have felt old sometimes, but he still had all his hair with no signs of gray. It was light brown and thick. He kept it short but stylish. He was in pretty good shape too; he worked out religiously, so his five foot eleven frame was lean but muscular. He did have a few crow's feet around his uniquely gold colored eyes and some smile lines around his mouth, but that just made him appear to be a happy guy. When you thwarted death, what was there not to be happy about? His entire outlook on life changed that day ten years ago. It wasn't always easy in his line of work, but he was the epitome of the optimist. He thought back to the day Mark saved his life.

There were several agencies involved in the operation. Carlo Bertelli was under investigation for multiple felony offenses including international drug trafficking, illegal arms dealing, and sex trafficking; not to mention numerous other illegal activities. There had been a deep undercover investigation going on for over five years, involving several undercover agents from various agencies.

It had gone surprisingly well in the five years considering so many jurisdictions were involved...mainly because no agency wanted to lose Carlo over glory. Everyone pretty much agreed at the beginning that all the jurisdictional crap could be sorted out after he was finally busted. It seemed that day may have finally come.

Mitch had been part of the team for three of the five years and knew this was their best chance. Four of their combined moles had given the same information on a delivery coming in by boat off Lake Michigan in two nights. The shipment supposedly consisted of drugs of various types, several different types of weapons, and sex slaves of various ages and nationalities.

They only had thirty six hours to put together the operation of a lifetime. They needed a lot of foot soldiers for their intent and had recruited a large number of Chicago PD for the efforts. Mitch had been in charge of directing one of the teams that was to secure the perimeter of the harbor.

Everything had gone well until one of the team members turned on them...of course Carlo would have spies of his own. Carlo's mole, one of Mitch's own men, pulled a gun on him and shot. If Mark hadn't seen it happening and got in the way of the bullet, who knows what would have happened. The rogue agent was taken down quickly by another team member, and Mark had taken a bullet to the shoulder.

Luckily for the operation, Carlo didn't have enough notice to cancel the shipment or turn it around. He did have enough notice though to make sure he wasn't on site. Unluckily for Mark, he had to spend several days in the hospital.

Mitch reflected on the operation. With enough circumstantial evidence, they were able to detain Carlo. Even with a hotshot high priced attorney, he had been held without bail. The rogue agent who had shot Mark testified. With that and other testimonies, plus all the evidence compiled in the five year operation, Carlo would be in prison for a long time to come. Bottom line though? He owed Mark his life and would do whatever he could to help him now.

Mitch shook himself out of the reverie and got down to the business at hand. On a quick perusal of the files, Mitch was able to eliminate two as possible connections. One had been found alive and well with her boyfriend in California a couple years after the initial report was filed. Another had become a closed murder case. The parents had been found guilty of Filicide, or the murder of one's own child.

There are truly some sick people in this world, Mitch mused.

Both those cases happened to be the two that didn't have dates coinciding with Jenny or the others on the list. The resemblances between all the girls left on the list were superficial at best, (blond hair, blue eyes, with ages ranging from fourteen to twenty) but sometimes that was all it took. Jenny was the youngest by over a year, but she was an early bloomer it seemed by her photo.

Kids these days are growing up faster than I remember. He didn't have any kids of his own, and had never gotten married. He was too involved with his work to make, in his mind, maintaining a relationship possible.

After making several phone calls to various officials in the surrounding areas, he found out all these cases had stalled almost immediately and been left open. Most hadn't been worked on in years. There was apparently never anything to work with.

Maybe if the connection Liz found had been found earlier, things would have been different. It seemed there was a possible serial kidnapper/maybe murderer at work in the boonies of Illinois. The timing and physical appearances just couldn't be a coincidence.

After another hour or so of reading through all the files, Mitch caught onto another similarity…the height of the missing girls. They were all very short. All the girls were between four foot eleven inches and five foot, even the two adults. He pondered on that for a minute. He thought about all the crazy people he had come across in his fifteen years with the FBI.

People killed for all kinds of reasons and not all of them always made sense. Not that it was ever okay in his mind to murder someone in cold blood, but sometimes you could understand why people justified it. Other times, it was the voices telling them to do it, and that was all the reason they needed.

He decided to head down to Jefferson and see what he could do to help. He'd call Mark on the way and check on the progress down there. It would be good to see his old friend in the process.

With what was going on in Jefferson with this Billy kid and the possibility of finding Jenny, he wondered if all these open cases would finally be closed when this played out. And, he couldn't help but wonder if there may be more; he called his boss, Carl Stope, to let him know he was going to need the next couple of days off. He gave him a quick rundown of what was happening and why he felt obligated to help.

"I have a feeling about this one though, Carl; I might be seeing you soon."

20

After they got out of town, Liz voiced her concern for Melissa. "Did you see the bruise?"

He didn't have to ask her what she meant. "Yeah, I was thinking about it too." Jeff glanced over at her. "It seems like Melissa may be having some troubles at home." He gripped the steering wheel tightly as he bit off the words.

"I've got it brewing in here." She tapped her head. "I'm going to talk to her and try to get her some help if it's needed. I've already decided, but right now..." She grabbed his arm to emphasize her words. "...we need to find Jenny. I feel like we're running out of time."

"I know what our priority, Liz. It's my niece who's missing!" he said with a little too much force. He saw her flinch out of the corner of his eye and softened his tone. "Sorry, it's just...that shit really pisses me off! She's just a kid...there's no excuse for it."

"You're right, and we'll take care of it as soon as we can." She leaned back in the seat and took out her notebook. "I'm moving back." She decided to change the subject.

"Oh yeah?" He glanced at her. "What about the paper?" He let the change of topic go; he was going to let it brew for a while too.

"Well, it ended up being so boring; I mean, who really cares about the stupid Cranberry Festival or which house has the best Christmas lights!" she replied testily.

Okaaaay...touchy subject, he thought to himself, but asked, "So, you quit?"

Liz just sighed heavily. "Not exactly." She told him about getting fired the day before, how Tom had cheated on her, and how everything had just gone to shit. And, how she just knew it was time to come home.

And, here you are once again right where you need to be, he thought as he listened to her rant about her life the past few months. Deciding to keep his thoughts to himself, however, he asked, "So, what are you going to do now?"

"Honestly?" She said after thinking about it for a moment. "I think I'm just going to go back to doing freelance. The pay is decent, and I can do it anywhere." She started doodling on her pad as she thought about it.

She talked about her thoughts and plans for a moment. She'd figure it out in more detail after they found Jenny. "But, it doesn't really matter; I'll figure it out," she finished. "So, what about you? How is being a hotshot lawyer?" she joked.

"I hate it." His answer surprised them both.

"Really?" Liz looked at him intently, clearly surprised. "I thought you loved it."

"I like being a lawyer, but somehow the last few years I got caught up in the politics of working for the district attorney." He made eye contact for a moment. "Someone sees you're good at what you do and starts you on a path, and it's exciting don't get me wrong." He shrugged and went back to watching the road "It's great being recognized...knowing your work is appreciated, but eventually you get caught up...until you finally realize the path your on isn't yours anymore...I don't know."

He shook his head. "Maybe I'm just burnt out a little, but I've been thinking about it a lot in the last year. It's all about winning cases and making the DA look good, not helping people anymore."

He thought about it for a minute then grinned. "I was actually thinking about taking over Harold Lawrence's practice. He's been retired for over a year, and I've already talked to him about possibly purchasing his old building; it's just sitting empty right now."

He was getting excited now that he was finally talking about it out loud. "The nearest attorney is at least twenty miles away, and it definitely would be less stress, better hours, and close to my family." He was glad she let him get it all out. It felt good to finally tell someone what he had been thinking about for so long.

"Looks like you have it all figured out." Liz continued to look at him closely.

"Not exactly, but it's a thought." He knew though. Especially now, with everything that was happening; he knew he needed to come home to stay. His sister would need him regardless of the outcome of their current situation.

They finished the ride to the country in silence, both lost in their own thoughts about their futures.

After a few more minutes, Jeff roused Liz from her ponderings by announcing, "Here we are...the Riley farm." He pulled in and parked near the house. "You ready for this?"

Liz nodded. "Let's do it."

Jacob answered the door and the smell of alcohol permeated the air. "Yeah?" was all he said.

"Hey, Jacob; Jeff Post..." He held out his hand. "...can we come in and talk to you for a minute?"

"'Bout what?" Jacob ignored Jeff's outstretched hand. He was still blocking the entrance to the house with his large frame.

"A local girl, Jenny Mitchell, is missing; can we ask you a few questions?" Liz didn't bother with pleasantries.

Jacob looked at her through bloodshot eyes, obviously just noticing her for the first time. He was slow to answer. "I think I heard something about that." He was a little unsteady on his feet.

You could almost see the gears trying to turn in his head through the fog of alcohol. "Right," Jeff said slowly. "Chief Henderson came out last night and talked to you about it," he reminded him. "We're just here to do a follow up."

A little light of memory glowed in Jacob's eyes. "Yeah, I sort of remember that." He opened the door wider trying really hard to act sober, over annunciating his words and trying hard to stand up straight. "I'll try to answer your questions."

As he turned to lead them into the living room, Liz looked at Jeff with a raised eyebrow and said under her breath so only he could hear, "He's drunk as a skunk."

Jeff nodded and furrowed his brow as he followed Jacob through the doorway.

There's no way someone who stays this drunk could have kidnapped Jenny. He thought to himself because clearly Jacob was drunk all the time. He could tell; everyday drunks had a certain smell about them.

But you never know I guess. He had to keep an open mind. Alcohol does crazy things to people, and some drunks were very high functioning. He'd seen it dozens of times over the years in court. One of the best defense attorneys he knew was a raging alcoholic.

Their interview didn't last long and produced no new information. Jacob was clearly three sheets to the wind. His responses to their questions were garbled at best, but they got the gist of it. He had been hammered when he left Hank's the day before, but he hadn't wanted to admit it to Mark the night before. He didn't really remember the drive home and barely remembered his conversation with the chief the night before. He had not seen the paper, and did not have any information to share.

After leaving the Riley house, Liz and Jeff sat in the car and talked about their observations.

"What do you think?" Liz looked at him.

"I don't know." He shrugged. "He was clearly drunk in the middle of the day, and admitted to as much from the day before."

"Right, I get that it's the norm for him." Liz shook her head. She didn't really drink much herself, and although she knew alcoholism was an illness, it was hard for her to comprehend.

"Yeah, me too." He started the car and thought about it for a minute drumming his fingers on the steering wheel.

Jacob had lost his wife young and that was hard he was sure; he couldn't even begin to imagine. His sister had lost Jack young, and she hadn't turned into a drunk over it. Maybe if Jacob would have had a child to take care of he would have been spared some of his misery through responsibility.

Jeff sighed; he almost felt sorry for the man. "He wasn't lying; I'm almost positive of that." Jeff looked at Liz. In his career he had become pretty adept at reading lies. "But, he clearly has some memory lapses. If he's involved or saw something, he just may not remember."

"I don't think he was lying either though," Liz added on her own sigh. "He was too drunk to be that good at it."

They were in agreement there.

Jeff glanced at the clock on the dash and put the car in gear. "It's getting late quick; let's talk to Jim and see what he has to say."

21

Laura had just got off the phone with her mom updating her on the progress or lack thereof. She wanted to kick something! She felt like nothing was being done.

Of course, since she was manning the command center, she knew that wasn't true, but it was her daughter missing; that made it seem like progress was slow and time was short. Mark reemphasized her thoughts when he came out of the woods with Mutt twenty minutes later.

She saw him look at his watch and shake his head as he came towards her.

"It's getting dark quick in there." He looked towards the west where the sun was approaching the horizon. "Mutt took me on a little detour." He patted the dog on the head. "I think we found where Billy and David came from. They entered the woods a lot closer to town. Once I realized we were heading that way, I decided to come check on you." He looked at her closely, choosing to ignore the frustration he saw on her face for the moment. "And, I wanted to call the hospital and check on Billy too. I don't have much of a signal in there." Mark gestured towards the woods.

He made the call to the hospital. It only took a moment; when he disconnected, he looked at Laura grimly. "No change."

Her heart sank a little. "I just feel like nothing is happening!" she said frustratingly. She kicked the folding chair she had just been sitting in, knocking it over. She cursed slightly at the pain in her toe as she did. She felt a little better though from doing it.

"I know, and we got a later start here than I wanted." He looked towards the woods, choosing to ignore her angry action; he felt like kicking something himself. "I'm going to have to call it for the night," he added reluctantly.

Laura started to protest, but he stopped her.

"Trust me! I want nothing more than to not stop until we find her, but we have over a dozen people out there, and I can't ask them to risk their lives..." He held up a hand to stop her again. "...and I'm sure that not a one of them wouldn't, but..." He grabbed her shoulders for emphasis. "...we might miss something in the dark.

"I'm going to get on the radio and have everyone mark their spots. We'll start again at dawn." He looked at the map. "It doesn't look like much on the map, but we've covered a lot of ground." He pointed to the edge of the woods on the other side. "Once we get to the fields, it'll go quicker."

Since they were still alone, he took her into his arms. "We'll find her, Laura." He put her at arm's length and lifted her chin with his finger so he could look her in the eyes. "We will, I promise," he said with so much conviction that she couldn't help but believe him.

She smiled a half smile and couldn't resist. She stepped into him and leaned up to kiss him softly on the lips. She kept her eyes on his and saw the flash. When she would have pulled away, he pulled her close and deepened the kiss for just a second then drew away.

He cleared his throat and took a shuffling step backwards. "I really need to get everyone in before it gets too dark." He turned away quickly, cursing himself for taking advantage of her vulnerability.

Mark depressed the talk button on the radio and announced, "All teams return to Base. Mark your spots. All packs should have either orange ribbon or orange spray paint. We'll start again at dawn."

There were a few return squawks of protest on the radio, but he was insistent. "It's getting too dark to do anything else tonight; it's not safe. Please return to base as soon as possible for a briefing."

Laura put her fingers to her lips; they were still tingling. She cleared her throat as well in order to find her voice. "Is there anything you need me to do?"

He looked back as he returned his radio to his belt. They locked eyes for a minute. She felt the heat even from several feet away, and her heart skipped a beat.

"We'll wait for everyone to come in, and we'll do a quick briefing." He couldn't take his eyes from hers.

"Okay..." She didn't know what to say. The intensity of his gaze was leaving her almost as breathless as the kiss. She broke eye contact and walked over to the table to appear busy.

Laura picked up the chair she had kicked over. She could still feel a slight throb in her big toe. She focused on that in order to get her wits about her.

As the first of the searchers started to appear from the edge of the woods, a Sherriff's car pulled behind Mark's cruiser.

Deputy Lee Miller, Marks friend from the Sherriff's department, got out of the cruiser and approached Mark and Laura. He was a tall man, probably close to six foot four inches, and skinny as a rail. He also had a prominent Adam's apple.

"Hey Mark..." He shook his head. "...sorry it took me so long to get here, man; we had an accident out on Route 27. It was pretty bad. We had to cut someone out of one of the vehicles."

"Anybody seriously hurt?" Mark asked with concern in his voice.

"Not sure yet, the one we cut out was fine though. Craziest thing; not a scratch just trapped." He shook his head in wonderment. "The other vehicle was an older lady and she was bleeding pretty bad from a head wound." He put his hands on his hips in indignation. "She pulled out in front of the other car, and probably shouldn't have been driving. There needs to be a mandatory re-test for anyone over a certain age!"

Mark just nodded; this was a topic they'd discussed before.

"I mean if you can drive, great, but if not...!" The deputy huffed out a breath. "I mean, Jesus; they'll give anybody a renewal!" Lee looked at Laura knowing who she was immediately. Mark had talked about her quite a bit over the years...especially after a few beers. "Sorry...sorry." He waved it off. "It's a sore subject for me; anyway, it seems like everyone will be fine." He looked back at Mark. "Tell me what's going on here."

"I just called everyone in. It's too dark in the woods to keep going tonight." Mark just shook his head in frustration. "We did get confirmation the boys were more than likely planning on being in this area though. Cow tipping...wouldn't you know it? Stupid kids and their shenanigans."

Lee smiled. "Yeah, I got talked into that once myself when I was about the same age; you learn." He laughed. "Any other news?" He was serious now.

Just then, Mark's phone rang. He held up his finger for Lee to give him a second. "Mitch, do you have something for me?" He answered seeing the name on the readout.

He listened for a minute. "Yeah, we'll be back at the station in about thirty or forty minutes." He listened for a few more minutes and disconnected.

"That was my guy from the FBI; he's already on his way in. He has some information on the other missing girls. He'll be here in about an hour." He looked at his watch again.

"Have him come to the house." Laura made a split second decision. She shrugged when Mark and Lee both looked at her. "Mom's making her red sauce, and there's plenty. Liz and Jeff will be back soon too, and we can have the meeting there." They would be comfortable, be able to refuel, and her parents could be involved as well. She looked at the Deputy and smiled. "My mom makes the best red sauce."

No wonder Mark is in love with her, look at that smile. Lee couldn't help but return it. He patted his stomach. "You don't have to ask me twice!"

Mark laughed. "Watch out, Laura; he may seem like he never eats by the size of him, but he sure can put it away. He might eat all the sauce, pasta, and any sides all by himself."

Lee tried to appear hurt by the comment, but there was laughter in his eyes. He looked at Laura imploringly. "Don't listen to him; I'll save you a little." He approached her. "I'm Lee by the way." He offered his hand, and she shook it. "You're Laura; I've heard all about you from Mark."

At that Laura looked at Mark, who was trying to appear busy. "Really?" she asked curiously.

"We don't really have time for this." Mark interrupted trying not to blush. "Let's get everyone together and get this briefing started." He was glad the teams had started to arrive, so he had an excuse to change the subject.

I never should have got drunk enough to tell Lee about Laura and my feelings for her after that conference a few months ago, he chided himself.

Having no choice but to let it go for now, Laura joined the searchers gathered by the table. The briefing was short. Unfortunately, other than Mark's wild goose chase with Mutt, there wasn't a lot to talk about. It was brought up they should try to follow the trail Mutt had found, but in the other direction to see if they could find where the boys ended up. Mark had already marked the trail thinking the same thing.

All the volunteers re-volunteered for the morning. Knowing it could be a long day, Mark promised coffee and donuts. It was supposed to be even colder tomorrow. He made sure to reinforce the importance of dressing for the weather. He hoped the storm would hold off long enough to finish the search. He knew the snow could really slow them down, if not shut them down completely. He kept his concerns about the storm to himself.

Laura called her parents, then Liz, to let everyone know they were having a dinner meeting at the house. They would start when everyone arrived.

22

Jim Cook's place was right next door to the Riley's, but that was equivalent to a mile or so of driving. They rode the mile in silence, both thinking about how little they had really accomplished.

Liz wondered if it wasn't all a waste of time that could have been better served somewhere else.

As if reading her mind, Jeff said, "We still need to cover all the bases and take all the steps. Every possibility has to be pursued and at least ruled out."

"I know." She sighed heavily. "I just feel like we're running out of time." He was right; she knew it, but she still felt like time was ticking by way too fast. She was starting to feel a little anxious.

As they turned down the lane, Jim Cook's house appeared black as night. Not a light shown from any windows. Neither said a word as they drove down the lane and parked the car.

"It doesn't look like anyone is home." Liz looked around as she got out of the car.

Jeff got out as well and looked over the car at Liz. "Let's find out." He walked towards the steps to the front porch.

It was eerily quiet and the darkness of the house out in the middle of nowhere was creeping Liz out a little. She shivered as they ascended the porch steps. Jeff knocked loudly on the door, ensuring the sound could be heard through the entire house. After a minute with nothing, Jeff knocked again. They were getting ready to leave when they heard movement from inside the house.

A light came on startling Liz. She jumped and laughed at herself a little, realizing it was just the porch light.

What an idiot! Quit being so jumpy! she silently scolded herself.

A moment later, Jim Cook opened the door and peered out onto the now bright porch. "Hello? What can I do for ya?"

"Jim? Hi, it's Jeff Post and Liz Metcalf. I don't know if you remember me; I've been out of town for several years, so has Liz." He gestured to the woman standing next to him. "I'm Laura Mitchell's brother, and we'd like to ask you a few more questions about Jenny's disappearance if you don't mind?"

A look of confusion then one of concern crossed Jim's face. "Of course, come in, come in. Sorry to leave you in the cold; I was taking a nap...I've been a little under the weather, probably with the roller coaster ride in temperatures we've been having lately."

He led them into a small living room. "Has there been any word? I was telling Mark last night that I saw her and a couple of her friends in town yesterday. It's a shame; she's such a sweet kid."

Jim gestured towards the furniture. "Have a seat anywhere. You know I volunteered for a few years at the Fire Department with

Jack?" Realizing he was starting to ramble, Jim shook his head. "Sorry, I just got up; I need a minute to settle. I'm going to get some water; can I get you guys somethin'?"

"Actually, I could use a cup of coffee if it's not too much trouble." Liz smiled at Jim. "I need the caffeine; it's been a long day."

"Of course, that might be just the thing I need for this headache I've had brewing all day." He looked at Jeff inquiringly.

Jeff took a seat in an old rocking chair. "Coffee sounds good, thanks."

As soon as Jim left the room, Liz's phone rang causing her to jump in startlement. Man, she was jumpy all of a sudden. She fumbled the phone from her pocket and answered on the third ring.

"Laura!" she exclaimed upon answering. "Tell me you found something." Jeff jumped up expectantly.

"Okay, yeah..." She motioned Jeff to sit again and shook her head. No new developments. She listened for another moment. "Sounds good, we're about to wrap this up. Yeah, we're at Jim's house now." As she listened to Laura, Liz started wandering the room. She couldn't seem to sit still. "Okay. We'll be back in town in thirty minutes or so I'm guessing...."

She looked at Jeff for confirmation; he nodded. "...yeah...okay. Love you too, Laura Bean." She disconnected and looked at Jeff. "She sounded exhausted." Liz frowned at her phone. "Dinner meeting at her house when we're done; your mom is making her red sauce." They both smiled at that.

Liz was perusing the pictures on the mantle when Jim came in a few minutes later with three cups of coffee, a canister of powdered creamer, and a bowl of sugar. "I didn't know how you liked it."

"Black is fine for me." Jeff picked up a cup and took a sip. "So, you knew Jack?" Jeff decided to pick up where Jim had left off.

Jim looked at Jeff but walked towards Liz "Yeah, it was a sad day when he passed. He was a good man."

"Are these your kids?" Liz was looking at a picture of him and two little boys at the beach.

Jim joined her at the mantle and laughed a little. "No, those little rats are my nephews...my brother's boys." He'd missed those little rascals since his brother had moved out of state for work. "My wife and I never had kids."

"Is this your wife?" Liz asked, indicating a picture of a younger him with a petite blond woman in her thirties.

"Yep that's her." He smiled and replied fondly.

"She's beautiful." Liz remarked. *And tiny,* she thought, but didn't want to appear rude.

"Yep, she sure is." Jim beamed as he handed her a mug.

"Thanks." She took the mug and sat on the couch adding a little sugar to her coffee. After taking a sip, she sighed. "Mmmmmm. That hit the spot." She smiled at Jim. "Thanks."

"You bet, now tell me how I can help." He perched himself on the arm of the couch. "Has there been anything new since last night?"

They went over everything again. He answered all their questions, but it was clear Jim didn't remember anything new. Jeff and Liz told him about Billy's accident, David's disappearance, and of their plan for tipping cows; both watching him closely for any sign of reaction.

"Is Billy going to be all right?" He set his mug down, clearly concerned.

"I just talked to Laura while you were in the kitchen; there hasn't been anything new." She was still feeling a little antsy and wished she was still on her feet. "He's still unconscious but stable."

"That's good." Jim nodded and stood to stretch. "He's a good kid; a hard worker." He sat back down and sipped his coffee. "This stuff isn't supposed to happen around here. Missing kids I mean; I kind of remember a missing girl several years ago from around here. I don't remember her name or anything, but that was quite some time ago.

"This world sure is changing." He shook his head. "Any idea where David might be? He's the little spazzy kid right, one of the hundred Minelli kids?"

Liz smiled at the description. "Yeah, that's him."

Jim nodded. "Cow tipping you say?"

"That's the story we got from David's sister."

"I've pretty much been in bed all day with this sinus crap or whatever it is." He pressed a hand to his temple to indicate his headache. "I never made it out to check on the cows, or I may have seen something. I rounded them up close to the barn yesterday morning though since it was supposed to get cold. That way they could come and go from the barn." He looked at Jeff. "We can head out there and take a quick look if you want."

"Where was the accident?" Jim asked curiously on the way to the near field. They could see cows from the house.

"Out on Central." Liz shivered from the wind. "Actually it was on the other side of the woods at the back of your property."

They told him about the search and how it was underway but stopping for the night.

"We'll start again at first light if you want to join, there's room for volunteers." Jeff figured they couldn't have too many volunteers.

Jim seemed eager to join the search the next morning. "I'm pretty familiar with those woods. I did grow up in them." Jim smiled thinking it might do him some good to be involved with something right now; to take his mind off things. "Hopefully the storm holds off."

The remark sent a shiver down Liz's spine, and she remembered what Laura had told her about her dream with Jack.

You have to find her before the storm. He had told her.

She shook it off as they approach the large barn. "Would you know if anybody was here without your permission?" She looked around. It didn't appear he kept the barn very secure.

"I don't know." Jim shrugged "But it can't hurt to take a quick look around."

Nothing seemed amiss to Jim. He took the opportunity to make sure the cows had plenty of feed and water. Jim and Jeff went into the field with the cows, but Liz decided to stay back, wanting to avoid the very large creatures.

Anna was right, how could you knock one of those things over?

They came back from their quick walk through the field. "I didn't see any foot prints or anything that seemed off." Jim shook his head. "I don't know if that means they weren't here or not, but this is all the cows I have right now." He gestured to the field he and Jeff had walked through. "I do have a few more fields I use for grazing a little farther out on the property. And the Riley's have cows too, and a lot more of 'em."

He looked out in the distance past the barn. "It's getting too dark to head out there even to just look around." He motioned towards the west where the sun was dropping rapidly to the horizon. "But, I can head out there and check it out in the morning before I join the search."

"That would be great." Jeff clapped the man on the back, grateful for his willingness to help. "We truly appreciate all your help, Jim."

"No problem." Jim returned the manly gesture.

As they headed back towards the house, Jim explained the whys of rotating the grazing ground. He tried to rotate the fields every few months to ensure regrowth.

"But I don't have a lot of cows right now, so I don't have to do it as often." They had made it back to the kitchen door.

Jeff handed him a card. "My cell is on the back. Call us if you find anything in the morning if you don't mind."

Sensing the visit was over, Jim walked them towards the front of the house. "Of course." Jim put the card in his pocket as Jeff and Liz got into the car.

The impromptu search of the field had made their visit last a little longer than expected. By the time Jeff and Liz reached Laura's house, everyone else had arrived, and the table was being set for dinner.

23

"You okay?" Jeff asked Liz as they pulled up to his sister's house. She hadn't said a word the entire ride home.

"Yeah I just need a minute." She could feel the tears starting to come. "It's just been a really long day." She put her head back on the seat and took several long calming breaths.

Jeff gave her the minute she asked for, exiting the car to let her have it alone. After a few minutes, Liz got out and saw Jeff waiting for her on the porch so they could go in together.

She smiled at him. "You didn't have to wait for me." She climbed the steps, but he was blocking the door.

"Yes I did because I needed to give you something before we go in." He bumped her lightly with his hip.

"Oh yeah?" She teasingly bumped him back, appreciating the lightness. "What's that?"

"This." He pulled her into his arms for a tight hug. He held on for a minute taking comfort even as he gave it. "It has been a long day." He pulled away with the smell of her hair still sharp in his nose.

She smiled up at him. "That was a good hug, thanks; I needed it."

Before he knew his intentions, he had her against him again, and his lips were on hers. He just couldn't resist; her smile was so big and bright and shone clearly in her eyes. It was over almost before it started, but it had sent a jolt right through him.

He cleared his throat. "Sorry about that. It just seemed necessary." He smiled a crooked smile to keep it light, but his heart was still in his throat.

Liz didn't know what to say. She hadn't been expecting it, had never seen it coming. But, damn him! She would be thinking about it now! It was a short kiss, but it had sure packed a punch. She had been ready to dive right in without a thought.

Thank God he had ended it before I made a fool of myself. She couldn't deal with anything else right now.

"No big deal," she finally remarked. "It's been an emotional day and you got caught up." She explained it away for both of them and opened the door.

Inside, the smell of pasta sauce and garlic bread permeated the air. Jeff, who always had an appetite, breathed deep and grinned at Liz. "Red sauce," he said with smiling eyes.

Everyone was centered in the kitchen/dining room. Laura and Katlyn were busy putting the final touches on the meal. Laura was taking the garlic bread from the oven as her mother tossed a salad.

"Hey guys," Mark commented as he saw Liz and Jeff. "About time you guys made it."

Laura looked up. "I thought you'd be here forty five minutes ago." She had started to get worried.

Jeff told them about their time with Jim Cook and the short search of his front field.

"He plans on helping at the search tomorrow and is going to do a quick look over his property before he comes out," Liz added, snagging a piece of garlic bread.

"He'd be an asset," Mark reflected. "He probably knows every inch of those woods."

"That's pretty much what he said," Jeff agreed as he took a beer out of the fridge.

Michael who had just finished setting the table announced, "Let's sit and eat. We can talk during dinner."

Mark introduced Lee and Mitch to Liz and Jeff, explaining everyone's reasons for being part of the meeting.

Liz looked at Mitch. "Did you find anything more about the missing girls?" She was anxious for his answer.

"Actually I did," he began, but Michael interrupted.

"There will be time for that in a minute. Let's say grace." He grabbed his wife's hand and one by one they created a connected circle around the dining table.

Michael bowed his head and began, "Dear Lord, thank you for the meal before us. Please bless this food and everyone who will share it. Please Lord; keep my granddaughter and David safe until they are found. Please aid in the healing of Billy Richardson and allow him a full recovery. Please honor your children who have given their time to help us through this difficult time. We believe in your plan for us, Oh Lord, and know that everything in this life is part of that plan. Thank you Lord for everything you do and are, Amen."

A chorus of Amens followed, and there were several tears in evidence.

Mitch cleared his throat after a moment of silence. "How's the shoulder treating you Mark?" He decided to break the ice.

Mark automatically rotated his arm. "Not a hitch. I got lucky though; it was pretty much a flesh wound. It still acts up a little when it's raining though." He grinned at Jeff. "I'll never be able to fulfill my dream of beating Jeff in tennis either."

Mitch laughed. "Don't let him fool you, folks. This man here is a hero. He saved my life." Serious now, he looked at Mark. "I owe you man."

Mark blushed a little. "Quit being dramatic; it wasn't all that."

Mitch got even more serious. "You saved my life, and I will always be thankful." He grinned at Laura. "Have you ever heard the story?"

She looked at Mark sternly. "No, I haven't." She returned her attention to Mitch and smiled. "But, I would love to hear it."

As they ate, Mitch told the story with flair. He embellished a little, but it made it a pretty good story. "Okay," he finished, "maybe I exaggerated a little, but that's still pretty much how it went down."

Jeff, who had visited his friend in the hospital at the time, remarked with a huge grin, "He didn't look like much of a hero in his hospital gown that night."

Laura looked at Mark. "Is that why you came back?" The timing hadn't escaped her.

He looked at her for a long moment, his gaze intense "That's one of the reasons." The undertone was obvious.

Laura got goosebumps from the intensity of his gaze and had to break eye contact. She got up from the table. "Does anyone need another drink?" She asked using her empty wine glass as an excuse to compose herself.

When Laura came back to the table, Liz looked at Mitch. "So, tell me what you found." It was time to get down to business.

He told them everything he had come up with earlier in the day. Two of the cases had been closed but the others still remained open. One thing he'd noticed that Liz didn't was the height of the missing girls.

"Their looks were similar sure, but blond hair and blue eyes are everywhere. But, factor in the height as part of the "kidnapper's" criteria and it really adds another level to the connection."

Laura couldn't help but interrupt. "Kidnapper? You seem pretty confident that it's a kidnapping," she challenged.

"Well, let's look at what we have. Several missing girls with similar physical appearance, including height, which under different circumstances…like if it was a five-five to five-seven height range…that could be chalked up to just average height. But," He held up a finger for emphasis. "Being in the four-eleven to five foot height range is a pretty dominant feature for a woman, as it would be if they were five-eleven to six foot."

He was on a roll now. "To me, it seems more than likely the same person is responsible for all of the disappearances. And, I'm not convinced there aren't more we don't know about yet." He had been thinking a lot about that actually. "Plus," he added. "The date range is hard to ignore.

"Most of the girls were reported missing between December 18th and Dec. 22nd. The one that wasn't was reported on Christmas Day when she didn't show up for dinner at her parents. She was one of the two adult victims, and I found out earlier today she hadn't been seen or heard from prior to that for days. It just wasn't a concern until Christmas Day. So, I think it's safe to assume she was also taken between those dates as well."

He looked at Laura and finished his explanation, "There are just too many signs pointing to kidnapping to think otherwise at this point."

"So, you think we're dealing with a serial kidnapper?" Jeff looked at Mitch intently.

"I guess you could say that," Mitch answered, not voicing that more than likely they were dealing with a serial killer since none of the victims had ever been found.

When Mitch was done sharing his thoughts, Liz got up so she could move while she thought. "Maybe we should run another article tomorrow morning. We can run all the pictures. Highlight Jenny..." She stopped behind Laura and put a hand on her shoulder for a moment. "...and David. It will grab the reader's attention since they are known in town. Show the connection to the community, but have all the missing girls on the front page.

"They're all from near enough by where they might be recognized by someone. And even though it's been fifteen years, someone may remember something from when Margery went missing. A lot of people around here will remember that. Jim Cook even brought it up earlier when we were out there." She looked at Jeff for confirmation.

He nodded and she continued.

"I'll write the article. We want it short but informational. We don't want people to not read it because it's too long. The pictures should grab the reader though. I'll work on it after we're done here." She turned to Mark. "Did today's article get any response?" She sat down again ready to pass the baton, so to speak.

Mark sighed. "Sort of…nothing helpful really, mostly just offers to help look…a lot of people who saw what we already know; but nothing new."

Jeff asked him, "What about the search? Any luck there?"

"Not really. We do know which direction David and Billy came from. Lester has one of his team member's coming in tomorrow to work with Mutt. We figure if we can get the dogs going on both trails it should lead us to something. We're going to give Mutt David's scent where he took me yesterday to verify he was even with Billy. Even with the dogs though, it's a slow process."

It was his turn to stand up and pace. "What do you think about removing lots 1 and 4 from the search?" He looked at Lee. "If they were going cow tipping, that pretty much narrows it down to lots 2, the Cook farm and 3, the Riley farm."

Lee answered right away, "I don't know. You have enough volunteers to cover it all. So, removing sections won't really speed it up, and there's no guarantee they ever made it to any cows. Lot 1 is the vacant property. That right there is reason enough to keep it in the search if you ask me."

"I'm going to have to agree with Lee on this one," Mitch said when Lee finished. "If we have enough volunteers, and it looks like we'll have more tomorrow, I say keep it in."

Mark slumped back into his seat. "You're right. I just wish there was some way to speed it up."

Lee, who had been involved in a lot of regional searches, added, "Once we get to the fields, it'll go a lot quicker. You've already covered a lot of ground according to Laura's shadings on the map." He nodded towards her. "You're practically to the creek in all grids, and once we get past that, the fields are practically in sight."

Mark nodded in agreement. It was good to have outside perspectives to keep them on track. "I know you're both right. It's just hard to stay patient on this one." The feeling of running out of time was with them all.

They talked about the search for a little bit more and refined the plan. Lee would take over Command allowing Mark the flexibility to come and go if needed.

At some point in the morning, Mark wanted to make it over to the hospital to check on Billy in person. He also wanted to be able to follow any leads the new article might bring in. He wanted to pay another visit to Jacob Riley at some point too and try to catch him sober.

Michael and Katlyn weren't large participants in the conversation and planning, but they were doing a lot of observing. Michael got up to clear the table. He sent his wife a meaningful look, and she rose to help.

When they were alone in the kitchen, Michael took his wife into his arms for a quick embrace. "What did you think about that exchange between Mark and Laura?" He liked Mark a lot, but he wasn't sure how he felt about him and Laura as a couple.

She grinned, thrilled at the idea of Laura and Mark showing an interest in each other. "It's been a long time coming if you ask me."

He smiled then, not mentioning he had indeed asked her.

She continued, not noticing his smile. "It's about time Laura started seeing someone; it's been over two years since Jack passed away. She can't grieve forever."

"She's been doing fine, Honey." Michael defended his daughter. He felt Laura was the only one who knew when she'd be ready to date again, so he changed the subject. "What about Liz and Jeff?"

"There's something there; I'm not sure either of them know it yet though." She had noticed the curious glances they had been giving each other all through dinner, but it wasn't nearly as intense as Mark and Laura.

The electricity in the air between those two had almost electrocuted her twice since they had arrived together before dinner. The sparks were practically visible. "But Mark and Laura, they're both very aware."

Even though she liked the idea of Laura and Mark as a couple, she worried over it for a minute (it was her daughter after all) then decided to let it go. It was none of her business anyway. "Let's get back in there so we know what's going on. It sounds like everything might be coming together."

They reentered the dining room; the discussion had turned to the weather and the impending storm.

"It looks like it's not supposed to start snowing until later tomorrow." Liz looked up from her smartphone's weather app. She looked at Laura remembering her thought from earlier. "Didn't Jack say something about the storm in your dream?"

Laura, who had just been thinking the same thing, looked to Lee and Mitch who clearly didn't know about the dream. She quickly and almost embarrassingly explained to them the dream she had that morning; leaving out the more personal parts.

"One of the last things he said was, 'There's still time, but you need to find her before the storm.'" The two men looked skeptical, so she continued, "He also told me that Liz would help, and out of nowhere she showed up this morning without even knowing what's going on." *Had it really only been that morning?* she wondered, feeling like it had been days since then.

That was met with silence. It was hard to argue with such conviction.

Liz shivered, and the uneasy feeling she had earlier returned. She had a feeling she was missing something.

Day 3

24

Jeff glanced at the clock for what seemed like the hundredth time that night...well, morning technically. He couldn't stop his mind from going over and over everything they had talked about at dinner. Even though he had a feeling Mitch may think differently, he was still confident they would find Jenny and find her alive. But that didn't stop him from over-thinking everything.

Jeff wasn't a stranger to sleepless nights, but they usually involved either a lot of work or a lot of sex. In college he would pull all-nighters studying or writing papers almost nightly, catching a few hours here or there to recharge. Now, they weren't as common, but during big cases he'd find himself working until dawn at least once a week. As for the all night sex...

Yeah right, when was the last time you've had sex like that? he asked himself. *Or sex at all for that matter.*

Maybe that's my problem, he thought as he threw off the covers, giving up on sleep. Why else had he made a move on Liz?

He sat up on the couch he was using as a bed, wondering why he hadn't crashed in Mark's spare room. *I mean, it was Liz for crying out loud!* He rubbed both his hands on his face and through his hair.

She was practically his sister. Well, not really, but their relationship had never consisted of anything other than friendship. Never. Not even a stray thought or an, I wonder what it would be like, kind of thing, at least on his end. Up until the exact moment he had kissed her, he had never thought of it. He wasn't even exactly sure what had happened, but there was no doubt he was thinking about her like that now.

UGH! The timing was horrible, and he wasn't sure if he even wanted any kind of relationship with her.

She sure as hell wasn't someone he could just sleep with and forget about either. He decided it was best to just forget about it until after they found Jenny...or maybe even forever.

He thought about getting in the shower, but he didn't want the sound of it to wake anyone who had managed to fall asleep. So, he checked his email and did a little work to occupy his mind. When he got up to stretch, it was a little after three and his stomach was rumbling.

A little leftover pasta would do me good, he thought, thinking he might be able to catch a couple hours of sleep on a full stomach.

He tiptoed up to the bathroom to use the toilet then headed to the kitchen to devour some food.

As he was rooting through the fridge, he was thinking about Melissa and what he and Liz had discovered earlier that day. Child abuse in his mind was an abomination. He believed in disciplining children and had no doubt a smack to the mouth could be deserved (he had received a couple of those himself through his teenage years), but the bruise on Melissa's face wasn't caused by a mere slap.

He had known Melissa for a long time. He thought back to the last time he had made it back to town. He remembered a snippet of conversation they had. He had recently finished a long tedious case and had decided to come home for the weekend to decompress. He was in the back yard; they were getting ready to grill out. He had popped a beer and sat down to relax.

Melissa came up to him and said, "You know you shouldn't drink; it makes you mean." He laughed and said, "Don't worry darlin'; I don't have a mean bone in my body." He didn't think anything about it at the time, but it was true what they said...*Hindsight was twenty twenty.* Meaning everything was clearer when you look back.

He had a suspicion her mom wasn't just abusing her but was also abusing alcohol. A plan started to form in his mind. As he put the container of pasta and red sauce in the microwave to warm, he heard some movement form upstairs.

Looks like I'm not the only one who can't sleep. He assumed it was his sister.

25

Liz couldn't sleep very well. Every time she woke up and looked at the clock, less than an hour had passed since the time before. After the fourth time she woke up, the clock reading 3:33, she decided she may as well get up and pee.

After she used the rest room, she felt wide awake. She knew she was missing something, but she just couldn't put her finger on it. She needed to leave it alone to stew, but she just couldn't get it off her mind. She had barely eaten at dinner; there had been too much discussion of the day's events and developments.

Maybe a little food will put me to sleep, so my brain can shut off long enough to figure it out on its own. She decided to raid the fridge.

As she came down the stairs, Liz noticed the kitchen light was on and wondered who else was up at this hour. She assumed it was probably Laura. If she couldn't sleep, there was probably no way

Laura could. She smelled the sauce being reheated in the microwave and realized she hadn't really eaten at all that day, not just at dinner.

As she walked in the kitchen, her stomach growled loudly. She was ready to make a joke about it but saw Jeff, not Laura, leaning on the counter in nothing but a pair of sweat pants and wool socks. He looked up as she walked in, and their eyes met instantly. She stopped short, catching her breath, debating on whether or not to just go back to bed after all.

Damn, he sure doesn't look like a pretty boy with his shirt off, Liz noticed as she recovered her wits and walked to the refrigerator. The look they had just shared had been pretty intense, at least on her end. Her mind automatically went to the hurried kiss they had shared earlier.

"What are you doing up?" she asked casually, pretending like the moment never happened.

"Couldn't sleep." He shrugged. "Too much running through my head." He couldn't take his eyes off her. She looked cute and rumpled. He shook his head; this was Liz. Neither of them needed this right now, but maybe they should talk about it. Maybe it would release some of the tension.

Liz sat at the table. "Yeah, I know what you mean. I just keep going over everything. I can't seem to shut it off." She rested her head on her hand. "I just feel like I'm missing something that's right in front of my nose..." She sighed. "...I don't know, but I can't seem to do anything but doze off for a few minutes at a time, and I thought maybe a little sustenance would help." She gestured towards the microwave. "Is there enough for two?"

Jeff looked at her for a minute, saw she was exhausted, and decided not to bring up what had happened earlier.

"Yeah, there's plenty." He got out another plate. "Will you pour me a glass of that?" He pointed to the milk she had gotten out of the fridge.

They ate in companionable silence despite the earlier tension.

Jeff got up and cleared both their dishes. After rinsing them in the sink, he turned back to Liz and leaned back on the counter.

"So, what are you missing?" He was hoping to catch her off guard enough that she'd answer automatically.

She smiled, understanding the ploy. "Nice try." Her smile faded. "I just don't know." She looked up squarely into his eyes. "But there's definitely something." She was daring him to oppose.

"I trust your gut, Liz." He assured her. "As a matter of fact, I have reason to know for a fact that's why you're here."

"What do you mean?" She was confused and a little unsettled by his statement.

"Don't you think it's a little odd that you showed up today of all days...unannounced no less, without any clue as to what was going on?" When she didn't answer, he continued, "Not to mention the huge impact you've already had on Jenny's case, plus the potential other cases that might be linked."

"We don't know that yet." She got up to pace. "I mean, what if none of it is related, and it's just wasted time?" She stopped and turned to face him.

"Is that what you think?" he asked her.

"No," she said with absolute conviction. "I think Jenny is in the hands of a maniac who preys on young women. I also think we're running out of time. But for some reason, I'm nearly certain there *is* still time." She looked at him pleadingly for a moment then sighed. "Maybe that part of it's just because that's what I need to believe. I'm worried, Jeff."

"Me too, but…I still think there's a reason you're here, whether it be instinct or a guiding hand." He looked at her for a minute and decided to tell her. "Look, the reason I know, without a doubt, that you are here for a purpose is because it's not the first time."

"What are you talking about Jeff?" He was starting to weird her out a little.

"It's not the first time you happened to be in the right place at the right time." She just looked at him waiting for an elaboration. "Okay, do you remember when I broke my ankle senior year playing soccer?"

"Of course." It had been bad she remembered. "You were in a wheelchair for weeks and on crutches even longer." She wasn't quite sure where this was going.

"Okay just bear with me for a minute okay? I've never told anybody this before." He waited for her nod before he continued.

"Well, I was in pretty bad shape after that, and not just physically. Did you know I had scholarship offers for tennis from four different colleges?" He didn't wait for a response. "After I won state junior year, I was approached. I could go anywhere; a full ride…as long as I maintained a 3.0 senior year and continued to play my game, and that was a piece of cake.

"I had been 4.0 solid through junior year, and my game was only getting better. I was riding high all summer thinking I was going to be a pro one day. That was my dream. I loved soccer. I even loved school, but tennis was my passion."

He could smile at the memories now because he was mostly content with the way his life had turned out, and he was excited about the new direction he was thinking about heading.

"When I broke my ankle playing soccer, I didn't think about tennis right away or the possibility that I may never be able to really play again. I had multiple surgeries in the first month to repair the damage. But, with all the hardware, my range of motion will always be limited. There was a lot of pain in my recovery." He stopped for a minute and looked at Liz; this next part was the hard part to talk about.

Sensing this was important to him, Liz remained quiet and waited for him to continue.

"They gave me some pretty strong pain medication. At first, I needed it because the pain was almost unbearable...especially after rehab." He shook his head remembering. "But after a while, when I realized the rehab wasn't happening quickly enough, I asked my surgeon if I would be ready by spring to play tennis. I'll never forget the look he gave me; it was so full of pity..." He almost felt like he was there again. "...anyway, he said to me, 'Son, your tennis days are over. You're lucky to be walking.' I was in shock.

"I went into despair after that. My dreams, which had been so close just months before, had been obliterated. I started taking more pills than I was prescribed, and I fell into a pretty deep depression." He looked at Liz, begging her with his eyes to understand how he had felt at the time. "Before too long, I was relying on my pills to get me through the day. At one point, I even contemplated suicide."

"Jeff no…" Liz got up to go to him, but he stopped her.

"Let me finish, okay?"

Liz sat back down without a word, knowing he needed to get it out.

Jeff took a deep breath. "Do you remember that day, back then, when I saw you by the bridge out on Cook Rd.? You were taking the long way home from school, which you never did; you hated walking. But that day, you took the long way home…do you remember why?" He'd always been curious.

It took her a minute to put herself there. She thought about his question seriously because she felt like her answer was important to him. She did remember that day, pretty clearly actually.

She was a freshman that year, and that day she had been pissed off at Steve, her boyfriend at the time. She had seen him talking to Sally Stivers in front of his locker after school. It had turned out they were talking about an assignment they were paired up for in English, but she hadn't known that at the time.

She hadn't even approached him; she just stormed off. She turned left out of the school parking lot instead of right for no reason. She assumed to walk off her mad, but she was curious as to what Jeff had to say about that day.

"I was pissed off at Steve for something he didn't even do," she answered finally. "I don't know why I turned left instead of right like I normally would; honestly, I never thought about it until now." She looked at him intently after she answered.

"I do." He looked away for a moment preparing himself; he had never told anyone this. "I know why you turned left. It was to save my life."

He sat down at the table across from her and grabbed her hand. Liz was absolutely stunned by this comment.

Looking her in the eye, he continued, "I didn't just contemplate suicide Liz; I planned it. I was on that bridge that day with a brand new full prescription of my pain pills. I was going to take all of them and jump off the bridge. At that time in my life, I felt like my life was over, so why not make it official, you know? What did I have to live for?

"Obviously, I wasn't thinking about my family or anyone else for that matter." He let go of Liz's hand and got up from the table; he needed to move. "The point is...you saved my life Liz; by taking the long way home that day, you saved my life!"

She looked at him still confused. "I didn't do anything; Jeff..."

Needing her to understand her importance in this, he stopped pacing and looked at her again. "Yes you did, Liz...you talked to me. You were pissed off at Steve, but I didn't know that until just now. You saw me and yelled to me right after I opened the bottle. I had a handful of pills when you came up to me that day. You didn't say a word about Steve. And, I'll always remember this too; you said, 'Hey hotshot,' you've always called me that, 'what are you doing out here?' I said, 'enjoying the scenery.' And, you just leaned on the rail next to me and said, 'It really is beautiful isn't it?'

"I looked around and noticed, for the first time in a long time, that it *was* beautiful. Then you asked me, 'so, what are you gonna do now, since you can't play tennis?' It was crazy; all I had been able to think about for weeks was not being able to play tennis, and here you were telling me, without even knowing it, that I had other options."

He pulled Liz up to stand with him. His gaze was very intent on her. He held both her hands as he finished. "You made me realize in that moment that my life wasn't over; it was just going to take a different path now. A path that could lead wherever I wanted." He squeezed both her hands and continued, "I answered you. I said 'I don't know, maybe a lawyer.' You laughed and said, 'perfect.' Then you pushed yourself off the railing and headed towards town. I was stunned; everything changed for me right then.

"I threw the pills over the rail, haven't taken any since that day either, and basked in the beauty of the day with my newfound perspective. You were several feet away when you turned and said, 'Are you coming?' I caught up to you, and we walked the rest of the way to town, me limping and you bouncing like you always do. Just making small talk and enjoying life." He smiled slightly.

"Don't you see, Liz? If you wouldn't have shown up that day, I would have eaten those pills and jumped. There is no doubt in my mind that you saved my life." His gaze got serious again. "And, I have no doubt that you're going to help save Jenny's."

Liz didn't know what to say; she was dumbfounded. She had always thought him so confident back then. She had never realized how his injury had affected him. And, his absolute confidence in her was a little unsettling.

"I don't know what to say," Liz managed.

"You don't have to say anything, but I never said thank you." Jeff pulled her close and she didn't resist. He had been thinking about that damn kiss all night. It was a big part of the reason he couldn't sleep.

Why had he done it? He had kept asking himself.

He didn't have an answer. He'd never thought of Liz that way before; he had always considered her more of a sister. But right then, it was all he could think about.

The look in his eyes changed, and the intensity she saw was clearly a different kind than a moment ago. She gulped and thanked God when she heard someone coming down the hall, so she could break free from his gaze and pull free from his grasp. She knew all too clearly what her reaction would be if he kissed her again, and she wasn't sure how she felt about it. She had never thought of Jeff like that before...ever, and she had known him her entire life.

He whispered, "I'll thank you later."

She shivered, with anticipation or maybe apprehension; she wasn't quite sure.

26

Laura awoke from another nightmare involving horrible images of her daughter. She forced the pictures out of her head and looked at the clock. It was just after four, and she debated for a minute whether or not to try to go back to sleep.

She was so exhausted; she couldn't believe her body didn't just shut down and force itself to rest. But she had been through this before, sort of, after Jack passed away. She went from not sleeping to sleeping all the time, back and forth, for several months after he had died.

She knew how well the body and mind could function, if necessary, on little to no sleep. She had still had her daughter to take care of then and had no choice but to go on with everyday life. Now, she had her daughter to find and had no choice but to function fully in order to accomplish that.

She laid there for several more minutes before throwing off the covers and getting out of bed. She'd just make some really strong coffee and have breakfast ready when everyone started to rise for the day. Not thinking that she might not be the only one awake at this ungodly hour, she headed to the kitchen and saw the light was on.

Immediately her mind went to Jenny, thinking she must be in the kitchen, but reality kicked in quickly enough for her to realize that if Jenny had come home, she would have heard her come inside. Her grandmother's bells hung from the front door and jangled every time it was opened. She had no doubt if they would have sounded in the night she would have woken immediately.

When she walked into the kitchen and saw Jeff and Liz at opposite sides of the room, she raised her eyebrows. There was definitely some tension in the air. She had felt it earlier during dinner but didn't pay it too much mind. Now though, she was a little more than curious about what was going on with her best friend and her brother.

"Hey guys," she said. "Looks like I'm not the only one who couldn't sleep."

Neither of them responded, so she just looked back and forth between the two a few times before heading to the cabinet that held the coffee. "So, what have you guys been talking about?"

In unison they both said, "Nothing." They looked at each other quickly, neither looking very happy.

Laura pretended not to see the look but was now even more curious. She knew they were both upset earlier about being paired together. She wondered if they had been arguing.

But she knew she wouldn't get any answers out of either of them until they were separated. "Well, I don't know about you, but I think my sleep is over for the night."

Jeff took the opportunity to get out of there. "Actually, now that I got some food in me, I think I might try to catch a couple hours." He quickly left the room but not without giving Laura a hug first. He gave Liz another long look over his sister's head.

Laura waited a few minutes, but once the coffee was started, she turned to her friend. "Spill."

Liz looked away too quickly. "There's nothing to spill."

Liz was being too fidgety, and Laura knew her too well. "Come on, Liz; I know you, and something's up. What's going on between you and Jeff? The tension has been high between you two since you got back earlier." She looked at her friend; her gaze so strong Liz couldn't look away.

"Look, Laura; it's not important okay. With everything that's going on it almost seems stupid."

"Maybe I could use a little stupid right now. Did you ever think that?" Laura asked seriously.

Liz didn't know what to say to that. She understood what Laura was saying, but she wasn't sure if she was ready to let Laura know she had locked lips with her brother and might have an urge to do it again.

"I don't even know what to say right now. I have to think about it a little first," Liz stated honestly.

Laura could tell Liz was uncomfortable and changed the subject deliberately. "We can talk about that later I guess, but since we're both up, why don't you finally tell me what you're doing here."

Liz smiled at her friend, silently thanking her for not making her "spill" just yet. "That I can do."

So, Liz told Laura all about Tom and his book and how he had quit his job. How she lost her job and how, now that she'd had time to think about it, she was actually happy. She told her about Tom and his affair. And, about how she just missed her Laura Bean and needed to come home.

"You've had a lot going on." Laura got up to pour some coffee. "No wonder you've been ignoring me."

She saw Liz flinch. She hadn't meant it to come out so harshly, but it still hurt. They had been best friends for so long, and her friend hadn't answered or returned her calls for months.

"Laura..." Liz felt horrible.

"No, it's okay Liz; I get it." Laura leaned on the counter and peered at Liz over her mug. "You were dealing with a lot. I'm sure I wasn't even on your mind." *Okay so maybe I am more pissed than I thought,* Laura realized.

"Of course that's not true, Laura. You can't think that." The thought devastated Liz. "I thought about you all the time. My life was sucking so bad; I just didn't want to admit it, and I knew once I talked to you, I'd have to." Liz had just that moment realized the reason she'd been so distant.

She walked up to Laura, took the mug from her hand, and set it on the counter, so she could give her a tight hug. "Laura, I have missed you something awful, and I'm so, so sorry for not being in touch the last couple months. But I'm here now, and I'm not leaving."

Laura hugged her friend back just as tightly, understanding and accepting the apology Liz was offering.

"I know, and I appreciate you staying until this is finished..."

"No, you don't understand," Liz interrupted. "I'm not leaving. Even after we find Jenny; I'm not going anywhere."

"What do you mean?" Laura pulled back from her friend, so she could look at her face.

"I'm moving back to Jefferson. I decided on my way down from Chicago this morning..." She glanced at the clock on the stove "...well yesterday morning," she rectified with a grin. "I'm going to do freelance work again.

"Honestly, I made about the same amount of money and could pick what I wanted to write about, *and* pick my own hours. Why wouldn't I stay? I can do freelance work from anywhere."

Her excitement was really starting to show. "And since I'm not working towards a job at the Journal, I can sell my stuff to any newspaper or magazine who's interested.

"I can travel if I want...I mean, I could go to Florida for three weeks and write from the beaches if I want." She looked at Laura seriously now. "But I want to be based in Jefferson. I miss you so much, and once we find Jenny, I'd be stupid to leave again. There's nothing in Chicago for me anymore, Laura. I only had one friend there, and I can visit him whenever I want."

"So, you're really staying?" Laura had tears in her eyes, almost afraid she'd heard it all wrong.

"Yes, I'm staying, and if Jeff moves back too..."

Laura stopped her friend then. "What? Jeff?"

"Well, he mentioned something earlier about missing out on too much while being a hotshot in Chicago...of course he didn't say hotshot...but I know he misses being around just as much as I do," Liz explained. "But, don't say anything okay? I'm not sure how serious he is about it," she added hurriedly. "But regardless, I've already made up my mind. As soon as all of this is over, I'll look for a place." *With two bedrooms,* she thought, another plan automatically taking form in the back of her mind.

Laura threw herself at her friend and embraced her so tightly Liz could barely breathe. Liz, knowing the past two days had been grueling for her friend, held tight.

After a few moments, Laura pulled back and looked her friend in the eye. "Okay, now spill."

Liz only intensified the gaze and responded with, "I will if you will." She remembered her friends flushed appearance when reentering the conference room after being alone with Mark. She hadn't looked pissed either; she had definitely looked flustered.

Laura, clearly baffled by the remark, looked at Liz curiously. "What do you mean?" Then the image of her and Mark, in his office and then again on the street during the search, flashed through her mind. She flushed, cleared her throat, and took a step back from Liz. "I don't know what you mean," she said in a husky voice.

As Laura turned to top off her coffee, Liz just laughed. "Right, you know exactly what I mean, so spill."

Laura never could lie to Liz. "Okay," she began. "Earlier today Mark and I were arguing in his office, and then all of a sudden we were kissing...It was crazy." Her eyes lost focus for an instant. *And very, very hot.* She got a slight shiver down her spine.

"You were just all of a sudden kissing! Who started it? What was it like? I bet he's a good kisser..." Liz looked at her friend when she didn't elaborate. "Well!"

Laura sat at the table with her coffee and laughed. It felt like old times. "Believe it or not, I started it...at least I think...it's still a little fuzzy." Liz joined her at the table, intent on getting the juicy details "It was indescribable...really; I don't even know...it was like feeling everything all at once. Just like an explosion of sensation and all of it good." She shook her head to clear it. Just thinking about it was making her a little lightheaded again.

"It's about time you guys hooked up anyway." Liz leaned back in her chair. "He's been all about it forever."

Laura laughed. "Whatever..."

"Come on, Laura. Don't deny it. This has been a long time coming. I remember just as well as you do the first time he kissed you. I'm your best friend remember?" She had known about it within hours. "It messed you up for a while." She remembered that all too well. Her friend had been an emotional wreck for weeks.

"It didn't mean anything to him. He left, remember?" Laura got up from the table to get another cup of coffee and leaned on the counter.

"I always thought he was just scared." Liz shrugged.

"What on Earth was there to be afraid of?" Laura asked defiantly.

"Gee, I don't know, maybe realizing you were in love with your best friend's little sister. Maybe he was afraid that you wouldn't feel the same way...you know, rejection? A lot of people are afraid of rejection. It's pretty common," Liz stated matter-of-factly.

"So, you'd rather just never know? It just doesn't make sense to me." Laura shook her head, unable to see that point of view. She had always gone after what she wanted, without thinking about the what-ifs, because if you go after it there aren't any. There is only what-is.

"I know what you mean, honey, but not everyone thinks the same way. And, not everyone is afraid of the same things." Liz gave her friend a sly look and got up from the table. "I mean, I'm sure Mark isn't afraid of spiders." Liz crawled her fingers up her friend's arm.

Laura shivered but couldn't help but laugh. "That's not even close to the same kind of thing, but I get your point. Not that it matters anyway; it was a long time ago. A lot has happened, and is still happening, since then." Laura couldn't help but think about Jenny. Everything came crashing back (not that it had every really been completely gone).

Liz noticed the change in her friend and knew exactly what had caused it. "We'll find her Laura; I'm sure of it." She grabbed Laura's hand, so she wouldn't turn away. "No, listen to me; we'll find her. We're close; I can feel it." She hugged Laura close.

She didn't tell Laura what she had told Jeff earlier, but she thought about it again.

I'm missing something. And it's important, damn it; I can feel it. It'll come to me. She was sure of it, *and when it does we'll find her.*

She just hoped it wasn't too late when they did. She had heard Mitch's unspoken statement loud and clear, and she could feel time running out.

27

*M*ark was back in his office with Laura, arguing about whether or not she should join the search. Everything was happening exactly as it had that afternoon until the part when they broke apart from the kiss. In this version it didn't stop there.

When she uttered the gasp, which in reality had brought him to his senses, in his dream he returned his mouth to hers instead and backed her up to the edge of the desk. His hands were all over her body, desperate to feel all of her, and hers were gripping his hips pulling him even closer. He pulled her jacket from her shoulders halfway down her arms trapping them to her sides.

He assaulted her now exposed neck with his mouth reveling in the taste of her skin. He removed her jacket completely wanting her hands on him again. He slid his hands under her shirt to feel the warm smooth skin of her back. He began to knead her muscles with his fingers, working his way upward. His mouth moved to her collar bone and traced it lightly with his tongue.

She was hurrying now to unbutton his shirt, so she could get her hands on his flesh. He grabbed her hands and put them over her head, so he could slide her shirt off easily. When her hands were free again, she slid them inside his open shirt front and ran her fingers through his chest hair, grazing his nipples with her fingernails.

It was his turn to gasp, and he attacked her mouth again, pulling her tight against him; flesh to flesh. The only barrier between their chests was her lacy bra. He was in too much of a hurry though to undo her bra; instead, he slid the straps form her shoulders and pushed it down to expose her breasts. He stopped for a moment to admire their perkiness. Slowly, with his eyes on hers he cupped her right breast with his left hand and relished its fullness.

He caressed her for a moment, circling the nipple with the pad of his thumb. She took a sharp intake of breath, grabbed his head, and pulled his mouth to hers. She pressed her body to his with an urgency she was daring him to match. He tore away from her lips, wanting his mouth on her breast. His hand still on her right breast he used his mouth on the left, circling her nipple with his tongue until it became taught. Then he took it in his mouth and suckled, grazing the rock hard nipple with his teeth ever so slightly before teasing it again with his tongue. She was holding on for dear life, her fingers in his hair.

He lifted her and sat her on his desk, and she wrapped her legs around his body bringing them even closer. He was rock hard and needed to take everything he could. She pushed him away but only long enough to undo his belt and the fastenings of his uniform pants. She slid them and his boxer briefs over his hips and exposed his fullness. She took him in her hands...

Mark woke up gasping for air...and with a bad case of morning wood. He couldn't believe it! He woke up right when it was getting good.

Maybe too good. He groaned. He may have been getting ready to embarrass himself in the dream with a little prematurity.

Mark squinted at the clock once he realized there was no getting back into the dream; four fifteen. He had slept better and longer than he would have thought. Unable to physically shake the dream, he realized it had been a long time since he needed to start the day with a cold shower.

After the shower, which had cooled him down some, he decided to go over the notes Liz had given him on her and Jeff's interviews the day before. He kept going back to the interview with Jacob Riley.

It seemed neither Liz nor Jeff felt that Jacob may be involved. *He just seemed too drunk,* Liz actually wrote in her notes. Mark felt like Jacob had been lying when he questioned him. They had already proved he had lied, at least about how much he had drank at Hank's. Maybe he had needed to think there was more just so he had a direction, but the more he went over his and Liz's notes, he had to agree. Especially after the profile Mitch had started to describe the night before. Jacob was like Liz said, too drunk to pull that off.

After going through all of his notes one more time, he found nothing new. Getting up to stretch, he decided to make coffee. While it was brewing, he thought again about the dream. He shook it off and thought about reality instead.

I'm taking advantage of her and the situation, he silently scolded himself. *I need to apologize and make things right again.*

He decided to deal with that first thing, so they could remove the distraction and have a productive day. With a determined nod, he poured a cup of coffee and got ready to face the day.

28

Mitch entered the hotel gym, which consisted of a treadmill and a Multi-Exercise machine.

His bathroom at home was bigger than this. He sighed, but shrugged. *Better than nothing I guess.*

He hadn't been able to sleep, and the exercise would get his blood pumping for the day. There were too many unanswered questions in his mind about this case. It was the why that was bothering him, or rather, the not knowing why. He thought about everything he had figured out the night before while his mind had been in overdrive. He went over his entire thought process again while he put his body on autopilot on the treadmill.

They had narrowed it down to seven missing girls, including Margery and Jenny, but he had added to the list the night before. He had been curious about why the "kidnapper" had seemed to be so sporadic yet seemingly consistent. He went for four years straight only striking within a four day span of December, but then took five years off before starting up again? But at the same time, the height and coloring of the victims varied only minimally? He wasn't buying it; unless the size and coloring were more important than the time period.

Or would that be vice versa, he contemplated. *Either way,* he decided, *the outcome would be the same.*

Basically, the "kidnapper" had four days or so, for whatever reason, to find a suitable victim, or his chance was lost 'til the next year. That was one possibility, but he couldn't assume that was the case.

Or maybe he didn't always find a criterion match locally, another possibility.

Sometimes he over-thought everything, but maybe that was why he was good at his job. He had moved into the Behavioral Analysis Unit seven years ago because he had a knack for being able to see all sides.

Even the fucked up ones, he thought as he upped the pace a little on the treadmill.

He considered that for a moment. He figured it like this; everybody had fucked up thoughts, and thinking it...or being able to imagine it, and wanting to act them out, were two different things. It was the acting on it that made you the bad guy. Otherwise, Stephen King and Robin Cook would be writing from death row.

He had already ascertained the "kidnapper" was local to the Jefferson area, especially with Billy as a possible witness.

Yeah, an unconscious witness.

Besides that though, it was a pretty sure bet that Margery had been the first. He had plugged in the physical criteria (age, hair/eyes and height) through ten years prior to her disappearance and searched nationwide. It had returned only two hits, and neither had the right dates. So assuming Margery Addison *was* the first, then the first and most recent victims lived in Jefferson. And, the other five girls Liz had tracked were within a two hour radius.

When he first noticed the gaps in the disappearances, he initially checked all jail and prison records in several of the surrounding counties and even states to see if maybe any Jefferson locals had served time. That would be a good reason to stop for a while. With no luck there, he had expanded the missing person search nationwide, not only the surrounding counties as Liz had done. He had to give her credit though; she was searching old newspaper articles online not a multistate database like he had access to.

He received six hits from his search, four missing and two dead. All four of the missing girls were reported missing within four hours of Jefferson in various directions. Both girls who had been found deceased were found mutilated and missing their hearts. One was in Kentucky just over four hours away. It seemed her body had been discarded like a bag of trash on the side of the highway. The other had been found in Arizona. Pretty far away, but other than that, there were too many similarities for it to be coincidence.

*The kidnapper had to have been traveling for the holidays that year…*it was Christmas time…*or some other similar explanation,* he concluded.

The date, age, height, and coloring all matched. And the missing hearts? It made him fearful for what his friend might find if he found Jenny.

So, with Margery and the other five initial victims, plus Jenny and the six he had found last night, they had thirteen missing girls in a fifteen year span. Leaving him to imply his original theory about missing the window was true, the other two potential victims were never reported missing, or the "kidnapper" had done some of his dirty work out of the country.

Regardless, now he had some things to work with. He had already sent the information to one of his colleagues in his unit. He would find out who in Jefferson had connections in Arizona, and potentially cross check that with international travel for the missing two years

Mitch glanced at his watch. It was almost time to meet up with Lee he realized, so he started his cooldown. He decided not to say anything to Lee just yet; he'd brief Mark on what he had found as soon as he saw him though. He trusted Mark with his life...literally.

Now if I could just come up with the why...

29

Laura had spent the last hour since Liz went back to bed thinking about her daughter and trying to think only positive thoughts. She wished desperately that she could talk to Jack again; that he could be there to help search for their baby.

Laura had finished almost an entire pot of coffee herself and was just starting another pot when she realized Liz hadn't spilled her story. *That dirty little bitch!* But, she'd get it out of her.

Actually, she was kind of glad she got to spill first. It had allowed her to think aloud about the situation she found herself in. And, it was good to hear an outside perspective. Liz seemed to think that Mark had always had a thing for her. If he had really had a thing for her for that long, he had been waiting very patiently to make it apparent to her. Not that she would expect anything less from someone with Mark's standard of morals; she had been married since she was eighteen.

He would never be able to justify to himself putting the moves on a married woman, let alone the wife of a good friend. Not to mention the sister of his best friend.

I guess it was pretty complicated! But, why did he leave without ever saying anything all those years ago? she asked herself.

She had run away from him she reminded herself. It was all too much to handle she remembered. She had never felt anything quite like it at the time...or really since, she thought.

Not that she hadn't been attracted to and turned on by her husband. They had learned a lot from each other and had become quite good at that part of the marriage, but this was something else entirely. It was like when their lips met nothing mattered but feeling more, until it was almost too much, but like you couldn't get enough at the same time.

It really was too hard to explain. It didn't even really make sense to her when she would think about it. But, it definitely made sense when she was feeling it. Nothing had ever made more sense.

Maybe after all this was over, they'd talk about what had happened the night of their first kiss. Or maybe after all of this was over, everyone's emotions would settle and everything would go back to the way it was. Honestly though? After experiencing it again, she didn't want it to go back to the way it had been. She couldn't imagine not feeling like that again.

As the fresh pot of coffee finished brewing, she glanced at the clock...five forty-five. She may as well start breakfast. Everyone would be stirring soon. Mark was supposed to be there by six thirty. Mitch, Lee, and all the volunteers were meeting at the search site at seven am. Sunrise was about seven fifteen, and they wanted to be ready to start as soon as possible.

She had checked the weather and it looked like the storm might hold off until the evening, but living here her whole life had taught her the weather in this area could not be predicted. There was supposedly even a small chance the storm could miss them all together.

She remembered what Jack had told her. *You need to find her before the storm.*

If that was true, she hoped it would miss them. The dream had comforted her the day before when she realized they had time. Now though, with the updated weather forecast, she recognized that their time was dwindling fast.

While the bacon was frying, first Liz and then Katlyn made an appearance. Both making a beeline for the coffee pot. Katlyn sat at the table and simply breathed in the scent of her coffee for a moment.

There's nothing like the smell of fresh coffee in the morning. She gained comfort from her morning ritual.

"How long have you been up sweetheart?" Katlyn, slightly more awake now, asked her daughter.

"A couple hours give or take a few minutes." Laura shrugged as the tears started to leak out. "I wasn't sleeping very well, so I decided to quit trying." She had been doing so well not crying while she had been alone.

Katlyn abandoned her coffee to go to her daughter at the stove. "Honey? Let me do this okay?" She tried to take over the cooking, but Laura declined.

"I'd rather keep busy if you don't mind. But, would you mind grabbing the paper, Mom? I want to read Liz's article."

After her mom left the room, Laura sighed. "It's hard to watch my mom not know what to do. She always knows what to do..." She looked at Liz; then after a moment her eyes narrowed.

Liz saw the look. "What?" she asked, not sure of what the look was all about.

"You never spilled!" Laura whispered emphatically, so as not to announce it the awakening house. "You said if I spilled you'd spill, and you never spilled."

Liz chuckled. "You scared me for a sec; I'll spill. I kind of want to talk about it anyway."

Just then, Katlyn came back with the paper followed by Jeff, who was fresh form a shower.

"Smells good, sis. Morning, mom." Jeff kissed his mother's cheek. He sat across from Liz and grinned wide. "Hey Liz; how'd you sleep?"

Before she could answer, Michael walked in. He took a look at his gathered family, automatically including Liz in the category without even thinking about it.

"You all look like shit." He walked to the coffee pot. "Looks like none of us slept very well." He poured a cup of coffee and looked at his wife. "I know I'm not supposed to have it, but one cup won't kill me, and I could use it today."

She didn't argue. She looked around; he was right they were a haggard looking bunch. "I'll set the table," was all she said.

Liz got up and started making toast. Jeff opened the paper and read Liz's article aloud.

When he finished, Laura turned to her friend with tears in her eyes. "Thanks for writing it; I know it couldn't have been easy for you." She gave Liz a one armed hug. Liz laid her head on Laura's shoulder for a minute in acceptance of the gratitude for her work. She was afraid to speak because she might cry.

The toast popping up broke the moment, and they both jumped a little then laughed a little. Jeff got the butter and jam and brought it to the table. They ate in silence, but for the first time in two days everyone, including Laura, cleaned their plates. It was bound to be a long day, and they would need all the energy they could get.

Promptly at six thirty, there was a knock on the door. Laura answered it to Mark standing on the porch. "You have a key," she said after letting him inside.

"I know, but that's for emergencies, like if Jenny locks herself out or you need your plants watered while out of town." He smiled brightly and whispered, "Where is everyone?"

"In the kitchen finishing up breakfast; are you hungry?" She was feeling awkward all of a sudden and didn't know how to act.

He lost the smile and looked at her with extreme intensity. "Yes, but not how you mean."

She swallowed but didn't know what to say; she just continued to look into his eyes.

Mark glanced around to ensure they were truly alone and pulled her close. He kissed her gently for just a moment. When he released her, he grinned again, said cheerily, "Thanks for the appetizer," and walked towards the kitchen. *Damn it! He was supposed to apologize not kiss her again.* He needed to control himself and do what was right.

Alone for the moment, Laura touched her lips and delighted in the fact that such a small kiss could cause such a large reaction. When she joined everyone in the kitchen, the men were nowhere to be seen, and Liz and her mother were just finishing the dishes.

"Leave it to the men to skip out on cleanup," Laura said dryly.

"Jeff had some things he wanted to talk to Mark and your father about." Drying her hands on a towel, Katlyn rolled her eyes, *Man's business.* "I'm going to take my turn in the shower." She hung up the towel, hugged Laura, and then left the kitchen.

After Liz put away the last dish she had dried, she turned to Laura. "I'll meet you at the search okay? I'm going to go pick up Melissa."

Laura looked askance. "Melissa?"

"Yeah, I told her she could help with the search today." She held up her hand to stave of Laura's protest. "Look, I'm not going to let her in the woods or anything, but we can find something for her to do, even if it's shade the map." She sighed. "I feel for the kid Laura; you went through it yesterday yourself. I know it's your daughter, and they're just friends, but who was the most important person to you at that age? Other than your parents?"

Laura saw where she was going with this. "I see what you're saying. But..."

Liz didn't let her finish. "Right, and if you were missing back then instead of Margery, I would have been involved. No one could have stopped me. And," she continued; "I kind of want to get her out of that apartment."

Laura was caught slightly off guard by Liz's tone on that last part. "What do you mean by that?"

"Does Melissa's mom hit her?" Liz asked bluntly.

"What!" Laura was taken aback by the question.

So, Liz told her about her and Jeff's conversation with Melissa the day before.

"It was pretty obvious to both Jeff and I; we even talked about it after." She shook her head. "Jeff was pissed; you could see it all over him. Anyway, I want to talk to her and let her know things can be done."

Laura cursed herself under her breath. "I never noticed anything." She thought real hard for a few minutes trying to remember anything that may have been a clue as to something going on. "But now that I think about it, the girls haven't spent the night over there in months, and Melissa usually ends up staying here all weekend most weekends. Plus, she comes home with Jenny after school most days too."

She looked at Liz. "I never really thought much of it; I mean, at that age you and I were together twenty-four seven it seemed like. They used to be a lot more back and forth like we used to be until a few months ago."

Liz looked at her watch. "We can talk more about it later; you guys are about to leave, and I need to head out."

As if on cue, they could hear the men approaching, so Liz grabbed her coat, gave her friend a quick hug and bolted. "See ya in a few." She really didn't want to see Jeff again right at the moment.

30

Mitch and Lee had agreed to meet for the free continental breakfast in the lobby of the hotel where they were both staying. They wanted to go over their outsiders' perspectives with each other.

"They sure seem like a pretty tight circle," Mitch commented as he put cream cheese on his bagel.

"They all grew up together." Lee shrugged, shoveling down his second bowl of cereal and chasing it with his third muffin.

The dude is skinny as a post and just ingested over two thousand calories sitting here without missing a beat. Mitch had seen him eat three plates of spaghetti and practically a whole loaf of bread the night before too. Mitch shook his head. All he was having was a bagel with fat free cream cheese. And, he had put in an hour at the hotel gym, if you could call it that, before breakfast.

"I think it's more than that." He looked at Lee. "You can feel the electricity between Mark and Laura. Hell, the heat almost burned me when I got close enough. Didn't you feel it?"

Lee shrugged. "Mark has always had a thing for Laura, so what?"

"Has she always had a thing for him?"

The question gave Lee pause. "Now that you mention it, the one time Mark ever really brought it up, it definitely seemed one sided."

"Well, it definitely didn't seem one sided last night," Mitch retorted. "I just hope it's not clouding his judgement. Mark is a great cop, but even great cops make mistakes if they don't keep their mind on the job."

"I think he's fine." Lee pushed his empty bowl away. "I know this is personal for him because it's like his family, but I went through everything last night when I got back here, and I don't think I would have done anything different.

"I probably would have even given Liz and Jeff the leeway with the interviews." He shrugged again. "They're both trained interviewers. She's an award winning journalist." Lee mentioned, referring to one of her freelance articles on mental health awareness. "And, he's a big time lawyer in Chicago. Probably even be the District Attorney one day."

So, Mitch thought, *Lee had done his research too it seems.*

"You're right. I just feel like something is off. Like…" He sighed and shrugged. "…I don't know; maybe it was the whole dead husband in the dream thing that's making me edgy. What's your take on that?"

He finished off his bagel, wishing he had Lee's metabolism, so he could have a little more.

"I don't know." Lee thought about it for a minute. "Seems to me she really had the dream, and Liz showing up without knowing anything...it does seem a little weird, but whether or not Jack was real, he's right. We need to find her before the storm rolls in. The snow they're calling for could put the search down for days."

They both thought about the truth in that for a minute as Lee went back to the breakfast bar for his fourth round.

When he came back with yet another muffin and a banana, Mitch shook his head. "Where do you keep it all?"

Lee looked at him sideways, not sure what he meant. When he realized what Mitch was talking about, he simply laughed. "My mom always wondered the same thing." His eyes got bright and he rubbed his belly. "Fast metabolism."

Mitch merely shook his head again. "What do you think about the search?"

"Gotta do it. Wish we had more to go on though. I mean, we're not even sure David was with Billy for sure or if Jenny is going to be at the other end." He put the banana peel in his empty bowl. "But, what else do we have?"

"Right." Mitch responded thinking about what else they did have. He wanted a little more information before he brought it up.

31

On the drive through town to Melissa's apartment building, Liz's nagging feeling from the night before returned. She had hoped leaving it alone for a few hours would help. She knew she had all the pieces; she simply didn't know how to put them together.

Don't think about it, she told herself once again. *It'll come.* She pushed it aside for the time being.

As she got out of the car in front of Melissa's apartment, Liz went over in her mind how to broach the subject of the girl's abuse.

*Be subtle, casually bring it up in conversation; you don't want to embarrass her, only help her...*All of that flew out of her head as Melissa opened the door before she could knock.

Melissa tried to slip past her, but Liz had seen the split lip. She grabbed the girl's arm to halt her progress down the stairs. "What the hell happened to your face?" she demanded.

Melissa flinched slightly from Liz's tone, but she didn't try to pull away.

She wouldn't meet Liz's eyes though. "I, uh, was changing the lightbulb in the kitchen..." She shuffled her feet and glanced at Liz. "...and I slipped off the chair, and uh, hit my face on the counter." She laughed nervously. "I'm kind of a klutz..."

"Cut the crap, kid. We need to talk." Liz gave her a steely look. "Does your Mom know where you're going?"

"She's still asleep."

"Well, wake her up; I'll talk to her." Liz suggested wanting to have a few words with the woman. *A fat lip? She'd give* her *a fat lip. See how she liked having to deal with someone her own size.*

"I wrote her a note."

Liz merely raised one eyebrow and crossed her arms.

Melissa hurried on, "I promise; I can show you. Please don't wake her up...please? That will only piss her off."

Melissa held her stare, so Liz could see the fear in the girl's eyes and a small glint of anger as well.

She should *be angry; it should be normal to wake your mother up to let her know you're safe!* "Fine; show me the note," Liz relented

Melissa hurried inside and returned a moment later with a handwritten note in hurried sloppy handwriting. Whether or not she hastily wrote the note when she ran in or if she had in fact pre penned it didn't really matter, because now there was definitely a note, and her mom needn't worry.

Mom,

With Jenny's aunt Liz, helping search.

Melissa

"Make sure it's somewhere she'll see it, and grab an actual coat instead of that jacket, and a hat. It's cold out here and we'll be outside. I'll start the car." She handed the note back to Melissa. When she got to the car, she took a moment to release her anger with a swift kick to the front tire, imagining a certain shin in its place. *AAAAAAAAAAAAAAHHHHHHHHHH*, she screamed silently and clenched her fists...*Melissa was not coming back to this house.*

She needed to talk to Jeff.

A few moments later, Liz appeared calm as Melissa, appropriately dressed for the weather, jumped into the front seat.

Liz didn't waste any time as she pulled onto the road. "How long has it been going on?"

Melissa froze in the act of putting on her seatbelt. "What do you mean?" Shit, shit, shit! She knew she shouldn't have come. She licked the spot on her lip automatically.

"I already told you once to cut the crap," Liz stated matter-of-factly. She looked over, and Melissa averted her eyes. "Look, honey; there's nothing to be ashamed of, okay?" She softened her tone and put her hand on the girl's knee. "Talk to me. There are resources; we can get you help."

"She doesn't mean it." Melissa started to defend her mother. "It only happens when she's drinking a lot."

"Okay, how often does she drink a lot?"

At that, Melissa looked away with tears forming in her eyes.

Liz pulled over to the side of the road and turned to Melissa. "Melissa...honey; look at me." After a few moments, Melissa looked over.

Poor thing, she is trying so hard to hold it in. Liz unbuckled her seat belt and slid closer taking the girl into her arms. "It's okay, sweetie; let it out." She stroked the girl's hair as she sobbed into her chest.

After about two minutes of clinging to Liz, Melissa felt slightly embarrassed but more relieved than anything. She could finally talk about it. She had hinted at it a few times with Jenny but was afraid to actually say it out loud.

She pulled back, wiped her nose on the back of her hand, and her tears on her shirt. "All the time," she finally answered Liz's question. "She drinks all the time. It wasn't so bad until she lost her job...that's when she started really hitting me.

"She started drinking not long after my Dad left...the bills were stressing her out, so she started drinking a glass or two of wine after dinner to relieve the stress. Eventually, that turned into a bottle which turned into two.

"Then when two bottles of wine became too expensive it was vodka; because she didn't have to drink the whole bottle. Since she lost her job, it's been the whole bottle and sometimes more."

She looked pleadingly at Liz. "She really doesn't mean to hit me, Liz. It's definitely the alcohol; I promise...she never did it before, never once." Melissa loved her Mom and wished she knew how to help her.

"I'm going to talk to her..."

"Please don't! Please, Liz." Melissa hated to beg but...

"You're not going back there unless she agrees to get help," Liz said with finality. "Do you want me to take care of this, or would you rather get Mark involved?"

Melissa tried to argue. "But..."

Liz stopped her. "No buts; we'll talk about this later. Right now, we need to get to the search. We're already late. Do you still want to help, or do you want me to take you to Laura's?" Liz asked before she pulled back onto the road. She'd have to whip a U-ie if she was taking her to Laura's.

"I'm helping. Let's go." Melissa sat back and faced the windshield with determination.

Liz smiled and put the car in gear. "Atta girl!"

32

Mark and Laura arrived at the search with coffee and donuts. There were twice as many people waiting to participate in the search than there had been the day before.

Lee had already taken charge and was assigning everyone their positions. He saw Mark and waved him over to the command table.

"I hope you don't mind; I went ahead and got started. Just about everyone was here, so…"

"No, that's great. Where are Lester and his buddy?" Mark looked around for the dogs.

"Already on their way to their starting points." Lee showed him on the map.

"Good. Actually, I'm not going to be here long. I need to talk to Mitch about a few things." He had gotten a call from him on the way to the donut shop. "Then I'd like to go to St. Joe's and check on Billy. You're good here?"

"Yep. Not a problem." Lee turned to Laura as she approached with a cup of coffee in each hand. She handed one to him with a smile.

Lee accepted the coffee with a grin. "Hey, Laura. Dinner was great last night; thanks again."

She flashed her dimple to Lee. "We barely had any leftovers." Her eyes were twinkling with humor.

Lee blushed slightly. "Well..."

Laura laughed, but sobered quickly. "Come on guys; let's find some kids."

Shortly after all the searchers entered the woods, Liz arrived with Melissa. She got out of the car and hurried to the command table. "Where's Jeff?" she asked without preamble.

"I don't know; he said he had some things to take care of and would be here about lunchtime." Laura looked at her friend closely. "Are you okay?"

"What we talked about earlier?" She nodded towards where Melissa was digging into the donuts.

"Yeah?" Laura glanced over at Melissa.

"Yeah..." Liz sighed. "We'll talk about it later okay?" Liz noticed the men looking at them curiously.

"Yeah..." was all Laura said.

"So, what do you need us to do?" Liz turned to Mark.

"He's in charge." Mark pointed over his shoulder to Lee. "But hold on...Where's Mitch?" He turned to Lee.

"He got a call from one of his guys and headed back to the hotel to check on a few things. You just missed him." Lee looked out over the woods. "I think there's something he's not telling me." He looked back at Mark. "Anyway, he wants you to call him."

"I think I'll just ride over there; I want to stop in and see Marianne too and then check on Billy." He looked at Laura and cleared his throat. "Can I talk to you for a minute?"

She nodded, and he led her back to his car. "We might as well be warm while we talk." They slid in on opposite sides and he started the car.

"What did you want to talk to me about?" Laura asked after a few minutes of silence.

He turned to look at her and quickly looked away again. A flash of his dream returning; he blushed. "I just wanted to apologize for what happened yesterday."

"Oh, I see..." Laura started. "It's fine, nothing to...No! Fuck that! Why are you apologizing to me?" She turned in her seat to face him more squarely.

He looked at her stunned. "I just...I thought...you're vulnerable right now...and..."

"Just shut up and listen to me for a minute, okay?" She didn't wait for a response. "I'm a grown woman; I kissed *you*, remember?" She was pissed! *Vulnerable! Who did he think he was?* "I'll tell you something mister! You are not taking advantage of me. The timing may not be the greatest, but what is happening here..." She gestured agitatedly between them. "...isn't something to be sorry about." She slammed her hand on the dash, all of her frustrations from the past couple days finally coming to a boil. "If you think you can run from this again..."

"Again? What are you talking about?" Mark asked confused, and then it clicked "Wait...?"

"Yeah back when you kissed me the first time and then left without a word? Remember that?" She was fuming.

"Wait a damn minute!" He gripped the steering wheel to try and keep himself calm. "You ran from me that night! I thought you were pissed or scared...I practically attacked you. You were just a kid...*you* ran from *me*." He was exasperated.

Laura interrupted, "Just a kid?" She was furious, but then it sank in, and she calmed a little.

She had *been just a kid and she* had *been scared.* She chuckled slightly. "I guess I was kind of scared, and I did run. But I wasn't scared of you, and I wasn't running from you." She sighed and grabbed his wrist. "I *was* just a kid, I guess. I had never been kissed like that."

She reflected back. "And, hadn't been again until yesterday." She smiled; dimple and all at that. "I was confused. The feelings it stirred inside of me did scare me, and I didn't know what to do. I had never felt like that before, don't you understand?"

Laura smiled again, slyly now. "I wanted you. But I didn't know what that meant." She laughed a little and scooted closer to him. "But I do now." She kissed him lightly on the lips. "Let's talk about this later, okay? We have some kids to find."

Mark was speechless. All he could do was nod.

"Call me if you find anything, okay?"

He nodded again.

"Are you okay?"

He looked at her intently then. "I love you, Laura."

Her heart jumped into her throat. "We'll talk about this later, okay?" She hurried out of the car and back to the command table to start shading the stupid map.

Damn it! Mark cursed himself and slammed his hand on the steering wheel once, then twice. *Why the hell did I tell her that?*

He started the car and headed to the hotel to talk to Mitch, cursing himself the whole way.

When Laura got back to the command center, Liz was the only one around.

"Where's Melissa?" Laura looked around expectantly.

"She's with Lee. They're walking the tree line looking for clues." She smiled at that. "Really, I wanted to talk to you about something. Lee can't sit still anyway, so I asked him to take Melissa for a walk."

"Are you ready to spill?" Laura asked, hoping for the distraction. Between Jenny still missing and whatever was going on between her and Mark, she was a mess.

"Spill? Oh..." Liz remembered her promise to tell Laura what had been going on the night before. "I forgot about that." The image of her and Jeff in a lip lock popped in her head.

Damn it! She blushed a little, flustered by the image. "Yeah, that. Can we talk about it later?"

"No, we cannot," Laura stated firmly. "You've already tried that, and now it's later."

"Fine!" Liz huffed. "Jeff kissed me last night, but..."

"What!" Laura was shocked; she had assumed Liz and Jeff had been arguing in the kitchen earlier that morning.

Liz sighed. "I know, right?"

"What!" Laura shook her head to clear it "Okay, now you *have* to spill. Tell me everything."

"That's it; there's really nothing to tell. He kissed me...when we got back to the house last night. I never saw it coming." She thought back, really trying to remember if she should have seen it coming. "I mean, there was nothing." Liz started to pace. "I've never thought about Jeff like that. I know a lot of our other friends did but we were just too close. You know what I mean?" She stopped pacing and looked at her friend imploringly but didn't wait for an answer. "I mean he's practically my brother!" Liz flung out her arms heatedly.

Laura, who was finally over her shock, simply stated, "But he's not your brother." She didn't know how she would feel about her best friend and her brother hooking up. On one hand, it would be great; she loved them both so much, but at the same time, she worried that if it didn't work out, it would be awkward for everyone.

She put her thoughts aside for the time being. "So, before dinner then...?" She pondered. "Then what did I interrupt this morning when you were in the kitchen?"

Liz cleared her throat...she didn't want to break Jeff's confidence by telling Laura what Jeff had been through all those years ago, but she had to tell her something. "He was going to do it again. You interrupted; thanks for that by the way." She was still feeling the relief from that morning. She had no idea what to do about any of this.

"Thanks? So, you didn't like it then?" Laura was feeling a little defensive of her bother.

"Oh no." Liz sighed. "I really liked it; I just don't know what to do about it yet." She started pacing again. "I mean, it was quick, but man did it go right to the gut...but it's Jeff...I don't know what to think...part of me wants to do it again, and part of me thinks it may just be because of heightened emotions, and even another part of me is afraid of what it might mean if that's not the case." She stopped and threw out her hands in exasperation then sighed. "I just don't want it to be weird."

"Then don't let it be." To Laura it was as simple as that. "Maybe you guys should talk about it." Liz nodded and Laura continued, "So if that wasn't what you wanted to talk about, what was?" Laura decided to leave it alone, knowing her friend would need to let it stew again for a while.

Liz, momentarily confused by the change of subject, raised one eyebrow questioningly. "Oh!" She remembered. "I want to talk to you about Melissa."

"Right!" Laura recalled their byplay earlier when Liz and Melissa had first arrived. She had forgotten all about it because of her conversation with Mark. "So, what's going on?"

Liz told her about Melissa's breakdown on the road and everything she had learned.

"She's not going back there, Laura. Not until Jessica gets her shit together. I'm going to get a two bedroom apartment, and she can stay with me until we figure it out." Liz was determined.

"I think there may be a little more to it than just not letting her go back." Laura held her fingers close together for emphasis.

"I know that; I'm already planning on talking to Jeff about it as soon as I see him. I want Jessica to get help; I'm not trying to take her kid away forever...just until she can get back on her feet. If she doesn't agree, I'll get Mark involved and go about it that way." She sighed, hoping Jessica would agree. "I really don't want Melissa to go into foster care at all though; I hope we can work something out."

The base radio chirped. Liz looked over. "Time for first check-ins. Let's find Jenny and worry about all this later." She hugged her friend close.

33

Jeff had every confidence that everything was being done to find his niece. He also believed wholeheartedly everything would turn out right. After his almost suicide all those years ago, he had vowed to always have a positive outlook on life. Sometimes circumstances made that very difficult, especially in his line of work. But with Liz involved and Jack's help from beyond, Jeff was sure of the outcome...Jenny would return to them safely.

Knowing he was needed more for support than anything else, he decided he would take the steps to ensure he would be able to fill that role for the long term. Instead of joining the search, he had contacted Harold Lawrence to look at his old office. Harold was in Florida, but after a little back and forth, Harold's son had agreed to show Jeff the place later that morning.

Since he had a little time before he was to meet Harold Jr., he spent some time on the phone with his office, tying up some loose ends and passing on his open cases. He talked to the District Attorney personally and explained everything that had been going on the last few days and his decision to quit. He would give a notice if necessary for an amicable separation but preferred to cut ties immediately. The DA wished him luck and assured him there would be no hard feelings. He admired Jeff for putting his family first.

When Jeff pulled in the parking lot of what he already considered his office at around nine forty five, he could immediately see the potential. The building was two stories with the office on the first floor and a two bedroom apartment on the second. He was walking around the outside when Harold Jr. pulled in and parked next to his car in the lot.

"Hey, Harry!" Jeff approached with his hand out and a grin on his face. "I appreciate you seeing me."

Harry was nothing like his father. He wasn't interested in law. He was an exceptional artist though. He had really come a long way from blowing glass pipes for his pot head peers in high school. His glass work sold for upwards of ten thousand dollars depending on the sculpture, but he was still a pot head. Jeff had a couple of his smaller pieces in his apartment in Chicago.

"Yeah man, no problem. I've been shut up in my shed working on something for days and really needed a break anyway." He shook Jeff's hand. "You're thinking about coming home then?" Harry nodded towards his father's vacant building. "Sick of being a big shot?" Harry grinned. They had been friends in School. Jeff had never bought one of Harry's pieces back then, but he'd shared one a time or two.

Jeff smiled. "I've been thinking about it for a while. And now, with everything that's going on, I need to come home to stay." Jeff's smile faded into grim determination.

"Everything that's going on?" Harry asked curiously.

"Jenny missing, and…" Jeff started.

"What the Hell! Jenny's missing?" Harry interrupted.

"Let's go inside, and I'll tell you about it why we look around; I've got some other things to take care of today as well."

Harry nodded still baffled. "Up or down first?"

"Down." He didn't care about the apartment so much. He could live anywhere. The apartment he owned in Chicago was tiny. He didn't spend a lot of time there because he worked so much. As long as there was room for a couch, a bed, and his fifty inch television, he was good.

Once inside, Jeff told Harry everything that had been going on.

"That's crazy, man." Harry was shocked. "Crazy shit!" He put his hand on his friend's shoulder in a comforting gesture. "Let me know if there's anything I can do, seriously man, anything."

"I appreciate it man, really. Now let's talk business." The building was exactly what he needed; it was plenty big enough, with a decent sized reception area, 2 offices, a small kitchenette, a small storage/copy room, and a half bath.

Just because Harry was a pot smoking artist didn't mean he was a dummy. Jeff and Harry haggled for a few before agreeing on a price. Harry was pleased because they agreed on five thousand over his father's bottom price, and Jeff was pleased because he got the office and apartment for less than what he could sell his apartment for in Chicago.

He wanted to move in immediately and agreed to pay the regular rent price for the apartment until closing, as long as the money was applied to the purchase. They shook on it and Jeff wrote a check right then and there for two months' rent.

"You sure you don't want to see upstairs?" Harry asked him as he locked the office behind them and handed Jeff the keys. "It'll only take a second. The couple who'd been living there just bought a house over on Miami."

"I'm sure it's fine. I'll come back later. I might even sleep here tonight." Jeff glanced at his watch. "I really need to go. I'll write up the contract for our agreement and bring it by later." He grinned at Harry and slapped him on the back before getting in his car.

On his way to his next stop, Jeff called Mark to check on the progress of the search. Mark had just left Mitch and was heading to the hospital, but he had just talked to Lee and there was nothing new to report, other than seemingly slow progress

Nothing new, Jeff thought as he disconnected. *Something had to break soon.* He could feel it

On his way through town, he stopped at the diner.

"Hey Sweetie, what can I get you?" the waitress, Lois, asked as he sat at the counter.

"A cup of coffee would be great." He smiled at her. "Is Joe here?" He asked after the owner/manager.

She set a cup of coffee in front of him. "Me and Lou…" She nodded towards the kitchen. "…is all you got today honey. Joe is out helping look for your niece."

"Can I ask you a few questions, Lois?" She'd been working there since he was in high school

"Only if one of them is to marry you." It was an old joke.

He only smiled. "What can you tell me about Jessica Rossi?"

Her smile faded. "A shame, that one."

"What do you mean?" He furrowed his brow.

"Such a sweet girl and a great worker; she always kept busy. If it was slow and there was nothing to do, she'd have this place sparkling." She leaned on the counter and shook her head. "Then her husband leaves her and that sweet girl of hers, and she loses herself in the bottle."

"How long ago was that?" Jeff asked curiously.

She thought about it for a minute. "He left her maybe going on two years ago now. She started showing up to work drunk a few months ago. Joe gave her multiple warnings but eventually had to let her go." She looked at him closely. "Why are you asking?"

"If I tell you what's going on you have to promise not to gossip." He laughed at her taken aback look. "I'm serious, Lois; everyone will know soon enough anyway. Let's not make it harder on Melissa than it has to be, okay?" She pinky promised, so he told her about his suspicions with Melissa being abused and the plan he had in mind to help Melissa and Jessica both.

When he finished, Lois had tears in her eyes. "You're a good boy, Jeff." She patted his hand. "Coffee's on me." She turned away fearful she might break down completely. When she came back a few minutes later, there was a five dollar bill on the counter. She smiled. *Such a good boy. He'll make somebody a good husband someday.*

34

Laura thought briefly about the last thing Mark had said to her.

I love you, Laura. He had been so intent. *Best not to think about it right now.* How could she not?

Lee had been the one Mark decided to keep in touch with at the search. Whether it was to maintain professional courtesy or to better avoid her, Laura wondered. The radio chirped and seized her away from her musings. Every time she heard it, she prayed for news of her daughter. So far, it had been a morning full of disappointments.

After another round of check-ins, *Ugh,* they took another look at the map and the seemingly slow progress. She had to admit though, from the end of the day yesterday to now, they had made pretty good progress.

Laura pondered while studying the map. "I wonder if Jim Cook found anything in his back fields this morning."

"Surely Jeff would have called us if he'd heard from him yet." Liz looked up from the map then towards the trees. She was getting the niggling again like she was missing something.

She turned her attention back to Laura. "He seems like a nice guy...he and his wife have a nice place out there." Liz looked out over the woods again towards where she thought his property was.

Laura looked confused "Who?"

"Jim Cook," Liz said in a *duh* tone.

"That's who I thought you meant, but he's not married." Laura shook her head confused.

"Sure he is. I saw a picture of them on the mantle. He wears a wedding ring." Liz had noticed that the previous evening.

"Oh..." Laura realized. "That must've been his late wife; I never knew her really, but she seemed sweet." Laura smiled slightly thinking about being a widow herself and wondering if Jack was with Jenny protecting her.

She shook off the thought. "She died several years ago. Jack and he were friends, sort of; Jim was a volunteer at the station and he's been over to dinner a few times. His wife was the love of his life though."

She remembered back to a conversation they had four or five years ago. "We talked after dinner one time; they were soul mates he said. He seemed content to be alone the rest of his life without her." She missed Jack and always would, but she couldn't understand that sentiment.

This seemed important to Liz. "When did she die?"

Laura thought about it for a moment. "I think we may have still been in high school, or maybe not. I don't really remember. I do remember feeling bad for him, but I didn't really know them that well." She shrugged. "Maybe ten or fifteen years ago."

Before she could think too much more about it, the radio chirped.

Laura jumped up. *We just had check-ins.* Her heart slammed in her chest.

"Go ahead, Lester." She heard Lee answer as he and Melissa made their way back from another walk. He was doing pretty well at keeping the girl occupied.

From somewhere in the woods, Lester responded, "We made it to Fox Creek shortly after we checked in the last time and we found something for sure."

They listened as he explained what they had found. When the dogs reached the creek, within minutes of each other from different directions, they became frantic at the spot where Billy had evidently fallen. There was some blood. They found fragments of his jeans on a broken branch at the top of the bank, a rock with some blood on it at the bottom, and a lot of marks that looked like he may have tumbled down the slope.

"The way the dogs are going, I'd say he was laying there for a bit," Lester finished.

"Any idea which way to go from there?" Lee asked into the radio.

"They've got the scent. We'll be heading north-east from here. We should be to the fields in less than an hour, maybe less if the trail stays strong…and the snow holds off. We'll check in again at the allotted time." And, that was it.

They found the spot on the map and marked it with a red ex. Based on the direction they were headed they'd come out of the woods right at the property line separating the Cook and Riley farms.

"When they get to the fields, they'll be able to cover ground a lot quicker," Lee reminded them.

Laura called her parents to update them on what was happening. After she disconnected, Laura decided to go get more coffee. Two sleepless nights in a row was wearing her down. "I want to run home and get some coffee; I'll bring back some sandwiches."

She smiled at Lee. "Lots of sandwiches." She turned to Melissa, who was looking at the map. "Why don't you come with me, kiddo? My mom and dad want to say hi."

"Okay." Melissa jumped up, anxious to get out of there. Helping was a lot more boring than she'd thought it would be. *Better than being at home though, at least I know what's going on, even if it is nothing.*

Laura stopped. "Crap! I rode with Mark. Can I take your car, Liz?" Laura turned back.

"Of course..." Liz handed her the keys, obviously distracted.

"What's up?" Laura could tell something was on her friend's mind.

The niggling in Liz's mind had become ringing bells. *I'm close,* she thought. "Nothing, just thinking; I'll see you in a few."

Ten minutes after Laura left, it hit her.

She was tiny! They were all tiny! She needed to get to the library. She had to know for sure.

35

Jeff thought about what Lois had told him about Melissa's mom Jessica. It was as he had suspected with the alcohol abuse. He had seen substance abuse ruin too many lives. It really was a shame. He was determined to help Melissa and hoped Jessica was willing to help him do that. After he parked in front of the apartment, he gathered some materials from the passenger seat and hurried quickly to the door.

It had gotten even colder since the sun had disappeared behind a seemingly endless dark cloud. Jeff looked at the sky; he hoped the snow would hold off just a little longer. He knocked.

Finally, on the fourth round of knocking, the door opened a crack. A small white face with squinting eyes peered at him from inside.

"Yeah?" Jessica looked up at him. "What do you want?" She recognized Jeff from gatherings at Laura's she and her husband had been to with Melissa in previous years.

"I wanted to talk to you about Melissa," Jeff said simply.

"What about her? Did she do something wrong?"

"Can I come in?" He didn't answer her question, merely looked at her expectantly.

"Why not? I'm up now." She pulled the door open wide and waved him in. She took a moment to notice the apartment was in some disarray and felt slightly embarrassed. She used to keep a pretty tidy house. "Excuse the mess; I've been busy."

Busy getting shlammered. He could smell the alcohol on her.

"No need to apologize." He sat on the couch. "I have a proposition for you." No need to beat around the bush.

Jessica looked confused. "I thought you wanted to talk about Melissa..."

"Oh, I do, but first, I want you to know that I know you've been beating your daughter," he stated matter-of-factly.

"What! How dare you come in here and accuse me..."

"I'm not accusing you of anything," he interrupted her with the same calm tone. "I'm telling you that I know." He saw her look towards what he assumed was Melissa's room. "And before you fly off the handle on her, she didn't tell me. I saw the evidence for myself. With that and a few comments, I put it together."

"What do you want from me?" The anger was turning into shame and a little fear.

"Like I said, I have a proposition for you. But first, I want to talk a little bit. Why don't you sit down?" As he set his things on the coffee table, he saw Melissa's note and handed it to her. "I assume you haven't seen this yet," he said, referring to her glance towards the bedrooms a moment ago.

She took the note and sat down. She had forgotten all about Jenny. She vaguely remembered the argument she and Melissa had the night before when Melissa told her she wanted to help find her missing friend. She flinched when she remembered striking her daughter in the face. The shame hit her hard, and she started to cry.

What has happened to me? Where did everything go wrong? But, she knew the answer. She had told herself she was going to quit drinking for months now, but she couldn't seem to quite make it happen. She had gone a few days without it a month ago or so, but she had found an excuse to start again.

Jeff let her cry for a moment before starting the conversation up again. "So, this is my offer." He pulled a brochure he had printed that morning from the folder on the coffee table. "You're going to go here for a thirty day inpatient rehab program."

She laughed sarcastically. "Yeah, because I can afford that!" She jumped up from the couch getting her ire back up. "Just because you're some hotshot lawyer with big bucks doesn't..."

"Sit down. And shut up." Jeff didn't raise his voice, but the authority was clear.

Jessica sat and shut up. Too astonished to argue, she only looked at him expectantly.

"I'm paying for it..." he started, but she interrupted.

"Why would..." She stopped when she saw his glare.

"I'm paying for it. Here's the plan. You go into rehab and take it seriously. You give up custody..."

"Now wait a damn minute," she interrupted again.

"Let me finish, or I'm walking out the door and calling the police to have you arrested for child abuse," he stated almost too calmly.

She could see in his eyes he meant it, so she sat and listened.

"You will give up custody to either Laura or myself or maybe even Liz; we'll figure out the details after we're in agreement. Anyway, you give up custody for one year with only supervised visitation. After your thirty days in rehab, you will come and work for me." At this, she looked shocked but was afraid to interrupt to ask any questions. Jeff continued, "I bought Howard Lawrence's law office today and will be starting a practice in Jefferson.

"I'm going to need someone to answer phones, take appointments, make copies, and do other general office duties. I will start you at a minimum base salary, but if it works out and you are proficient, we can discuss an increase. I will require you to take an alcohol swab test at the start of each shift. One strike and you're out. No chance of regaining custody. And, you will have to attend some kind of support group, whether it be AA or private therapy will be up to you. After one year..."

She interrupted him; she couldn't help it, "Why are you doing this?"

"Because you both deserve better," was all he said.

She broke down then, sobbing hysterically. This time he comforted her. After a moment her, sobs lessened. She pulled away from him, frantically wiping at the tears on her face. "I don't know how it got so bad...I really don't...I never meant..." She broke off in a sob. "I can't lose Melissa; she's all I have."

"It's not going to be easy, but if you really want to help yourself, and Melissa, we'll make it work."

His phone rang. He saw Liz's name on the readout and answered immediately. "Hello?"

"Jeff? Where are you? I need a ride to the library now!" Liz exclaimed through the phone.

"What? Where are you?"

"At the search site...she was tiny! Don't you see? She was tiny!" She was clearly excited.

"Liz, what are...?"

"Just come get me; we need to hurry." She disconnected. He didn't question it. He trusted her instincts to the bone.

He looked at Jessica. "I need to go; think about all this. I have some other things for you to look at." He handed her the folder. "I wrote up a sample guardianship document as well as an explanation outlining the terms of our agreement. It will be like a contract. And, like a contract one hundred percent binding," he explained. "The thirty days starts tomorrow. I've arranged transportation and will make sure you can see Melissa before you go. I suggest you start packing. You leave at eight am." He turned to leave, assuming she would take the deal.

He turned back to her, grabbed her shoulders, and looked her in the eyes. "Your life starts today, Jessica; make it a good one." He opened the door to leave but turned to her again. "Go dump it down the sink right now, and don't get more."

She merely nodded, unable to speak.

36

Mark arrived at the hospital. He was thinking about what Mitch had told him. There were more missing girls.

Two dead.

He couldn't stop the next thought from coming.

They're all dead. If they are all truly connected, then they're all dead. Not Jenny though, not yet.

He believed it one hundred percent, but they were running out of time. The newest weather report was calling for the snow to start in less than an hour, with whiteout conditions possible starting around one o'clock. He glanced at his watch. Eleven-thirty.

As he got on the elevator to Billy's floor (he had been moved to a private room from the ER the previous night), he said a silent prayer. When he reached Billy's room, he found Billy with his leg elevated and wearing one of those walking boots to support his ankle. It was not broken, but there was severe ligament damage. He may eventually need surgery.

The primary concern was the apparent head trauma. Until they figured out why he wouldn't wake up, no procedures involving anesthesia would be performed. The CAT scan had shown nothing indicating any kind of hemorrhaging or brain damage. Billy was just in a very deep sleep. He was unresponsive but not comatose. A neurological specialist was coming in from Chicago that evening to do a consult.

After talking to Sally, who hadn't left Billy's side, and the Physician on duty, Mark was granted a private visitation with the boy.

Billy looked so young and fragile. He was covered in bruises and scratches from his run through the woods. They had found where he had fallen at the bank of the creek and the rock he must've hit his head on at the time.

"Hey, Billy." He waited for a response; hopeful.

After a moment, Mark cleared his throat preparing to have a one sided conversation. "I wanted to say thanks for showing us where to start finding Jenny and David. We haven't found anything yet, but thanks to you we're looking. We could really use your help again. If you could wake up and tell us where they are, that would be great."

He felt like an idiot but continued, "We have found out a lot of information since you've been in here."

He told Billy about the search and how the dogs we're tracking his trail, but it was slow moving. He told him he was impressed that he was able to keep going after he had fallen and hit his head by the creek, and on a badly injured ankle to boot.

He could see the movement behind the boy's eyes and wondered what he was dreaming.

"You're a hero, Billy." He squeezed the boy's hand. "But we still need your help." Mark could feel the tears building. "Wake up...wake up...please, Billy," he pleaded. "We still need your help."

Billy kept reliving it in his dreams. Seeing David slashed and Jenny chained. Hearing the laugh and running. Over and over he experienced it, always ending with the squeal of tires on pavement. He knew it was a dream, but he also knew it was real. He couldn't wake up from it. He knew he had to help but couldn't seem to get out of the dream. It was on a never ending loop...until finally everything changed...

He was in a field. It was very bright; he had to squint his eyes. The previous dream had been dark and scary. He looked around, this was peaceful and colorful. Everything was so bright and intense; it was almost too much to take in. From across the field, someone approached him.

In the other dream, he would have fled from anyone that came near, but this was different. He could feel the goodness coming off this person in waves. At first, he thought he might be dying and this was Jesus come to take him to heaven, but then he recognized the figure coming closer.

"Mr. Mitchell!" He ran to the man, and everything about Jenny came crashing back. "You have to help her! Jenny's in trouble!"

Jack smiled at Billy; the boy was so eager to help his daughter.

"That's why I'm here," he told him.

"She's not here; she's..."

"I know where she is; I've already been to see her. You are the only one alive who knows exactly where she is, Billy."

He took the boy by the shoulders and looked him in the eye. "You need to wake up, so you can tell them. She's running out of time, Billy; she needs your help."

"How? How do I wake up? I've been trying, and I can't!" Tears were shimmering in the boy's eyes.

"Now that the nightmare has stopped, just wake up."

Suddenly, Mr. Mitchell was gone, but he could still hear him as from a distance.

"Wake up...wake up...please, Billy. We still need your help."

Billy turned his head to the side...that sounded like Chief Henderson not...

Billy opened his eyes.

"Billy?" Mark was shocked

All Billy could do was groan. Immediately, a nurse rushed in followed closely by the Dr. They pushed Mark aside and attended to the boy. The Dr. was using a light to look into Billy's eyes and was asking questions.

They must've seen something on the monitors. Mark was shuffling his feet and looking over the shoulder of the Dr. He was impatient to talk to the boy.

"Excuse me, sir; you'll have to step outside," the nurse stated authoritatively.

"I need to ask him a few questions," Mark insisted.

"That will have to wait," she responded, ushering him out the door.

"It can't wait; he's a witness to a crime, and I need to know..."

She shut the door in his face.

37

In his hotel room, Mitch was on the phone with one of his team members.

"What about the international travel?" Mitch asked as he paced the small hotel room. "Nothing? Are you sure?" He stopped pacing and looked out the window, noticing the sky had become quite overcast.

"And you're sure there are only these three connections in Arizona?" He glanced at the names he jotted down earlier. "I know you're the best, Pete...sorry...no really, I didn't mean to offend you. I'm just...I know...yeah...I owe you one, buddy." Mitch rolled his eyes to the ceiling as Pete disconnected on a huff.

Pete Monroe was an ace on the computer; he really was the best, but man he was sensitive. Mitch looked at his watch; it was already after eleven. He tried to reach Mark on his cell phone, but it kept going to voicemail. On the third try, he left a message.

"Mark, it's Mitch; I have some new information. I'm going to wrap up a few things here and then head to the search site. I should be there before twelve thirty."

Jeff squealed to a stop in front of the command table and jumped out of the car. He almost had to run Kyle over to get through.

"Liz!" he called to her. She and Lee were walking towards him from the edge of the woods.

"Thanks, Lee." He heard her say. She gave him a big hug and a kiss on the cheek before running towards him. A jolt of jealousy shot through him.

Quit being ridiculous, he scolded himself. *It was a kiss on the damn cheek!*

Liz jogged to where he was. "Thanks for getting here so fast." She headed towards his car. "Laura took my car, and I can't take Lee's cruiser." She smiled at him brightly. "Where have you been anyway?"

He slid in the driver's seat, obviously agitated, and waited for her to get in before he answered. "I had some things to take care of." He was slightly miffed about the way she had hung all over Lee for a minute.

Liz raised an eyebrow at his tone. "I'm sorry if I interrupted your all-important day," she remarked sarcastically. "You can drop me off at the library, and I can have Laura pick me up if you need to get back to it." She looked out the window, set on ignoring him.

"I'm not dropping you off," he said haughtily, gripping the steering wheel a little too tightly. "What are we doing at the library anyway?"

Liz simply stared out the passenger window.

"Come on, Liz; what's going on? You sounded excited on the phone." His curiosity was getting the better of him.

She slanted him a look. "I'll tell you...*but*...only if you tell me what crawled up your ass today."

He didn't want to tell her about the jealousy burning a hole in his gut but couldn't help but ask. "So, you and Lee looked cozy...is there something going on there?"

She looked at him, dumbfounded for a moment, before she realized what he was talking about. "You're jealous." The thought of it made her chuckle inside.

"What?" he asked, trying to sound shocked but sounding more embarrassed than anything. He even blushed and squirmed a little in his seat.

Liz laughed out loud. "You are!" The laughter died pretty quick though. "Jeff, I think we should talk about what happened last night."

"Last night? What do you mean?" He tried to play it off cool like.

"Cut the shit. You know damn well what I'm talking about." When he didn't answer, she continued, "I have never once thought of you like that before..."

"Look it's no big deal, okay?" God, he felt like an idiot.

"Will you let me finish please?" She waited for him to nod before continuing. "Okay...so, I have never thought of you like that before, but ever since last night when you kissed me, it's hard to think of anything else."

She looked at him seriously. "I'm really not sure how I feel about it honestly, but that one tiny little kiss kicked me square in the gut. I keep thinking it's probably just all the emotions running rampant because of everything that's going on...but what if it's not? And that's what really has me scared, Jeff; what if it's not?" she asked him earnestly.

He knew exactly what she meant. It looked like they were pretty much on the same page. "Yeah, that's pretty much exactly the way I feel." He glanced at her now. "We're only two blocks from the library; let's put this aside for now. I take it you finally figured out what you've been missing."

"I know who it is," she said. "At least I'm pretty sure; I just need to check out a few things first to be certain."

Laura was at her house talking to her parents about Melissa's situation and what Liz wanted to try and do for her. They were in the kitchen making sandwiches for Laura to take back to the search site. Melissa had fallen asleep on the couch almost as soon as she had sat down. Laura had removed the girl's shoes and covered her with a blanket.

"That seems like an awful lot to take on," Katlyn remarked.

"I thought so too, but once Liz gets a hold of something, she doesn't usually let go." She looked towards the living room where she left Melissa. "And I have to agree with her; if it's getting that bad, something needs to be done...Thanks, Dad." Laura took the thermos her father had filled up for her to take back.

Michael smiled. "I think it's a great idea. Liz needs something in her life; maybe this is it." He shrugged. "I think it would be good for both of them."

He didn't tell them Jeff was pretty much thinking along the same lines, even with Liz as the potential guardian. They had discussed it that morning before everyone had left. The men had promised to keep it a secret from the "womenfolk" until Jeff had seen to a few things.

Laura nodded. *Looks like my Lizzy Bear is really serious about coming home.*

They talked about the search and the progress in the investigation. It had seemed the night before they were getting somewhere. But today with the storm set to arrive any minute per the newest winter storm update, it seemed like they were stuck in mud.

"If you don't mind, I'm going to leave Melissa sleeping on the couch and head on back to the site with all this," she said to her parents.

"Of course not, honey. Bring Jenny home with you, okay?" Michael said, trying to be positive.

Laura managed a half smile. "I'll do my best."

In the library, Liz and Jeff read about Marie Cook's tragic accident fifteen years ago.

Fifteen years ago today, Liz noticed. The picture in the obituary was the same pretty blonde in the picture on the mantle.

"I want to check something else real quick."

She hurried to the local history section and found the yearbook for Marie's graduating class. Within minutes, she found Marie's senior picture. At first glance, it could have been Jenny looking out at her, or

Margery, or Sasha, or any of the other girls. She looked at Jeff over her shoulder, speechless.

He grabbed the book, put it back on the shelf randomly, grabbed her hand, and said simply, "Let's go."

They ran through the library, ignoring the harsh glare from Mrs. Jones. When they got outside, Liz was already dialing Mark's cell phone. It went straight to voicemail. Every time.

They had been in the library for less than thirty minutes, but when they came out, the snow was falling.

"Stupid voicemail!" After the fourth try, she left a message. "It's Jim Cook; Jeff and I are on our way there!"

Jeff dialed his sister's number. "Maybe he's at the site."

Mark had been pacing outside Billy's room for over twenty minutes. The nurse had allowed Sally to enter a few minutes before to see her son.

After a few more minutes, Sally opened the door and motioned to Mark. "He's asking for you."

Mark started to push past her, but she didn't budge. "Be easy with him. He's obviously confused and very upset."

He placed a hand on her shoulder. "Don't worry, Sally. I'm not going to beat anything out of him, but we're running out of time." He had seen the snow falling through the window in the hall.

She nodded and stepped out of his way.

He entered the room to see Billy sitting up in bed with a lot less tubes and wires connected to him. His eyes were closed.

"Hey, Billy..." He knew he needed to hurry, but he also knew he needed to be gentle. The boy had been through hell...literally.

Billy's eyes flew open. "Chief Henderson! He killed David and he's going to kill Jenny if you don't hurry!" The boy became almost frantic when he saw Mark.

"Who's that?" he asked, anxious to know the answer.

The boy started crying hysterically. It was all just too much to think about. After a moment, he managed, "Mr. Cook," through sniffly tears.

He wasn't as surprised as he thought he'd be to not hear Jacob Riley's name, but Jim Cook did come as a shock.

"Are you sure, Billy?" *Jim? What?*

"It looked like him, but not exactly," Billy tried to explain. "His voice was a little different and his eyes..." At that, the boy shivered.

"Tell me what happened, if you can." Mark put his hand gently on the boy's arm.

Billy started from the beginning.

Ten minutes later, Mark was running down the stairs to the parking lot.

When Mitch got to the search site, the only one there was Lee. "Where the hell is everyone?" he asked, approaching the command table.

"Well, Laura left to get some lunch and coffee to bring back, and Jeff and Liz ran to the library." He shook his head. "That girl is a spitfire! She was all excited about something. She was rambling so fast, I could barely keep up. She asked me to take over the map and pretty much just bolted. That was 'bout thirty minutes ago or so. Haven't heard from Mark since he got to the hospital; that was close to the same time."

Mitch took the opportunity to catch Lee up on everything that had happened since they talked last. Including the information he hadn't shared with him that morning.

"Hmmmm," Lee considered. "So, there are more? I was wondering about that; the gap in the dates seemed off."

A car pulled in behind Mitch's SUV. "Is that Liz?" Mitch asked, recognizing the car.

"Nah, it's Laura; she took Liz's car because she rode in with Mark. Liz took off with Jeff in his little hotrod."

Laura got out of the car carrying a large paper bag and two thermoses. Mitch hurried over to help her.

"Thanks. Where's Liz?" she asked Lee as they walked up to the table and sat down the supplies.

"She and Jeff ran to the library a little bit ago; she had something she wanted to check out." Lee dug into the bag containing the sandwiches, and Laura grinned at him.

"Anything new?" she asked to neither in particular

"Actually I was just telling Lee," Mitch answered. "I'm glad you're here."

He told her about the other missing girls, leaving out the horrid details of the murders. It started snowing as he told her the rest.

"I had a buddy of mine check on any familial connections any residents of Jefferson may have in Arizona." He pulled the paper from his pocket to read the names, even though he had them memorized.

Before he started, Laura's phone rang. "It's Jeff."

She answered, "Jeff, I'm with Mitch; he thinks he might...."

Jeff didn't let her finish. "It's Jim Cook, Laura; we're leaving the library now and heading there."

"What? Jim Cook? Are you sure?" She was dumbfounded.

Mitch took the phone from her. "Jeff, it's Mitch. What's going on?" Jim Cook was one of his three names; his brother lived in Arizona. He listened as Jeff explained how they came to the answer.

"I'm on my way." Mitch hung up and handed Laura her phone.

"What's going on?" Laura followed him to his SUV.

"Jim Cook was one of the three names on my list, but it looks like Liz narrowed it down to one," he explained as he got in his vehicle.

Laura hurried to the passenger side and jumped in before Mitch could take off.

Mitch simply looked at her. "What do you think you're doing?"

"Do you want to waste time by trying to physically remove me from this vehicle or are we going?" She clearly meant it. The look on her face was pure determination.

He looked at her for a moment. She was right; they didn't have time to argue. "Put your seatbelt on." He faced front and floored it.

38

Jim woke up after noon, feeling like he had slept for days. He had taken three sleeping pills the night before to ensure he would get some sleep. He looked at the clock and realized he'd slept for more than 12 hours or so. At least he hoped; any portion of that time could have been a blackout.

He felt refreshed though, better than he had in days. He ate a big breakfast consisting of three eggs, half a pound of bacon, and three biscuits with jelly. He had completely forgotten about his promise to help in the search that morning.

Today is going to be a good day. Jim smiled to himself realizing there was no headache.

Finally, he got the paper from the front porch determined to be lazy today. He opened the paper and saw nothing but the date. He frowned and realized it was the anniversary of Marie's death. Instantly, the good day turned sour. He tumbled into grief. After sobbing violently for several minutes, he tried to recover his good mood. He opened the paper to read it and start his day over. But he saw the article with all the pictures on the front page.

Images flashed quickly through his mind, each accompanied by a jolt of pain. The images were gone too quick, and he wasn't quite sure what was going on. The breakfast he had eaten soured in his stomach, and he barely made it to the sink retching, practically turning his stomach inside out.

When he was finished with the violent emptying of his stomach, Jim was afraid to look at the paper again but felt he must. He picked up the paper and saw Marie...his heart stopped, and the headache flared again.

On a scream and a searing pain through his head, "he" came forward.

She deserved it every time! He had some work to do, he remembered suddenly.

She never should have left them. He walked out the door, leaving it open. He walked down the back steps and through the snow flurries to where Marie was waiting for him.

Jenny knew it was daytime because she had seen the sun shining through the cracks in the old barn walls. A few minutes ago though, the light faded drastically, and she could hear the wind pick up outside. She thought about what her father had said to her.

Tell him what he wants to hear. What did that mean exactly? How was she supposed to know what a crazy person wanted to hear?

She decided to try and rest. Almost as soon as she laid her head back, she heard the barn door creak open and then slam against the barn from the wind. The light in the outer room came on. She sat up straighter and listened carefully. She heard heavy footsteps approaching the room she was in.

Please don't stop; please don't stop, she silently begged, hoping he'd go past like he had yesterday after she'd heard the voices.

No such luck. The light came on, and she got a strong sense of déjà-vu as the man approached her

"Don't worry, Marie…"

Marie? He thinks my name is Marie! "My name is Jenny."

"Now, Marie; let's not be silly."

Marie? Who is Marie?

It was happening exactly as it had the day before she realized, and that almost ended very badly. She tried to think.

Tell him what he wants to hear. The thought drifted to her from somewhere not in her mind, and she knew it was her father reminding her. She remembered her thought from the day before.

"I'm sorry…you're right…it is me…Marie." She needed to be Marie; it was her only chance. Marie had left him. She needed to make him think she came back for him.

The man looked confused at this.

"Why did you leave us, Marie?" he asked angrily.

"I…um…I didn't want to leave you," she managed to stammer; she was more scared than she'd ever been in her life.

The man yelled, "YOU NEED TO BE PUNISHED, MARIE!"

She needed to try and reason with him. "No, please; I didn't want to leave you. I had to," she said hurriedly before he could do anything to punish her.

"What do you mean? You had to?" he asked, suddenly curious with what she had to say.

She didn't know how to answer, so she said simply, "It doesn't matter. I'm here now, and we can be together again. Forever."

"Forever? You won't ever leave me again?"

"No, of course not..." She gulped, hoping it was working. She had to buy time her father said. "I love you." She almost choked on the words. "Why would I leave?" She could feel the sweat pouring down her back. She was terrified.

He sobbed and went to his knees in front of her. He held her closely for a moment. With her wrists still restrained, it was a very awkward embrace.

"Please, unchain me...please?" she nearly begged. "We can be together, but you need to untie me."

Jim held on for a moment, and then he got up and removed a key hanging from a nail across the room. It was right there the whole time. He undid the shackles on her legs then her hands, but before Jenny could grab the knife, he took both her hands in his and pulled her to standing.

"I've missed you, Marie." He pulled her close, and although she was horrified being so close to him, she needed the support. The blood rushing through her extremities was painful and she gasped.

"Marie, did I hurt you?" he asked with concern in his voice.

Yeah, you smashed my head into a truck, chained me to a wall for days without food and water, and almost killed me! she thought angrily. "No...no...I'm fine...just a little lightheaded." It wasn't even a complete lie. She was dizzy.

Gently, he walked her to a chair on the other side of the room and sat her in it. "Here, sit..." He kept her steady with his hands on her arms.

This man had eaten dinner at their house, had been friends with her father, and had talked to her dozens of times over the years. Why did he think she was this Marie lady? He was obviously insane, going from wanting to punish her to being concerned about her well-being.

She decided to call him by the name she knew him as and hoped it would help her be Marie.

"Thanks, Jim; is there...?" She was going to ask for water because she desperately needed it, but at the mention of his name, he changed. Like he had on the road but in reverse.

"Jenny?" he asked, recognition in his now somehow sane looking eyes. His eyes changed again. "Marie?" He shook his head trying to clear it. She saw the anger flash. "YOU LIE!"

The headache seared through his brain...he let go of her to put both hands to his head. She didn't know if he was talking to her or the other him, but she wasn't going to wait to find out. As soon as he released her, she jumped up.

That's my purse! I don't know you! A scene from *King of the Hill* ran through her head as she kicked him as hard as she could in the balls.

Run, her father had said, and she did.

39

As he fishtailed once again, Jeff cursed his sporty little car. He didn't dare slow down though; the storm was here. They were out of time.

The road conditions were too hazardous to even have a conversation. Liz just held on to the oh shit bar and kept her eyes glued to the road.

They were minutes away, but it seemed like hours.

When they finally pulled down the driveway and skidded to a halt in front of the house, they both jumped out and ran to the door.

Locked! Damn it! Jeff threw himself against the door; one, two, three times when they finally heard a cracking. He kicked it now, concentrating his power near the lock. On the fourth kick, the door crashed in.

"Stay close," he said to Liz.

They searched the house. It was empty. In the kitchen, Liz picked up the paper lying on the floor and saw the pictures of the girls staring up at her. The back door was wide open and quite a bit of snow had made its way into the house.

"Let's check out the barn," Jeff suggested.

Mitch had four wheel drive on his SUV and was making good use of it. He was flying down the country roads. When they arrived at the Cook farm, they saw Jeff's car in front of the house with a thin layer of snow already covering it.

"Stay here," Mitch said to Laura.

"Fuck that!" she retorted and jumped out with him.

He looked at her, realizing it would waste time to argue; besides, he really didn't want to leave her alone. "Fine, but stay close."

He drew his weapon from a shoulder holster under his jacket and approached the house cautiously. They found the front door busted in and entered the house. Mitch held one finger to his lips, indicating that Laura should stay as quiet as possible.

They crept through the house, and Laura nearly jumped out of her skin when she heard a door slam open in another room. Mitch held up a hand, halting their progress down the hall.

They heard Jeff's voice. "Damn it! Where is she?"

Laura couldn't remain silent anymore. "Jeff!" she called out and hurried to the kitchen where his voice came from.

When they were all in the room, Jeff told them they had searched the entire house and the barn outside.

"Don't these old farmhouses have outside storm cellars?" Mitch asked. The house he had grown up in had one.

After a few minutes, they found a raised area off the back of the house completely covered in snow. After wiping away the snow, they found an old wooden door. Jeff pulled it open and the hinges creaked badly. It was dark, with only the top few steps visible.

Mitch pulled out a flashlight. "I'm going down. You stay here," he said, giving Jeff a look that clearly stated 'stay with the women'.

After a few minutes, Mitch returned with cobwebs in his hair and a frown on his face. "Nothin' except lots of canned food and bottled water." He looked frustrated. "No sign of anything amiss in the house and nothing but cows in the barn!" He kicked the cellar door.

"They have to be here somewhere. Jim's truck is out by the barn and Jenny's here; I know it; I can feel it," Liz stated confidently.

"Where? There are forty six acres on this farm!" Laura had the plot map committed to memory. "Where do we look?" She was so sure they would find Jenny when they got there.

Wait a minute, Jeff remembered, *there's another barn!*

Just then, Laura's phone rang.

Mark, with sirens blaring, called Lee as soon as his phone booted up after being off inside Billy's hospital room.

"Lee, I know where she is." He told him what Billy had said. "Is Mitch there yet?"

Lee told him everything that had happened in the last twenty minutes or so, including calling off the search. "The snow just made it impossible to keep going. The dogs were losing the scent and they were doing too much backtracking. With the conditions worsening, I had to call it."

"It doesn't matter. I know where she is. I hate to ask this of you, but could you go to the Minelli place and let them know what Billy told me? Tell Marianne I will be there as soon as I can with any new information."

Before Lee could answer, Mark dropped the call. He tried to dial back, but it was no use; this had always been a dead spot.

He dialed Laura's number a few minutes later when he got through the dead spot. He had lived there long enough to know exactly where that was.

She answered on the first ring. "Mark where are you? We know who it is."

"I'm on my way. Billy woke up; I know exactly where she is. I'll be there in two minutes." He disconnected, wanting both hands on the wheel, and sped up a tad more

Within the two minutes, he came flying down the lane. He had turned his lights and sirens off to ensure Jim didn't hear him coming. He didn't want to prompt the man to do something he may haven't already done.

He parked on the other side of Jeff's little toy, extremely glad to see Mitch had a Government Issue four wheel drive SUV present.

He saw his four friends at the side of the house and ran over to them. "Okay, Mitch; we'll take your vehicle since it has four wheel drive. Jeff, you stay here with the girls..."

Laura interrupted, "I'm coming."

"Laura, it could be dangerous; we don't know what he may be capable of," Mark tried to explain his reasoning.

"My daughter is out there, Mark. I'm coming." Her tone left no room for arguing.

"I called an ambulance while Laura was on the phone with you." Jeff shrugged when all heads turned to him. "I figured we better be prepared. I'll wait here and tell them where to go."

"You know where?" Mark asked him.

"I'm guessing the old horse barn." He looked between them all. "Mark and I used to bail hay for Jim. I just remembered about the old barn right when you called Laura." He looked at Mark. "What are you waiting for, man? Go get her."

"I'll wait with Jeff," Liz said, not wanting him to have to wait alone.

Mark, Laura, and Mitch piled into the SUV and headed through the field. The snow was accumulating fast.

Liz walked up to Jeff and planted one on him. It wasn't a quick kiss this time, but it was another shot to the gut.

"What was that for?" Jeff asked her when she finally broke contact.

She shrugged. "I'm still not sure about it, but it seemed like the right thing to do under the circumstances."

Liz looked in the field where the taillights had been swallowed up by the snow. "I hope they find her in time." She held out her hands in the snow. Clearly, they hadn't found her before the storm.

"They will." It was as simple as that to Jeff. "I want to talk to you about Melissa." He turned to her after a moment.

"Oh yeah? Well, I want to talk to you about Melissa."

Jeff told her what he had been up to that day, and she laughed. "What's so funny?" he asked, clearly offended.

"Nothing." She just kissed him again.

Suddenly, she was a little more sure about it.

40

Run, was all she could think. The short walk across the room had gotten the blood flowing in Jenny's legs enough to allow her to move a little easier. By the time she reached the door to the outside, she was managing a stumbling half run. When she made it outside, the wind hit her full force, and she stumbled to the ground.

Snow, she thought when her hands hit the cold fluffiness. She scooped up a handful and put it in her mouth on instinct. She groaned in relief, took another, and then scrambled back to her feet. Even that small amount of hydration gave her the energy she needed to really run. She couldn't tell where she was going because the snow was coming down so thick. She just knew she couldn't stop.

I hope I'm not headed for the woods, she thought, remembering what her father had told her. Behind her, she heard Jim scream

"MARRRRRRIIIIIEEEEE!" He was coming for her. She pushed herself a little harder.

Don't look back. Don't look back. She repeated it over and over in her mind.

It was slow going through the field. He had four wheel drive sure, but the visibility was nil.

"What can you tell me about this barn?" Mitch risked a glance at Mark.

"I haven't been in it for fifteen or twenty years..." But, he closed his eyes to picture it. "Large main room with maybe four or five horse stalls on each side. There's a hay loft on each side over the stalls. A large tack room off the back and a small storage room on the right past the last stall.

"There might be a small bunk room off the tack room." He opened his eyes. "Jim would stay with the horses when they were getting ready to foal. He liked to stay close; I remember that about him." He still couldn't quite believe Jim Cook was responsible for Jenny's disappearance, not to mention for everything else they had learned.

This was the longest ride of Laura's life. She felt like they could have walked faster! Her daughter was out here, the storm was in full force, and they might be too late.

No! She's alive; they weren't going to be too late. It simply wasn't an option.

"Can't we go just a little faster?" Laura was practically in the front seat; she was leaning so far forward to peer out the windshield.

Mitch couldn't see five feet in front of the vehicle. He couldn't risk a random tree or boulder jumping out at him. He had grown up on a farm. He knew all too well what a grazing field could consist of, and that was just about anything.

Even the shell of a fifty seven Chevy like at his grandpa's place. He and his sister used to play in it as kids. There was also a giant boulder (well, it had seemed giant at the time) they used to climb. They called it the big rock.

"Oh my God!" Laura said jolting him out of his reverie. "It's Jenny!"

Before Mitch could completely stop, she was throwing open the door and running to the tiny figure coming toward the SUV.

"JENNY!" Laura ran to her daughter who collapsed in her arms, sobbing uncontrollably. "Jenny…" Laura fell to her knees in the snow oblivious to everything else around her, her face in her daughter's hair, rocking her back and forth.

Mark hurried up to them, hesitant to interrupt the reunion but knowing they still might be in danger. "Let's get her in the car and warmed up," he suggested. He leaned over to lift Jenny to carry her to the SUV, but Laura wasn't ready to let her go.

"I've got her." Jenny's arms were around her mother's neck already, and she was holding on for dear life.

Mitch had blasted the heater and had retrieved a couple blankets from the back of the SUV. Laura climbed in with Jenny, and they wrapped her in the blankets. Mitch closed the door and turned in time to see a large form appear out of the snow. Jim Cook was coming up behind Mark and fast.

"Mark! Behind you!" he yelled out in warning. Mark turned, the shout saving his life. The sickle, which had been descending towards his skull, caught his shoulder instead. The arm of his leather jacket was sliced, and he could feel the warmth of his blood trickling down his arm. Unknown to him, the leather had saved him from an amputation.

He didn't feel the pain, not yet. He lowered his other shoulder and rammed it into Jim's gut with his entire body weight, taking them both to the ground in the snow. When they hit, Jim lost his weapon. Mark punched him in the face, again, and again...

"Mark, that's enough. Mark!" Mitch had to pull him off of the man, and it took quite an effort. Mitch checked Jim's pulse to make sure Mark hadn't beaten him to death.

Mark approached Jim again, but Mitch got between them.

"I'm good, man; I promise." Mark's blood had already started to cool. He was starting to feel the slice in his arm too. "I just want to cuff the bastard." Mitch nodded and let him by.

Mitch called Lee to let him know what was going on and asked him to have a four wheel drive transport unit come get Jim Cook. After disconnecting, he looked in the distance; he really wanted to get a look at this barn.

Back in the car, Laura was on the phone with Liz, Jenny asleep in her lap. Laura was unconsciously stroking her daughter's hair as she slept. Jenny had finally stopped shivering.

"She's fine...a little beat up, but she really seems to be fine." Laura couldn't take her eyes off her daughter's face. Tears were leaking out of her eyes and down her cheeks, unnoticed for the time being.

She got off the phone, hugged her daughter to her chest, and took a moment to thank Jack for all his help. Mark had told them what Billy had said. And, before Jenny had fallen asleep, she had mentioned that her dad had told her to run.

We miss you honey, every day. But, it was different she realized. It didn't hurt anymore.

She watched Mark through the windshield as he approached the vehicle; she was oblivious to what had gone on outside after she and Jenny had gotten in the vehicle.

When he climbed in the passenger seat, she gasped. "You're bleeding! What happened?"

He told her about the attack and how Mitch had saved his life. Laura shivered, thinking how close behind Jenny Jim had actually been. Once she had seen her daughter, everything else ceased to matter.

She was horrified. "How bad is it?"

"I don't think it's too bad…it is starting to hurt a little though." He winced and gasped in pain as he tried to take off his mutilated jacket.

"Here, let me help you." She laid Jenny gently across the back seat and got out of the car. She went around to the passenger seat and opened the door. "Get out; it'll be easier to get off if your standing."

She helped him out of the car realizing now how pale he looked. When they got the jacket off, she breathed in sharply. His shirt sleeve was cut and soaked with blood, the cuff dripping at the wrist; his arm just below the shoulder was laid open, the wound clearly deep into the muscle. He swayed, and she eased him back into the passenger seat just before he passed out.

"MITCH!" she called loudly and he came running.

"What is it?"

"Mark...his arm; it's bad. He passed out." She took off her jacket, intending to use it to staunch the flow of blood.

"I've got something better." Mitch hurried around to the back and grabbed a couple towels. He tried to close the wound as best he could and had Laura roll up a towel and press it firmly to the wound. "Hold it tight." He got out his knife and cut the other towel into strips to tie the rolled towel in place as tight as possible.

"I just talked to Liz," Laura told him as they finished. "The ambulance is on its way back."

The visibility hadn't gotten any better, so Mitch turned on his hazard lights. He went back to the cargo area one more time and got the flare gun. After the third shot from the gun, they saw the ambulance's flashing lights coming towards them.

While Jenny and Mark were being tended to, Mitch went and checked on Jim. He was just coming to and was struggling to sit up in the deepening snow. "What? What's going on...?" Jim looked around and then up at Mitch. "Who...what...?"

"You're under arrest..." Mitch started then saw the man wince in pain and then change.

Jim glared at the man in front of him. "Where's Marie? She needs to be punished."

Mitch merely nodded. "Can you tell me why that is?"

"She left us. She promised to never leave us, and she lied. SHE RIPPED OUR HEART OUT!" he yelled. "And now, she needs to be punished." He spat it out, the anger evident. He looked into Mitch's eyes and said quietly, "We're going to rip her heart out like she ripped out ours." The insanity in the gaze was almost enough to drive him mad.

Then, Jim laughed...

Mitch got a chill down his spine at that and broke eye contact. *Well, at least now I have the why...*

A Note from the Author

I just want to take a moment to thank you for reading my book. I hope you enjoyed reading it as much as I enjoyed writing it. *Before the Storm* is my first novel, and I have learned so much about the process of making the story into a book. I'm sure I didn't learn it all though, and I apologize for any grammar and formatting errors I may have missed during the long grueling processes of editing and formatting. Hopefully the story was gipping enough that it distracted you from any such mistakes.

I'm looking forward to writing more and hope you'll check out my next story when it's finished. And, if you love Liz as much as I do, you'll be pleased to know there's a good chance she'll be back.

If you wouldn't mind, please take a moment to email me at mhansenauthor@gmail.com, visit my website: maggiehansen.com, or visit my Facebook page: facebook.com/maggiehansenauthor, and let me know what you thought of *Before the Storm*. I would appreciate any feedback, positive or negative…you can never stop learning and improving, and why would you want to? We can only get better and grow from here.

Thank you so much,

Maggie

www.ingramcontent.com/pod-product-compliance
Lightning Source LLC
Chambersburg PA
CBHW061129200626
46817CB00016B/440